'As a detective, I often deal with the bizarre. Sometimes involving murder. Always involving mystery. Deep down though, I'm a Pragmatist, bent on finding practical solutions to claims of perculiar activity.
Even when I fail, I think I come pretty damn close . . .

. . . I'll let you be the judge.'

Cameron Josey

James William Davis

Book 2

Mind Set
©

James William Davis

Mind Set

Written by James William Davis

Published by James William Davis
17 Wedgewood Crescent, Beacon Hill NSW 2100

Copyright 2012, James William Davis
International Standard Book Number
ISBN 978-0-646-99152-8

National Library of Australia Cataloguing-in Publication entry
Author: Davis, James W.

Title: Mindset/ James William Davis.
ISBN 978-0-646-99152-8
File: 013 G Book 2 Mind Set 001-2023 G.doc
Cover: 024 9780646991528-Perfect Mind Set B2.pdf

Cover Design and Layout by James William Davis.
©

iii

James William Davis

Born in 1944, James William Davis first branched into writing due to his involvement in the film and television industry. Story telling became a driving force in his working life, albeit mostly with a camera or an editing device.

Now, he likes to hone his craft using the written word—that essential step prior to all other forms of expression.

Books by
James William Davis
In a planned series of 13

THE IMMORTALITY CONNECTION

MIND SET

ZEROZONE

HOLIDAY HORROR

GHOST WRITER

OVERKILL

WITHOUT SOPHIE

James William Davis

MIND SET
Established Attitudes

Pregnant and out of wedlock, eighteen year old Montana Pritchard is badly injured in a car crash while texting.

Her unborn daughter, Monty, lives on in the womb of her comatose mother, kept alive by Doctor Walter Pritchard, the woman's father.

At the age of three, Monty begins to sense her dead mother is reaching out to her about the circumstances surrounding the accident . . .

Detective Josey is called in to investigate what *really* happened, eventually discovering the horrific truth about the death of Monty's mother.

CHAPTER ONE
The Incident

On the night of her eighteenth birthday, driving through the glistening lights of her hometown city of Brisbane; Montana Pritchard should have had the world at her feet.

Her wealthy father had acquired an entire yacht club for a huge party with friends and family; the genesis of which had grown over three weeks of intense planning. In spite of the outcome ending affably, there remained a deep sadness in Montana's heart that couldn't be erased or ignored.

It was hard to imagine that this vibrant young woman, who at a glance seemed to have so much going for her, could find herself in such depths of despair, a pretty girl with the looks of an angel. She aught to have been excited about getting together with her girlfriends and an undeniable myriad of male suitors, but she was dreading it.

Only two people on earth knew that she was harbouring a damnable secret, a secret that would tear her family apart. Her eyes welled as the terrible memory seeped into every dark corner of her being.

How was she ever going to disguise her feelings in front of everyone? Surely they would notice that something was wrong.

She took a deep breath and wiped away tears with the back of her hand.

'Clean up your act girl,' she demanded of herself.

The melodious tone of her cell phone permeated her thoughts. Her eyes cut to the illuminated screen and saw it was her brother calling.

She cleared her throat and acknowledged him, failing to disguise her mood. 'Yes, Andrew?'

'Hey, *Sis*; how's the party girl?'

'Never better,' she lied.

'Listen; I might be slightly held up; nothing too serious. Do me a favour and let Meredith know the address, she rang the hospital earlier and I forgot about it. Do you have her number?'

'Yes Andrew. I have her number.'

He picked up on her mood. 'You okay, *Sis*?'

'I'm fine - get off the phone,' she told him as lightly as she could muster.

He chortled and said, 'Hope you cheer up before you get to the party.'

She cut him off.

'I'll cheer up when this is over,' she whispered

while reaching to the touch-screen of her mobile phone.

Tap, tap, tap; with her left hand.

Meredith's details appeared.

Quick check of the road - lights coming up a block away—green.

Eyes back on the touch-screen . . .

> *Tap, tap, tap, tap, tap, tap, tap, tap—*

Eyes back on the road—still clear all the way to the green light at the next intersection.

Meredith's phone finally rang out.

Montana's eyes fell to the screen.

One of these days I'll get voice-recognition, she thought as she selected messages.

> Tap, tap, tap, tap, tap - *Check the road; –* tap, tap, tap - *Check the road—*

As she did, a truck came out of nowhere on her right.

'Shit!' she screamed ramming her foot on the brake pedal—

If the truck hadn't run a red light, she may well have made it through the intersection unscathed. As it was, she couldn't have been in a worse position when the two vehicles collided.

Time slowed to a crawl as she watched her door cave-in under the massive weight of the relentless truck—

Everything went mercifully black for her at that moment.

For the horrified onlookers, there was no such

mercy. The truck continued on its destructive path, slicing its way into the cabin of the car, ripping and pushing the interior—and the unconscious rag-doll passenger—completely to the opposite window. The doomed little hatchback was scooped across the intersection and slammed harshly into a power pole, shattering the driver's window into a halo of glass that tore and ripped into Montana's head.

The deafening noise of the crash sank sharply into a steely quiet as witnesses stood stunned . . .

Montana's brother Andrew, who was just four years older than herself, yet already a practicing Neurosurgeon at *Pooles Private Hospital* in Archerfield, came out of ER and headed straight to the bosses office. He knocked once and entered the door labeled, Director Walter Pritchard, in gold letters. The director looked up as the surgeon strolled in and stood at the edge of his desk. He gave the young man a brief moment of recognition and continued on with what he was doing.

'Dad; we need to go.'

'I know, Son,' he said with an exasperated sigh.

'I suggest we not be late. She's not in much of a mood.'

'Tell me something new.' The director sounded edgy.

'Can we drop all that shit,' the young surgeon protested, 'just for tonight if it's not asking too much.'

His father looked up sharply at the gainly young

man and released another exasperated breath. He pulled his glasses off and threw them on the desk. 'All right,' he said as he stood and gathered his coat from a stand, taking his time under the glare of his son. 'I'm coming.'

It wasn't hard to tell they were related, people often said Andrew looks a lot like his father. Walter had clearly passed on his genes to both siblings – in part at least. The passage of time had sedately painted a degree of age into the director's face, yet he remained quite hansom for a man in his late forties. The light stubble that he liked to keep didn't detract; it suited him. His full head of dark hair, which was void of grey and looked set never to fall out, carried reflections of his youth.

The way that he carried himself at six foot one; aided by a strong chest and a no nonsense persona, projected authority, not just over his family, but over the entire hospital. He demanded and received respect from everyone, right up to the hospital board. His aloofness was his most notable downfall.

Andrew on the other hand had a more familiar approach with his colleagues, and was well liked for it. Photos of Andrew at twenty could be mistaken for his father at the same age. He was taller by a couple of inches and had the lanky-look of the modern generation, a sprinkle of ginger in his hair presented the major aesthetic difference between he and his father; his locks were acquired from his mother, Margaret, who was a natural honey blond, derived from her Scottish descent.

As they neared the door that led out of the office, it opened with urgency. The nurse who was standing there looked ashen.

'What's wrong?' the director asked bluntly.

The fifty year old matronly looking nurse held her mouth open as if waiting for the words to form; then announced. 'It's your daughter, Sir. Montana has been involved in a bad car accident.'

Andrew's face dropped. 'What? I just spoke with her.'

'How bad?' Walter asked the nurse urgently.

Nurse Sullivan shook her head and handed him the phone she'd walked in with. 'The guy who called it in is still at the scene.'

Walter snatched the phone and put it to his ear. 'This is her father speaking. What's the situation there?'

Is that the best you can come up with, Dad?

Andrew turned to the nurse and spoke quietly. 'Who have we got on this?'

'Jacobs, the only paramedic left. And he's already got another job.'

Andrew pulled the phone away from his father before he had a chance to object, which the young man considered no ruder than the way his father snatched it from Nurse Sullivan. 'An Ambulance has been dispatched from Marta,' she hastened to tell him as he strode into the corridor taking over the call.

Neither one of them saw the distress creeping onto the director's face. 'Is she breathing?' he demanded from the guy on the scene.

Sullivan teetered, not sure whether to follow Andrew or stay with his father. The director's scowl drove her away; she opted to follow the young surgeon.

'I, I'm not sure,' Andrew heard the man on the line stutter.

'Put your ear to her mouth,' he instructed sharply. 'Are you in a position to do that?'

'Yes.' The caller sounded nervous.

The phone crackled.

'Sir; are you checking if she is breathing?'

No answer.

Passing the nurses station, the surgeon ignored the attention from the staff and slipped into a jog. 'Sir; answer me. Are you still there?'

The phone crackled again, then, 'Sorry. Yes, yes, I'm here. She is breathing.'

'Okay, listen to me. You're doing great. I want you to keep talking to her. Don't let her sleep. Keep her awake till the ambulance arrives. It's on the way. Check your phone's good.'

Crackle.

The surgeon blocked his other ear to drown out extraneous sound. The man on the scene seemed to be taking too long—

'Sir?'

'Yes, I'm here. Battery's good and plenty of signal.'

'Good man. Stay on the line; all right?'

'Yes. I'll stay.'

Paramedic, John Jacobs, switched on a serious face as he bounded out the door at the same moment Andrew reached the ambulance station.

'Hey, doc. Sorry about—'

'What's the status of your patient?' the Surgeon asked over the top of him.

'Lacerations; minor.'

'Stabilised?'

'Yep; he can wait. We can go to your sister first; no problem.'

'Right; let's go.'

'I'm told an *Ambo's* on its way from Marter,' Jacobs said as they broke into a light sprint.

'Correct.'

The two men joined the rest of the crew waiting in the ambulance bay. Within two minutes they were heading out with siren blaring.

The last thing they expected to see was the director running out from the hospital and placing himself in their path, frantically waving his arms.

'Don't stop,' Andrew demanded of the unsettled driver.

Andrew's enraged father stepped out of the way as the baulking ambulance recovered and increased speed. The director formed a fist and threw a punch into the air, 'Keep me informed you little shit,' he yelled over the siren as they sped past.

The ambulance driver glanced at Andrew and shook his head.

Ignoring the disapproval Andrew picked up the conversation with the *Good Samaritan* at the scene.

'She has stopped breathing!' the man announced sounding out of breath.

'Shit,' Andrew cursed, sweeping the phone away from his ear momentarily . . . 'How long?'

'Pardon?'

Panic.

He shouted at the man. 'How long has it been since she stopped breathing?'

'I'm sorry; I'm not used to this—'

'No fucking kidding,' Andrew responded with the phone at arm's length.

The guy still heard him. 'You don't have to swear at me. I'm doing my best.'

Andrew checked his watch.

'Listen to me. I need to know how long it's been since she stopped breathing, please focus—'

'Just now!' he snapped.

The ambulance crew saw the surgeon was losing it. Paramedic John Jacobs decided to pull the reins. 'Ease up, *Doc*—'

Andrew took his advice and backed off. 'I'm sorry. What's your name?' he asked in a more amiable voice . . . *My sister is dying; and I have to act nice?*

'Robert,' the man told him, sounding a little relieved the caller had calmed down.

'*Robert*; my name is Andrew. Listen carefully to me.' He realised his voice was beginning to rise again, and he once again adjusted his tone. 'The girl that's been injured is my sister. Okay, I'm going to tell you how to clear her airway. Do it now Robert. She only has two minutes.' He tapped the face of his watch looking at the paramedic behind the wheel of the ambulance. The driver indicated five minutes with splayed fingers.

Andrew's next instruction was more urgent. 'Robert, place your hand under her neck, carefully lift up a little, until her head is arched back as far as it will go. Do you understand?'

There is dead silence.

'Robert . . .?'

No answer.

Surgeon Andrew Pritchard's expression told the driver they'd lost their man at the scene. Robert was gone.

They were on their own with no time to spare. They would need to hurry if they were to save the Surgeon's Sister.

Montana Pritchard was probably going to die on the very day of her birthday.

As the Pooles' Ambulance pulled in, they noted the accident site looked like any other that they'd attended. Fire trucks, cops with their cars parked at all angles, and of course onlookers held back behind police barricades. This time the Marter Ambulance was on standby, and the bright yellow SES chopper that had settled fifty feet from the wreckage had Paramedics already working on the trapped victim.

Andrew wondered if his man at the scene had been relieved of his duty by these guys, *probably the best thing that could have happened.*

A police officer saw the Pooles ambulance arrive

and shunted members of the public out of the way to wave it in. Andrew left the vehicle before it came to a stop and ran towards what was once Montana's smart little hatchback; now a crumbled wreck.

The sight of it shocked him.

'We need to keep the Doc out of their way,' the ambulance driver warned his fellow officers.

'Roger that,' Paramedic Jacobs agreed as he made his way out the back to take chase.

A second cop that hadn't noticed Andrew alight from the Pools' ambulance saw him running in the direction of the crash site and called out for him to stop.

One of the SES guys looked up and recognised it was the girl's brother that the officer was yelling at.

'Get Pritchard *out'a* here!' he yelled to a paramedic nearby.

Andrew made it past the strong-arm copper, but got bailed up by the SES guy just ten feet from the carnage. Outraged by the interference he threw a wild punch that collected and broke free, rage and fear consuming him.

This sparked action from two cops to rush in and overpower the surgeon.

'Is she breathing!?' Andrew shouted out to the bloodied paramedic attending to Montana.

'Alive and breathing, Doc!' he yelled back. 'Stay away! You don't need to see this right now! We've got the situation in hand!'

The police sensed the *Doc*' as he had been referred to was no threat, and loosened their hold enough to ascertain if he was prepared to behave himself. He eased off struggling and they reacted in kind.

Shock was setting in.

The paramedics from the Pooles ambulance moved in to replace the police, who gladly let them take over.

They walked Andrew to the ambulance and sat him on the access step on the passenger's side.

The SES Paramedic with Montana was battling to fit her with an oxygen mask in the limited space available, her head was sandwiched between the left and right side of the car, her features hardly visible behind the blood.

He couldn't be sure how truly hurt she might be, but her head injuries were substantial—that much he knew; probably fatal.

'All right, she's stable for now!' he shouted, stepping back out of the way. 'All yours, Timmy.'

Timmy—the SES guy holding the massive jaws-of-life, moved in and began prizing the crumpled metal apart.

Montana saw none of this.

The paramedic who had stabilised the victim stood wiping the blood off his hands while talking with one of his fellow officers. They could see the boys from Pooles-Private standing by their ambulance with the victim's brother, who undoubtedly would be suffering from shock.

'Between you and me, Stew,' the other SES man asked, 'do you think she'll make it?'

Stewart looked across at the victim as her head

was slowly being released from the plies-like vice she'd been held in for the past fifteen minutes and said, 'Not a chance.'

CHAPTER TWO
Bad News on Bad

Margaret Pritchard arrived at Pooles Hospital in a complete state of panic.

Her husband Walter had called her with the news while she was at the Gym. She arrived in her leotard with a light cotton skirt over the top. In her mid-forties, a couple of years younger than Walter, she appeared to have worked at keeping herself in shape, but in fact it was the gift of family-genes once again. The Cohens had a long line of *Slimsters*, as her husband jokingly called them.

She was the type of attractive wife a wealthy doctor might expect to have, but of course he carried his own, even without the more-than-comfortable monetary status. Margaret could be described as shapely rather than thin. Like Walter she appeared to be carrying the weight of the world on her shoulders.

It wasn't just the present situation she found herself in that gave her that look, there was more to it than met the eye. On the main she was a glass-half-empty kind of person with a slight nervy edge to her.

All the way to the hospital, Margaret had been expecting the worst; given that she was told her daughter had very serious head injuries. What she didn't expect was to see her husband openly arguing with her son in the hospital corridor, right outside where Montana lay hooked up to tubes and life support.

'Dad, all I'm saying is you could have let me know you called the SES. I had a guy on the line that disappeared right after telling me she'd stopped breathing. I thought I'd arrive to find Montana dead.'

'But you didn't!' the hospital director enforced loudly. 'That should be all that matters!'

Margaret was stunned, unable to comprehend how they could be so disrespectful—

'Stop it!' she had to shout to raise her voice above theirs.

They immediately turned and saw how wild she was. Walter attempted to console her, but she opted to brush past him to look in at Montana, so terribly injured. Her head had been shaved, her skull and face a patchwork of sutures and bruises; testament to what may lie beneath the bed covers.

Her voice quivered when she spoke. 'How badly is she hurt?' she asked her husband with tears welling.

Andrew joined them at the observation window in

time to hear his mother's question. 'I've put her in an induced coma, Mum.'

She looked at him questioningly. 'Will she be all right?'

'If we can get the swelling down in time, she has every chance.' He was doing his best to keep a professional tone, but it wasn't quite working.

'Every chance?' she echoed; 'At what?'

His mother's distressed face stunned him into silence. His father stepped up and answered, 'At life, Margaret.'

She looked past her husband and watched Andrew as he walked over to a chair and sat down with his head in his hands. 'What were you two arguing about?' she asked with her voice lowered.

'Sorry you had to walk in on that.'

She was waiting for an answer . . . '*Well?*'

'My fault–while he was on his way to the scene I called in the SES, but didn't let him know. For ten minutes he thought Montana was without help; without air.'

Margaret could see it was hitting her son hard; Montana and he were good mates–most of the time. She looked back in at Montana lying in the hospital bed.

'What actually happened?'

Disappointment swam over him. 'A truck ran a red light.'

She waited for further information. She could see he was hesitating.

Finally he told her, 'She was texting Meredith

16

Northey.'

Margaret's shoulders sank and she let out a saddened breath, *how often had young people been told not to text while driving?*

Margaret herself had tried to drum it in.

Why would Montana take such a risk?

'How do we know it was Meredith she was texting?'

'Meredith rang Andrew earlier at the hospital, but he was in theatre. She didn't leave a number, so he called Montana. Montana couldn't get Meredith on the line, so she decided to text. The text was half finished, presumably at the moment of impact. Meredith phoned me just after we learnt what had happened.'

Margaret glanced over and considered her son sitting alone, still with his head in his hands.

'He's blaming himself,' she decided.

'You might be right. He's pretty upset.'

Margaret huffed at her husband's comment and walked over to sit with her son.

On the ground floor, Meredith Northey walked up to the nurses desk looking like she was carrying huge bags of blame, like someone had just tore her heart out. She was about the same age as Montana, slightly heavier and shorter by a few inches, which she compensated for with maximum high heels. Her peanut coloured hair and blond fringe was swept to one side.

The colour's probably added a nurse thought as she dutifully looked up.

'Hello, can you tell me where I'll find Director Pritchard?' Meredith inquired of the young girl, 'he's expecting me.'

'Your name?'

'Meredith, *Meredith Northey*.'

'Oh, right,' the nurse said picking up a phone. 'I'll have him come down.'

The director took the vibrating phone from his pocket, answered and listened . . .

'I'll be right down,' he told the caller.

He walked past his wife and son and told them *Meredith had arrived*, and continued on out of sight.

When the Director arrived at the nurse's station, Meredith put her arms around him and gave her condolences. It was right then that the usually unfaltering Walter Pritchard broke down for the first time since the accident. The staff was slightly taken aback at seeing their boss sobbing in the arms of a teenage girl. There were a few frowns from those who didn't know what was going on, but mostly they returned to what they were doing until the couple had left the area. Then it was open-slather. Tongues-wagged and rumours sprang into being.

Walter returned to intensive care with Montana's friend and met up with Margaret and Andrew at the observation window. Meredith was feeling uneasy, unsure about what their reaction would be to her being the recipient of the phone text at the moment of the accident. She began to weep bitterly and Walter wrapped his arms around her, encouraging Margaret and Andrew to do the same. Embraced for several minutes, they all shed some heartfelt tears.

In the hospital coffee shop an hour later, after they'd had time to breath, and to cover all the aspects of the accident, Margaret focused on Meredith's friendship with Montana.

'Meredith,' she hedged, 'I have to ask. Do you know why Montana seemed so out of sorts lately?'

The question unnerved the young woman . . . She was hiding something.

'Meredith?' Walter probed.

Her voice shook. 'I made a promise; not to tell anyone.'

'Meredith,' he repeated, 'you have to tell us everything you know. It might have a bearing on the accident itself.'

Visibly trembling, she gathered herself to answer; 'Montana tried to tell you guys,' she revealed, 'but just couldn't talk about it.'

'Sweetheart, it's okay,' Margaret assured her. 'I'm sure our daughter would want us to know about it now; with what's happened. At least this way she won't have to agonise over telling us later.' *Please god, let there be a later*.

Montana's mother is struggling, Meredith thought. 'I'll tell *you* Mrs. Pritchard,' she agreed taking Margaret's state of mind into consideration. 'I'll leave you to tell the others.'

Margaret got up from the table. 'All right, let's take a walk.' She took Meredith by the arm and began leading her away.

'Margaret; stay,' her husband demanded softly, 'I

think we all need to hear this.'

'Leave it, Dad,' Andrew told him, 'I already know what Montana's secret is—'

'Secret?' Walter barked. 'I take it you mean from Mother and me.'

'I only found out myself an hour ago . . . It showed up on x-rays.'

Margaret's shaking hand rested on her throat. 'Dear Lord, has she got cancer?'

With the pressure suddenly off her, Meredith elected to announce the assumed secret. 'No Mrs. Pritchard, she's pregnant.'

Margaret was about to ask to who, but Andrew was already adding to the story. 'Not just one pregnancy; two—'

'What?' His mother had morphed from shock to profound surprise. Under such dire circumstances, the news was considered to be both good and bad, and Meredith looked just as astonished, confirming she hadn't known her friend was carrying more than one fetus.

'Twins,' Andrew confirmed.

Margaret finally got her question out, directing it at Meredith. 'To who?'

'I have no idea,' she told everyone with a shrug, 'she wouldn't tell me.'

'How far along?' Margaret asked Andrew.

'About a month.'

'About the same time she hasn't been herself,' Margaret mused. At least now there was a reason for Montana's recent sadness. 'Was she seeing anyone?'

The question was directed at Meredith.

'There was one guy, but I'm not sure I should say, he's someone you know.'

'Not an option I'm afraid,' the director told her. 'Please tell us.'

'It's not an issue, Dad,' Andrew reasoned. 'We can't do accurate DNA testing yet anyway.'

Walter dug his heels in. 'Now!' he told Meredith again.

The few awkward glances that bounced around the table projected general discomfort over Walter's bully approach.

'If we can't do DNA testing,' Andrew repeated pushing his point, 'there's no reason to stir the pot.'

His father glared at him.

Heedless, his son said, 'Following DNA we can approach whoever this guy is, see if he matches and take it from there—'

'Brian Appleby!' Meredith cut in.

Walter's expression changed from annoyance to surprise.

Meredith's sudden disclosure effectively ended the dispute cold. 'Look, I need to go okay . . . I'm sorry, but Montana swore me to secrecy. I shouldn't be saying anything.'

This brought the meeting in the coffee shop to an end. Margaret's expression told her husband he'd been rude. His expression was one of acceptance. 'Meredith, I'm sorry,' he called after Montana's friend.

'Forget it,' she told him curtly as she rounded the

exit and left.

'I have to go to the bathroom,' Margaret said as she marched away from the table.

Andrew looked set to leave too, but Walter asked him to stay and talk things over.

With the women now out of ear shot, Andrew said, 'Obviously I wouldn't have done an x-ray if I'd known she was pregnant.'

Walter had relaxed enough to give his son a little credit. 'And you didn't follow protocol because being your sister; you thought you would have known about her being pregnant. I understand.'

Andrew felt bad about the oversight.

'Forget it, Son. We're all under a lot of pressure. We just have to hope, assuming all goes well with Montana, and the babies go full term, there will be no damage done.'

Walter's forgiveness did nothing to alleviate Andrew's gloom. They would both have felt a whole lot gloomier if they'd known Kristen Poole was within earshot the whole time, hidden from sight at the side of a large drink machine. As the name suggests, Poole was the owner of the hospital. A short plump woman in her early fifties, she looked every bit the iron ruler. Her short hair and lack of makeup made her appear slightly masculine; perhaps a deliberate attempt at equality with the male staff, which she definitely had, but not with all. These characteristics intensified her demeanour.

Her attitude to the Pritchard family, although born out of events of the past, would soon be amplified by what the Pritchards would eventually set in motion at her hospital. Montana's Coma was set to become a medical minefield.

CHAPTER THREE
Assessments

Instead of staying at their home in Peachester, Walter and Margaret settled into the director's personal accommodation at the hospital. The small unit consisted of a self-contained kitchen, living area with TV, and one bedroom. Margaret hardly ever slept there, opting to stay by Montana's bedside in the Intensive Care Ward. Long stays by visitors were usually not permitted, but being the wife of the Hospital Director provided special privileges.

Kristen Poole dare not object, unless prepared to face the wrath of Walter. For three days Margaret sat and talked to her daughter as though she could hear every word. An excellent chatter-box at the best of times, she was happy to do all the talking, but would gladly have shut-up if her daughter suddenly came out of her coma and spoke.

On the third day, Walter stood watching from outside the observation window. He was extremely worried for his daughter and his wife; specially his wife. If Montana were to die, he couldn't be sure Margaret would be able to handle it. For that matter, he wasn't sure how he would handle it himself. In the past the Pritchards had not always been the perfect happy family unit. Now they were thrown together for the long haul, a journey that had the potential to either bring them closer, or drive them further apart.

'Dad?'

Walter turned and saw the look on Andrew's face. 'What's wrong?'

'I need to talk to you.'

'Go on.'

'In private.'

Walter took Andrew by the arm and led him away from the window, out of Margaret's line of sight.

'What is it?'

'Montana's head injuries don't look good.'

'Show me,' he instructed as they strode off down the corridor toward the x-ray room.

Andrew spread Montana's film across the light-box for the director's inspection.

'You can see damage to the Skull and cervical are incredibly marked,' he said without needing to point at the damage.

With arms folded his father massaged his chin thoughtfully. 'What else?'

'I'm not done with all the protocols.'

'Have you been able to determine absence of intracerebral filling?'

'No, but that's just one of the obstacles as you can imagine. I've tried EEG, ICU, nuclear-scans, bilateral-absence, plus Doppler ultrasonography. None of the confirmatory tests were reliably conclusive.'

'So brain stem reflexes and apnoea tests are too difficult?'

'Correct.'

'Painful stimuli?'

'No activity.'

Walter shook his head with deep disappointment. 'Are we calling this irreversible-coma yet?'

'My guess—yes,' Andrew sighed, but then added, 'I'm Sorry, Dad. I really think she might already be beyond saving.'

Walter turned to face him and told him solemnly, 'From here on out, any tests you do on Montana are between you and me.'

'Are you sure that's wise?'

'Trust me, just do it. I want no mention of her being brain dead.'

Andrew looked at the ghostly images of his sister, considering if it would be even possible to hide the facts from other doctors, or from the occasional switched-on nurse.

'She's family,' Walter expressed emotionally, 'how we handle her case is our prerogative.'

Andrew knew secrecy would not sit well with the board of directors if they ever found out about it, especially Poole, but he also knew better than to argue with his father when it came to hospital politics.

'Whatever you say, Dad.'

Over the following month, their secret that Montana may already be brain dead, and the fact the paternal father was ostensibly unknown, was successfully kept under wraps. A few of the staff had touched on the subject, but were quickly encouraged to drop their inquiries on the basis of privacy. The quarterly board meeting was due however, and the facts might not be so easily masked.

The board of directors consisted of five people, including Walter and Andrew. The meeting about Montana, which was officially called Case 15-999, was far more personal for father and son than any trauma cases they'd previously dealt with. Andrew was especially stressed given certain statistics were being withheld from the other board members.

Kristen Poole, the only woman on the board and the outright owner of the hospital, would be the hardest to deal with. She had already been in trouble with the medical board however, and felt she was still on some sort of unofficial probation, even though the serious run-in had been more than two years ago.

'Doctor Pritchard,' she said to Andrew seeking confirmation, 'your finding is that the patient has been determined to be, *unresponsive*, is this the best medical description you can come up with at this point?'

Walter elected to answer. '*The patient*,' he said, echoing her insensitive terminology, 'is unable to undergo certification due to the critical level of her cranium and her serious cervical injuries. Or in other words, yes.'

Poole gave the subtlest snarl imaginable and went to say something else—

'Yes, all right Kristen,' the chairman Geoff Lyons interrupted, 'we're not here to discuss Montana's present condition in detail. We're here to nail down legal aspects of the case.' Lyons, a thin little man with a drawn face, grey diminishing hair and blue eyes, looked his age at seventy and had a soft yet strongly commanding voice that claimed attention. His rimless glasses went on and off routinely. The habit of removing his glasses as he made eye contact was his way of saying, you had better listen; I'm not saying this twice.

Poole's power was somewhat watered down when it came to the board, as opposed to her rule over the nurses and doctors.

Lyons looked at his watch. 'Nicholas Hawser, will be here any minute, and I'd like to clear up a few things with Walter before he comes in.'

Kristen tried her best to make a forced smile look genuine as she focused on the director rather than his son, who had mostly been left to answer questions under the watchful eye of his father. 'Sorry Walter,' she said pathetically.

Walter dismissed it with a wave of his hand, and focused back on Lyons to hear what else he had to say.

'We all appreciate that this is a most difficult time for you, Walter,' the chairman told him with the utmost sincerity.

He thanked him with a nod.

'My immediate concern is you and your family, but that doesn't alter the fact there are some extremely taxing questions that must be addressed in relation to your wishes, if the worst were to happen. Complicated by the fact Montana has been carrying not just one, but two fetus, a little over two months in utero.'

Lyons looked around the room. 'We have three lives in our hands people, all balancing on a delicate Legal Line. Not to mention between life and death itself.'

He gave everyone a moment to absorb his words.

'Walter, can I ask; what view of the pregnancies would you and Andrew take if Montana is finally found to be beyond the point of no return; if clinical death is irrefutably confirmed?'

'I would be in favour of saving the babies. After all, they are my grandchildren.'

'Of course; and Margaret would feel the same I assume?'

'We haven't discussed that yet. She's too upset.'

'Understandably,' the chairman agreed once again.

Kristen recovered. 'Have you spoken with the father?'

Andrew shot Walter a glance, wondering if he would mention they don't know for certain who the father is.

Poole hadn't been able to restrain herself since overhearing the Pritchard's conversation in the cafeteria–she had openly admitted to Walter that she had eves dropped–chillingly expressed in a way that was void of apology, or embarrassment. For her the information was fodder to be utilised. 'I understand the pregnancies are illegitimate, how does the father feel about the babies?'

He ignored her. *You know damn well he might not even know they exist.*

He kept his focus on the other board members; he could see the news had rattled them . . . 'The father feels the same as I do.' The lie came out without a flinch, and still without as much as a glance in Poole's direction.

The conversation lulled.

He finally gave in to a quick glance. Her wild expression lingered below the surface, confirming she was feeling deprived of power—

The in-house phone murmured next to Geoff Lyons elbow, interrupting further discussion. 'Yes?' he said with his finger on the PA button.

'Nicholas Hawser is here, Director; will I send him in?'

'Yes, thank you, Mel.'

They all remained silent as they waited for the hospital solicitor to enter from the reception area just outside the room. He knocked and entered carrying a small leather case, which he placed on the table in front of his usual seat.

'Morning gentlemen, - Kristen.' He opened his case and stared in at its contents. He habitually fiddled with a smoke stained moustache that had become misshapen by the life time tick. His physique gave off the appearance of a series of varying size spheres sitting on top of each other, which somehow didn't make him look fat. He had beady eyes that arguably would have looked better behind thick prescription glasses.

The attendees gave their individual responses as they shuffled around to face him.

'Got some reading matter for you,' he said as he walked around the table handing out their personal copies. 'This is stuff I've dug up on the ethics of fetal development in a brain dead mother.'

'My daughter's not brain dead,' Walter told him sharply.

Hawser looked embarrassed as he caught the eye of Burt Simmons, the only board member who hadn't as yet spoken, and ostensibly Howser's hospital liaison. 'I thought this was the information I was asked to provide; was I wrong?'

'No, no,' Simmons advised quickly to alleviate the solicitor's discomfort, 'you're quite right — I do apologise.' He then faced the director to add, 'I'm sorry, Walter, I think someone other than you needs to handle the legal matters, you do understand you're much too close to this one.'

Walter understood there was no beef with Burt Simmons; he was a likable man with a kind face and a shy personality, not the sort to evoke an argument

– so, he kept his focus on the others. 'I'm as close as I can get,' he quantified. 'That's why any decisions made about the condition of my daughter and her babies will be mine.' He studied the somewhat stunned faces. 'I sincerely hope you all have that straight.'

'Having it straight,' the solicitor chipped in as he reached his seat, 'might turn out to be far more complex than the hospital board wants it to be.'

'What's that supposed to mean?' Andrew asked rejoining the conversation.

'It means you better take a good hard look at what I've just given you. That is, unless you want the hospital to face a possible lawsuit.'

'Who's suing? I'm not! None of my family is,' Walter assured them.

'What about the other party?' Poole reminded everybody, trying to sound impartial. 'The father should be brought into this surely.'

There's that bloody question again, Walter thought, absent of an immediate response.

Hawser looked around at the faces. 'Can I go on?'

'Please,' Simmons agreed . . .

'Right; the first point is that there is considerable variation in the laws, not just around the world, but right here, between each and every state.'

He relaxed back in his chair and rattled a case off by heart, concluding with, 'Some states have no relevant legislation at all, while a small number allow women to state positive wishes about pregnancy in their advanced-care-plans. In the case

I've outlined on page one, you'll see that the hospital in question, who believed they were covered legally from all angles, were sued because the father objected to continued life support on the basis that his daughter's advanced wishes were not to sustain life in such circumstance as the one she unwittingly found herself. In other words, being brain dead and carrying a child out of wedlock.'

'Whether my sister is in or out of wedlock should have no bearing,' Andrew snapped locking eyes on the owner of the hospital.

The solicitor gave an equally snappy response. 'I could ask, *is she*, but that would be none of my business.'

'Dead right,' Walter said, weighing back in. 'If all this is too hard for you gentlemen to handle, I may have to make other arrangements for my daughter.'

No one responded, perplexed by Walter's tone. The director stood and made his way to the door to leave.

Kristen Poole didn't miss noticing she had been lumped in with the *Gentlemen* in his concluding comment, yet she was looking somehow pleased at the director's virtual dummy-spit – evidenced by her pencil thin almost undetectable smile.

At the door he turned and took a couple of paces back into the room to present them one last thing to digest. 'Maybe I'll just abort my damned grand-children. End of problem, right?'

Reverse psychology.

Or was it?

Judging by the dumbfounded expressions he received, they all clearly thought he was losing it.

He left, and Andrew hastily followed without adding anything that might inflame the situation more than the burning-house that it already was. He understood the power his father had over every single person left in that room, including hospital solicitor Nicholas Hawser - and hospital owner Kristen Poole.

'I take it that was a bluff,' Andrew suggested to his irate father as they strode back toward intensive care.

'The abortion was; - maybe.'

A chill ran through the young surgeon. 'And *other arrangements?*' Andrew asked with raised concern about his father's intentions.

'Definitely not a bluff, but that can wait till the time's right. Right now my only concern is keeping Montana and the babies alive.'

'What happens when *the time's right?*'

'Like I said—I'll make other arrangements.'

Andrew recognised his father was being evasive, not wanting to involve him in whatever it was he was planning. He decided to put the matter on the back-burner.

Over the next few days, Walter kept away from his usual hospital duties as much as possible. Most of the staff—most of the time—gave him the space he needed. Andrew carried on with his scheduled operations. There was no one else at the hospital that could take care of Trauma Injuries like he could. Margaret remained at Montana's bedside, talking and praying.

Following a gruelling twelve hours in theatre, Andrew came out of the ER still in his coveralls, obviously very tired. An anxious nurse intercepted him and apologised for bailing him up. 'Sorry Doctor, it's Montana,' she warned.

Without a pause, he led the way to intensive care in a rush, his tiredness forgotten. 'What's happened?'

'I think she's lost one of the twins.'

'Has my father been notified?'

'Yes.'

When they arrived in ICU, a very distressed Margaret was standing beside the raised bed with her head on Montana's stomach; sobbing.

Realising the surgeon would want to listen for heart tones, the nurse handed Andrew her stethoscope.

'Take my mother to the waiting room,' he told her.

Hearing his voice, Margaret raised her head to face him. She looked pitiful. 'Andrew, sweetheart, what's going to happen to Montana now?' Her voice was thin and laced with worry.

'Montana's fine, Mum. Actually, this may even strengthen her chances.'

Not a medical diagnosis . . .

'Will the other baby die too?'

'Not if I can help it.'

She gripped his arm as she was being ushered

away by the nurse.

'Give me back Montana,' she pleaded. 'I don't care about the baby.'

His mother's blunt ultimatum shocked him, but he didn't show it, giving her his assurance with a simple nod, at the same time indicating to the nurse she best continue with her task to take his mother out of the room.

After they'd gone, he placed his hand on his sister's abdomen and felt for movement. There wasn't much, but he knew it could only be coming from the remaining embryo, which perhaps now had a better chance at life—at least while Montana lived. He knew losing the remaining twin was of no benefit to Montana herself, but he suggested it anyway for his mother's benefit.

'Is she all right?' Walter asked as he entered.

'No change,' Andrew divulged. He listened with the stethoscope. 'But we've definitely got fetal-demise in one of the twins,' he confirmed handing his father the scope.

Walter had a listen. 'Too early to abort you realise.'

'I'm thinking another month. It should give the viable twin time to mature a little more.'

'Ordinarily,' he agreed, 'we can be thankful their not in the same sac.'

Montana's brother released a gentle breath.

Reaching across and wiping her brow with his hand, Walter suggested, 'It'll all be hypothetical if our girl succumbs to her injuries.'

'A bridge too far, Dad.'

'A bridge perhaps closer than we think,' his father countered. 'Further down the track we may be faced with weighing up the risks involved in a preterm delivery. If the baby puts too much of a strain on Montana, we may even have to consider aborting.'

'That's a hell of a call.'

He sighed and gave it deeper consideration. 'Your right;' He gave his daughter a kiss on the forehead then led Andrew to the foot of the bed. 'Leave it to me to fill your mother in,' he said. 'I'll tell her tonight. If she quizzes you, just tell her the main thing is that Montana is still doing okay. Don't go too deeply into it.'

'I hear you.' Andrew affirmed as they began their exit.

If they had stayed another few seconds, they might have thought twice about what was to be said in front of their so called comatose patient.

Walking out into the corridor they missed seeing the faintest of a flicker in Montana's eyelids; and, a profound movement from within the womb.

CHAPTER FOUR
Coma

For the past month, there had been no change in Montana's condition, except for the fact the deceased fetus was gradually being resorbed, and hopefully would be gone by the time the other twin reached full term. The live fetus had not benefited however, as expected it might, but rather continued to grow weaker by the day.

Margaret's bedside vigil continued. She talked to Montana constantly, forgiving her for not disclosing the pregnancy, forgiving her for everything, for every single little thing that she had ever done wrong in her short life.

'I want you to know, sweetheart,' she continued to say in the usual whisper she had adopted while at her bedside, 'when you get better, things will be different at home, I promise. Your father and I will do better. No more arguments about who's right and who's wrong.' . . . She clasped Montana's hand and pleaded, 'Please know that your father and I love you very much.'

Resting her head onto the bed sheets, she sobbed out the words. 'Please God, bring her back to us.'

She cried convulsively for several minutes—

I'm here Mum . . . Why can't you hear me?

Margaret didn't stir.

Stop crying and listen to me!

Void of the ability to read minds, Margaret was totally incapable of hearing what her comatose daughter was saying.

What she immediately did react to though, was a squeeze from Montana's hand. She jerked her head up from the bed and saw her daughter's sad eyes were wide open, looking straight at her . . .

Relieved, Montana said, 'Thank God, you see me,'

She not only saw her, she *heard* her.

Although Margaret couldn't believe what was happening, she knew damned well there was nothing wrong with her senses. 'Of course I can see you,' she said, puzzled and scared. 'I can see you are awake.'

'No Mum—I'm not.'

Margaret sprang to her feet and stepped back from the bed. 'You're frightening me, Montana,' she warned her daughter. 'What's happening?'

'There's nothing to be afraid of. You're seeing what I'm thinking, not what I'm doing . . . I'm still in my coma, but I can hear every word you say . . . Please tell Andrew my brain is not unresponsive, I know everything that's happening.'

Margaret wanted desperately to understand and believe that her daughter talking to her was real–that this was a wonderful miracle–however, her belief in miracles wasn't enough to dispel the absence of logic.

This is not possible, I must be dreaming.

Another voice emerged from deep inside her mind.

'Mum, wake up—'

Consciousness descended on her as heavily as a crushing cloud.

Her son's image swam to the fore; gently shaking her shoulder.

Tear soaked sheets pressing hard against her face brought her to realize her head lay on the edge of Montana's bed, where she must have fallen asleep while crying.

The dream had been so real . . .

She straightened and faced her daughter, half expecting to see her wide awake, but she lay still - eyes closed, helplessly trapped in her comatose nightmare. Her face remained a pasty grey – her lips, the same pale lifeless hue.

Worried, Andrew asked, 'Are you all right?'

She grabbed his arm. 'Son, promise me you won't turn off her life support after her baby is born.'

He could see the dream had really unsettled her. 'What were you dreaming about?'

She turned back to Montana.

Was I really dreaming? . . .

With eyes fixed on Montana she told him, 'She spoke to me . . . It was so incredibly real I still can't believe it didn't happen.'

Hiding skepticism he asked, 'What did she say to you – in the dream?'

'She said to tell you, her brain is not, un, *un* something.' Margaret was trying to remember the term Montana had used.

'*Unresponsive?*' Andrew cautiously asked with a furrowed brow.

'Yes. That's exactly what she said. She said to tell you she knows everything that's happening around her.'

For Andrew, it was curiously unsettling that his mother would solicit the phrase, *unresponsive*, because he and his father had only ever referred to Montana's condition as being a *coma*.

Tears glistened on Margaret's cheeks. 'Andrew, sweetheart; is it possible you could be wrong?'

He hadn't told his mother that the comatose state was in fact threatening to advance way beyond *unresponsive*, even as far as to perceivably register complete brain dysfunction. He was beginning to wish the truth about her daughter's worsening condition hadn't been kept secret.

For weeks, only Andrew and his father had known about the young woman's demise and they wanted desperately to keep it that way. But little more than a week following Margaret's dream–in spite of their efforts to keep it under wraps–it became common knowledge among those on the hospital board that Montana was brain dead.

Following Kristen Poole's constant badgering, Montana had been deemed brain dead by both the hospital board - and the medical board. Her brain death had been officially confirmed. According to Poole, the process for Brain Death Certification had been carried out to the letter. Her written report stated that *Physical Examination* findings had provided a clear etiology of brain dysfunction. Also, exclusion of Cortical or Brain Stem Function was undeniably found; Neurological Examinations were completed; Brain Stem Function studied; And last but not least, Brain-stem Reflexes came up nil. All this was to have been done behind Walter and his son's back, but they got wind of her plans and ended up joining forces with the other doctors.

None of this could adequately be described to Andrew's mother, but he gave it his best shot, keeping it as simple as he could so that she would understand. He was astounded at how well she took it. He considered her supposed talk with Montana, in her dream, might have skirted all disappointment, raising hope in the face of hopelessness. At the very least, the dream provided her with one final conversation with her beloved daughter. Details of Walter's *other arrangements* still hadn't been mentioned to her.

'Let's put it this way, Mum,' he said with guarded assurance, 'Dad and I haven't given up on the baby.'

Margaret presented no emotion when she heard this.

Although basically pandering to his mother's belief she had spoken for real with Montana, he couldn't shake the feeling his mother aught not to have known of the term, unresponsive . . .

Why would her mind conjure a word that no one had ever used in front of her?

When Walter finally told them what his other arrangements were, Andrew put the subject of Margaret's dream to rest. Knowing the extent of the arrangements was strangely comforting, but not without some mixed feelings.

Over the next six months, Pooles Private Hospital settled down to the routine of watching the fetus growing inside its clinically dead mother; not just a fetus now, but a daughter, granddaughter and niece.

Poole herself kept a beady eye on every procedure that took place, and seemed to spend a lot of time with the hospital solicitor, Nicholas Hawser, presumably passing on the details so they could continually assess the hospital's legal position. The whole time, not one word of compassion from Poole or Hawser about the inevitable death of Montana, had been directed towards the family. This suited Walter; he didn't want anything to do with either of them.

Eventually everyone at the hospital felt that

Montana's condition was irreversible; any thoughts to the contrary were not spoken of. The hospital staff was instructed to continue monitoring her as closely as they did her remaining live fetus. The mechanical ventilator and the other critical Care equipment were the only things keeping mother and baby alive long enough for Montana to reach full term.

Organ donner-ship had been brought up with the family, but rejected on the basis it hadn't been discussed with Montana, her wishes were unknown. Pool believed the family was playing on what the solicitor had told them about a patient's unsolicited wishes, *to deliberately annoy her* she thought, and because they believed body parts might be taken before the machines were turned off.

Policies and practices were also being monitored by the medical board throughout the whole term. Neither Walter nor Andrew could have scratched their noses without it reaching the ears of the authorities. *Life* marched on, while Montana laid waiting for it to end.

Waiting with her for that inevitable day, was Margaret. Her only conciliation in the whole sad affair was the expected birth of her first grandchild, juxtaposed as it was to dealing with the death of her only daughter the same day. It never left Margaret's mind that Montana was somehow inside her lifeless body, trying to escape; trying to communicate. Her dream had helped her hang onto this idea, albeit subservient to the suggestion she may have had a paranormal experience. In fact she harboured the fantasy unashamedly, choosing to believe strange and impossible things sometimes happen for a reason.

In spite of finally being told Montana would never recover, Margaret decided she would continue talking to her daughter, repeating key moments in her short life.

On one occasion she said to Montana, 'When we brought you home, two days after you were born, Andrew was so excited to have a little sister. He was three. We called you Montana, because we were in *Montana* with your father. He was working there as a surgeon at the time. Little did we know Andrew would turn out to be a surgeon as well, he must have got his brains from your father.' She released a light laugh even as her weak smile was fading . . . 'Do you remember the time you fell off your bike? You split your head open and needed some stitches—'

She broke off and sobbed over the memory, placing her hand across the dome that now shaped the bed linin—

Montana's abdomen jumped violently.

Margaret gasped in shock, robbing her of the air to breathe, let alone cry.

She cautiously cast her eyes toward the monitors that were allowing her to witness the activity of the fetus; wriggling about restlessly in unison with the movement beneath her hand.

Is the baby listening . . . ?

The fetus bent its head back as if to look up.

What a strange movement?

Her dream came back to mind. 'Are you really brain dead my sweetheart?' she said out loud to her daughter. Then, against all logic, asked, 'Montana, speak to me again; I will hear you.'

On the ultrasound, the fetus once again looked up*; to the sound of its mother's voice, or mine?*

Excited by this, Margaret tried several more times, waiting for the baby to settle before further testing the miracle. Only once did the baby not respond in the same way as expected. All other times, when Montana was prompted by Margaret, there was a short delay before the image of the fetus would move its head back - as if responding to a voice resonating within the womb.

Am I dreaming again?

She went out to the corridor and was immediately seen and spoken to by a passing nurse. Everything seemed perfectly normal . . .

She returned to Montana's bedside and waited to see if someone came to wake her. An hour went by and no one did. This was either a very long and realistic dream, or what she saw had actually happened. Then, a chill ran through her.

What if I am beginning to hallucinate?

She needed to know. Standing and leaning across the bed, she pressed her cheek against the baby-bump and sang, fighting the tremble in her voice.

Part of her wanted to shout out her experiences. Another part, the part that thought she may be losing her mind, decided to keep the event to herself, and to just sing to her baby daughter and granddaughter.

CHAPTER FIVE
Birth

One month later, the day everyone both dreaded and desired, finally arrived.

It wasn't usual for family members to be present for a caesarean birth, but these were extraordinary circumstances. Not only was the assistant surgeon the patients brother, but her father was the director of the hospital. Margaret could have opted out of watching the operation, but chose to be present.

She cried throughout the whole ordeal.

Andrew came in at the start with the surgeon who was to perform the operation, both dressed in their coveralls and gloves after scrub-up. Most notably amongst other masked faces in the room was Kristen Poole, who said she just wanted to observe, but in effect was there to make sure the Pritchard family didn't break any rules. Little did she know they had already planned to break hospital rules in a bigger way than she could ever have thought possible.

Andrew spoke with his distressed mother before getting right down to business. 'Are you okay if we start, Mum?'

It had taken an hour to calm her to this point.

She nodded, unable to speak.

Earlier, she had been in a real state, demanding that things be done properly, insisting her daughter be given an epidural. Those involved in the procedure knew full well, that in cases where brain dead women are to give birth, it isn't necessary to administer any form of pain suppressant.

The hospital staff couldn't get Margaret to say why she wanted it done, especially given she had been made aware Montana wouldn't feel a thing. She refused to give in; all she would say was—*just do it*.

She remained tightlipped with the staff about her so called paranormal experiences, but Andrew and Walter understood that's what was driving her.

Andrew let her have-her-way, quietly explaining to the anaesthetist that his mother was dangerously stressed and needed to be humoured. Satisfied his mother was reasonably settled, he indicated to the surgeon to go ahead with the caesarean.

Margaret turned away at this point. Walter stayed with her and kept her held close, thankful to have his back turned as well.

Andrew would have preferred to perform the operation himself, but working on family members was generally against most hospital protocols, in

Poole's case it was mandatory – he decided it was the one concession he would allow the woman to have. The designated surgeon, a doctor well known to the family, agreed to respect Mrs. Pritchard's wishes, conscientiously keeping a steady hand as he guided the scalpel along the bikini line, only ever an aesthetic consideration, but for Montana aesthetics were completely uncalled for, except by Margaret.

Margaret's ultimatum, to treat her daughter as a normal non-comatose patient, was partly due to Walter insisting on not turning off the life support immediately after the baby was born. He never made it clear to his distressed wife whether or not he believed there was a spark still glowing inside the mind of his daughter, but he knew she believed it, and that was enough to convince him to proceed with his *other arrangements*.

Walter's arrangements, which had been divulged to Margaret to give her a little peace of mind, were primarily about *time*. His decision to go ahead with his unorthodox tactic—in the face of expected opposition—would be his only chance of allowing his granddaughter to at least become aware of her mother's existence. Maybe even get to know her a little. He, along with his son believed it was worth doing for the child's sake, if not for Margaret as well. But if the plug were to be pulled, it wasn't going to be Poole doing it.

The surgeon reached the end of the incision into the epidermis. The nurse wiped his brow before he began to cut through the dermis, exposing the fat cells below. Careful not to penetrate too deeply—and accidentally cut into the embryonic sack prematurely. He guided the blade with deft hands, ever mindful that Andrew's unborn niece was millimetres away from the blade.

He turned to the nurse and she dutifully cleared away sweat.

Andrew fixed his eyes on what he could see of Montana's lifeless face beneath the ventilator mask. All outward signs indicated she was completely unaware of the drama surrounding her, but he couldn't help wondering if that were true. He was unable to put his mother's beliefs out of his mind. True or false, he hoped Montana wouldn't be feeling any pain . . .

It was time to meet the new arrival. The surgeon felt for the position of the baby, to make sure she was safely cushioned away from the scalpel, and began to cut. The Embryonic fluid seeped from the sack in increasing waves. Now able to reach inside the nine month old abode of the baby, the surgeon motioned for Andrew to make the delivery. Kristen Poole took a step forward as if to object, but got such a look from Andrew that she abandoned her protest.

Andrew gently took hold of the head of the baby and began lifting his niece into the world.

'You two might want to see this,' he called to his parents.

They came to watch; to see the beautiful new life being ceremoniously introduced to them. Margaret broke down at the very moment her son severed the umbilical cord, separating the baby from her mother once and for all. Andrew cradled the infant in his left forearm and applied a quick burst of compressed air against her chest, forcing the child to open her lungs and let out a resounding wail.

'Meet your granddaughter,' he told the proud grandparents with more than a little of his own pride.

As the surgeon began closing up, the family followed Andrew and the baby to an interim crib, whereupon she continued to exercise her lungs. The sight of Montana's little child, alive and well, filled Margaret with immense joy. She looked over her shoulder at her unconscious daughter and spoke to her. 'She's just perfect, Mummy,' then joined the baby in a deep cry that emanated deep from within her soul.

'Take your niece to her mother,' Margaret told Andrew through the tears.

Curious eyes from all the masked faces flashed around the room, but Andrew did as he was asked without question. As he laid the infant across Montana's chest, Kristen Poole shook her head as if wishing to put a stop to the most outrageously useless thing she had ever seen.

Margaret and Walter came to the side of the bed and joined Andrew and the baby in a group cuddle with Montana, rejoicing in the deafening sound of the baby's newfound voice.

The hospital staff set about cleaning up. The baby,

at Walter's request, was assigned to Nurse *Patricia Heath*.

Poole hovered around like a crow waiting for the traffic to clear before moving in to feed on road-kill - to turn off the life support machines. 'Shows over folks!' she called out on top of her voice.

A few attendees blanched to the shrill order.

Walter was a whole lot more countered. He came right up close, invading her personal space, and delivered a resonate message. 'Get out!'

She drew air indignantly. 'I peg your pardon?'

'You heard me. Leave! . . . My family and I would like some privacy to say goodbye to our loved one.' He stared at her until she left the operating room.

'The rest of you,' he said quietly to the theatre staff, 'finish up as quickly as you can.'

This was the director talking. They moved about smartly and were gone inside of two minutes; all except Nurse Heath, who by now had the baby cleaned and wrapped in a cocoon of swaddling. A plump young woman with enormous brown eyes, Patricia was Walter's favourite. Margaret liked her too, which was a key requirement in being chosen to take care of the child. She began gathering up boxes of drugs that had been prepared and placed in a cupboard in preparation for their departure.

Walter's game-plan swung into action.

'You all know what to do,' he told those involved. He was in charge of the mobile ventilator, which would insure the supply of oxygen to Montana's blood;

Margaret took charge of the defibrillator for her heart function; Andrew controlled the hospital bed, which carried all the other paraphernalia such as tubes, lines, drains, catheter bags and a suction pump.

The door to ICU swung open with a crash, and Kristen Poole sprang off a seat in the corridor as she saw the ensemble emerge carrying Montana. Nurse Heath was cradling the crying baby; this incited the fury of the hospital owner more than anything, prompting her to lash out.

'Heath!' she screamed, 'If you help these people I'll see to it you never work in another hospital.'

Patricia ignored her, forcing the irate woman to focus on the Head Surgeon. By the time Poole drew level with the traversing bed, it had already moved halfway toward the elevator.

'What do you think you're doing?' she shouted at the doctor.

'We're taking her out of here. What's it look like.'

'It looks like you're heading the right way to get the sack, director. Don't think that can't happen.'

'Save your breath, Poole. I've already quit.'

'Me too,' Andrew told her as they arrived at the opening doors of the elevator.

'If anything happens to that baby I'll have your head, Pritchard . . . Where the hell do you think you're taking them . . .?'

They were all staring at her blankly as the lift doors began closing. 'That's for us to know, and you to find out,' Walter summarised as they disappeared from sight. The baby's wailing could still be heard coming from inside the elevator shaft, diminishing with each floor that they passed on their way to the ground.

Poole marched straight off to the offices of Burt Simmons and Nick Hawser, to see what could be done to stop this inexcusable affront to hospital authority.

Walter knew, getting Montana out of the hospital without being seen wouldn't be possible, so doing it in plain sight was the only option. He didn't know if he was breaking any laws, but he didn't much care.

Moving patients to other hospitals is a common enough practice, but as they exited the front entrance of the hospital and began transferring Montana to the waiting transport vehicle, a few people nearby were attracted to the sound of the newborn's incessant wailing, who's cries seemed more extreme than one might expect—given the infant was wrapped up so snugly. It was beginning to worry Margaret as well. So much so that she was compelled to mention it. 'I think something's wrong.'

Walter and Andrew were already thinking the same thing. 'She's in pain, Margaret,' Walter confirmed. 'We need to get her to Carmel-Care quickly.'

Although he had the option of taking the baby straight back into the hospital for immediate attention, there was nothing that was going to stop him from extracting his daughter from Pooles

Hospital. He had no interest in a confrontation—which is what would happen if they delayed their departure—and with the baby not well, it had become even more urgent to keep moving. Time was of the essence, but he was comfortable in the fact Carmel Hospital wasn't that far away.

'Is Bruno all set, Tom?' Walter asked the driver as they began manoeuvring the bed into the special vehicle.

'Everything is ready. He knows about the baby.'

'Good.'

'I'll call ahead,' Andrew announced as he put in the number.

The casters slid into the appropriate place, and Tom strapped the whole arrangement down tight, ready for transit. He didn't need to ask why they were so worried about the baby; the infant's distress was indication enough. 'Let's hit the road,' he said as he closed the double doors and rounded the vehicle.

Walter joined him in the front seat of the duel cabin. Margaret and Nurse Heath sat in the back with the baby. Andrew remained at Montana's bedside.

By the time Kristen Poole showed up to put a stop to Walter's plan, along with her solicited entourage of protectors, consisting of Hawser, Simmons and Lyons, the transport vehicle was already making its way along the driveway toward the main gate.

'Daniel,' she barked into her *CBR*. 'This is Kristen Poole - there's a white transport heading your way carrying an unauthorised patient dispatch. Do not let them through.'

Geoff Lyons snatched the handset from her. 'Danny, this's Geoff Lyons. Forget that order. Let them through.'

The look Kristen Poole gave him could have sliced through metal, but Lyons wasn't at all intimidated. He handed her back the hand-set and reentered the hospital, wanting nothing more to do with her protest. Simmons shrugged at her and followed. Infuriated, she had one more thing to say to the man at the gate. 'Did you get the Van's number?'

'Of course,' he responded as though she'd asked a stupid question.

His answer gave her reason to smile. 'This's not the end of it,' she told Hawser as he stepped up beside her.

He knew her reputation for keeping hold of the-tiger's-tail. 'You could be wrong about that,' he told her.

'What?'

'He may have every right to take her.'

'I'll have him disbarred; he's a director of this hospital, resigned or not.'

'No,' the lawyer corrected. 'Right now—he's a father.'

Poole's ego slumped to an almighty low, and she let out a raspy, disappointed groan.

With siren blaring, the transport vehicle travelled out of the city carrying its comatose patient and her sick baby.

They passed through a platitude of outer suburbs to reach Carmel, a small private hospital nestled among rows of family homes. Owned and run by Walter's longtime friends, Doctors Bruno and Carmel Borcheck, the hospital itself was once a home belonging to the Borcheck family.

Bruno, a stout little man with a thin moustache and a Friar Tuck hairdo, seemed to be eternally smiling, even if he'd say he wasn't. His wife Carmel, who the hospital had been named after—at forty six— was half his age and a few inches taller with short black hair.

With polite expertise, she met the ambulance at the entrance and personally ushered the entourage inside. She was already made aware of the added urgency in dealing with Montana's baby. Carmel relieved Margaret of the sick little girl; then whisked the child away to surgery.

The consensus was that she was suffering from a twisted bowel. While hospital staff took care of Montana and Margaret, Walter and Andrew scrubbed up ready to operate. An hour after arriving, full of the expectation they may have to face the worst, Montana's baby was sleeping peacefully; the operation a complete success.

In the following weeks, Montana and her family were given everything they needed to continue with around-the-clock supervision of their patients, available to them until the time came to move on to the next phase of Walter's ultimate plan. Poole's hospital bed and medical equipment was returned by fast delivery the day after Montana was resettled at Carmel-Care. Margaret practically lived by Montana's bedside for two weeks, talking and hoping for another experience that would convince her Montana was still inside. The family stayed together in a small flat provided for them on the hospital grounds. The baby, who Margaret insisted on naming *Monty*, remained under constant intendance in the intensive care ward . . .

'Yours for as long as you need it,' Bruno had told them when they first moved in.

Although they ended up staying for a month, giving time for baby Monty to get better, it wasn't long before a newspaper article appeared on the front page of the Sydney Morning Herald under the headline;

HOSPITAL
DIRECTOR
ABDUCTS
DAUGHTER

'This's Poole's dirty work,' Walter said throwing the newspaper on the table in disgust.

As was often the case, Bruno and Carmel would join their guests at meal time, with perhaps a glass or two of something at night. He even joined them occasionally for breakfast. They were all having breakfast together the morning Walter and Andrew decided Monty was well enough to be moved.

'What happens if Poole causes real trouble for *you*?' Margaret asked their gracious hosts.

In a sense, that had already happened. The press had been circling the hospital since the story broke, but didn't look capable of advancing beyond annoying.

'I don't think she will,' Bruno elected to say. 'If she had the nerve, she would have done so already. And anyway, I can handle Kristen Poole. She's got more to answer for than anyone when it comes to hospital ethics.'

The Pritchards had no doubt that if it came to a war, Bruno would win hands down. Two years ago he had been surreptitiously invited by the prosecution to give evidence against her in the medical board's *Improper Medical Practices Case*, which saw her hospital fined two million dollars. If he had divulged all that he knew about her *tendency to-take-shortcuts*—in relation to *Internal Disease Control*—Pooles Private Hospital would have been closed down; still could be if he chose to make it happen.

'Well, we're leaving,' Walter announced. 'It's time to move Montana to where they'll never find us.'

'Is your place ready?'

'Not quite, but good enough for now.'

'I will make arrangements to get you there without you're being followed. You can set off early in the morning; if you're sure you are ready.'

'Andrew?' Walter inquired of his son.

'Sooner the better; I've just about had a gut full of hospitals.' He glanced at Borcheck apologetically. 'No offence.'

'None taken.'

'Thank you so much Bruno,' Walter told him. 'You're a true friend.'

'I will have the air ambulance ready and waiting at four-am.'

Kristen Poole was feeling excited about the negative response Walter Pritchard was receiving following her newspaper story. She took the trouble to drive out to the director's house in Peachester—a short hop west of Brisbane City—to see some of the action. She came onto the twenty acre property expecting to see reporters swarming everywhere. She wasn't disappointed. That is until she got out of her car and saw the less than happy faces of the press swarming over the lush green lawns like lost sheep.

Making her way up to the house she pushed her way through the crowd gathered near the front entrance and saw the reason why—SOLD!

The massive two story home, with its verandas surrounding both floors, and its huge expanse of land, that had an uninterrupted view of *Glasshouse Mountain* in the distance—had been passed to new owners.

Her fleshy cheeks took on a subtle pink glow.

'Shit,' was all she could think to say when she saw

the revealing sign.

She walked further into the front yard of the property and stopped a reporter who was retreating from having knocked on the door.

'Wasting your time,' he told her, 'they're long gone.'

Her shoulders slumped. '*Shit*,' she repeated.

Poole vetted her anger without restraint. She rang Borcheck to give him an earful for helping the Pritchards to get away, demanding to be told where they had gone to after leaving his hospital. It was quickly apparent he wasn't about to tell her a thing. He had been fully expecting her to call, because once the getaway ambulance had been identified, the Pritchard's first port of call quickly became well known, leading all-and-sundry to focus on Borcheck's hospital. He had no hesitation in telling her to back-off; otherwise she would find herself fronting the tribunal for a second time.

Poole never gave up though; she continued to search for the Pritchard family for months after they disappeared. Her first thought was to contact the new owners in the hope they, or their realtor - *slash – solicitor*, would know where the Pritchards went. The new owners were uncooperative, and extremely Chinese, pretending to not speak good English. The realtor referred her to the solicitor. The solicitor was bound by an affidavit not to divulge any information.

Any normal means would never have allowed her

to find them, Walter had seen to that. First, he opened a new mail box at the Peachester post office and had all mail redirected to another post office. His friend, Doctor Bruno Borcheck, had the mail collected from there, then packaged and sent once a month to the family's new abode.

The parcel was addressed to Patricia Heath, who had become Montana's full-time nurse. Patricia was being paid a thousand dollars a week for her services and her silence; a handsome fee for a nurse. This kind of money was nothing to Walter Pritchard. It was an understatement to say he was well off, given he was actually a billionaire; a billionaire who had no need to continue working at Poole's hospital, or any other. Now of course he had a new job, looking after his family; not the least being one very brain-damaged daughter and her four month old baby. So far they had successfully remained in hiding, once again with Borcheck's help. So long as they kept a low profile, they would never be found.

Margaret's insistence on calling the child Monty, avoided confusion in the house. The little child was in the constant care of Margaret and Nurse Heath. She was a healthy little girl and extremely bright for her young age; she had begun talking at twelve months. At age two, she could carry a normal conversation with a full adult vocabulary, albeit with some limitations in the area of adult subjects; but those kinds of subjects were few and far between while in the toddler's presence. She never questioned why there were no other people about, other than her family. And, she never questioned why her mother, Montana, never woke up - or why she needed so many strange machines attached to her in her bed. For Monty, life went on, albeit draped in the only normality she knew.

There was nothing normal about her mother's life of course. Montana was unofficially being kept clinically alive by her brother and father, away from the prying eyes of the world.

The massive house that Walter had purchased for this secret endeavour, a private acquisition between the Borcheck's and himself, rested on pastoral land a thousand kilometres from their city of Brisbane, well outside a country town called Trundle. The house had five bedrooms, giving each person their own, except for Margaret and Walter who shared the main bedroom. Montana's room was more than a bedroom; it was an entirely self-contained hospital.

Countless tests performed by Andrew and Walter still could not technically conclude that Montana was *totally* brain dead, and time had not given them any proof that she wasn't. They might have, under normal circumstances, switched off all the machines and put her soul to rest, but Margaret's continued insistence that Montana had responded to her in hospital while non-responsive, prevented them from making such a final decision.

It wasn't only what Margaret was telling them, they too had seen what looked like responses for themselves whenever Monty was in the room with

Montana, usually in the presence of Nurse Heath, if not Margaret.

The most profound thing they witnessed was on one of her many chaperoned visits—talking to her mother, just like Margaret would. Baby Monty suddenly said out of the blue, 'Why did you take your eyes off the road, Mummy?'

It was as if she were expecting an answer.

The bizarre comment made everyone question what they thought was going on between the two of them.

That wasn't the only thing; the bigger question was, how did she know to ask the question, when *the cell phone incident* had never been mentioned in front of her—

No one admitted to doing so anyway - when asked . . .

There were many other strange things that took place. One day Monty came to her grandparents and said, 'Do you love Grandma now, Grandpa?'

They both froze on the spot, unable to comprehend such an adult-like question from such a little mind. It was even deeper than that; there was an element of *understanding* in the question. It was as if she knew what had happened years before the accident, before she was even born, at a time when her mother was only ten years old and her parents were having personal problems.

Andrew thought to ask how she knew about his father's extramarital affair, but decided *Maybe that's not what's she's talking about - how could she even understand something like that?* The incident was unsettling in one way, but uplifting in another. Both Andrew and Walter were starting to believe in Margaret's stories of paranormal communication between baby Monty and her so-called *brain dead mother.*

It strengthened their resolve to not give up on Montana.

CHAPTER SIX
Passing

On the day of Monty's third birthday, she had other children in the house for the first time in her life. Margaret had pointed out that sooner or later Monty would have to attend school—would *need* to attend school and meet with other kids her own age—to aid in her development.

Walter finally gave in and invited some close relatives to a party for his granddaughter. They were all sworn to secrecy, including Monty—who had been asked to make believe her mother had passed away—because if outsiders were to know the truth, it would be too upsetting for them, and for her mother, Montana. Nurse Patricia Heath was the only one not invited to the gathering; she was left to stay at Montana's bed-side. Montana's hospital-bedroom remained locked until the party was over and all the guests had left. None of the relatives were aware Monty's mother had been in the house, and they were asked not to talk about the location; due to the unwanted media attention it would bring if found out. They were led to believe Montana had died nearly three years earlier in a very convincing way. A week before the get-together, Walter had erected a lavish fake grave-site with marble headstone and all, right next to the house. Several people had paused there on the way in and offered a moment of prayer.

The epitaph read;

Our Loving Daughter, Montana.
Taken to God Too Soon

Visitors to the house that day amounted to six adults and ten collective children ranging in age from three to thirteen. Monty had a great time; she joined in on the fun and was the most normal Margaret had ever seen her. It was heart lifting to see her concentrating on something other than her sick mother.

At the end of the party, around three in the afternoon, the family stood at the top of the stone stairs that led down to well-kept gardens, waving goodbye to their relatives.

'Bye, Natalie,' Monty shouted as the last carload headed off down the gravel driveway. She looked sad as the cars moved out of sight, toward the main gate a kilometre away.

'Did you have a good time, sweetheart?' Margaret asked.

She didn't respond at first, but then said, 'I want to

go and see Mummy now.'

She'd said it with such chilling conviction that it gave Margaret a fright. Her mood had changed as suddenly as a slamming door in a gust of icy wind. The others noticed the change too. They felt compelled to follow her back inside the house without asking why. Her demeanour was disturbing, delivering unshakable feelings of dread.

Outside Montana's door, Monty waited patiently with the others while Walter knocked.

The door unclipped from the inside and was opened by Nurse Heath. She was a little surprised to see the whole family standing in the hallway, but recovered quickly, beaming at Monty to ask, 'How was the party, darling?'

Monty strolled in without a word, and walked straight to the bedside and stood on the stool that had been placed to allow her to touch and talk with her mother. Looking back over her shoulder at the nurse, who had remained at the open door with the others, she said, 'You didn't need to lock the door, Patsy.' Her indignant tone was startlingly adult. 'It wouldn't have mattered if our friends had seen her,' the little girl added.

Margaret elected to deal with Monty's troubling indignation. 'Why do you say that, sweetheart?' She moved into the room to be at her side.

Monty turned and faced her grandmother so soulfully it rendered Margaret speechless, the little girl's penetrating gaze shifted to the faces of her family, gently moving her eyes from one to the other as they all made their way into the room. A deep fear rose in their hearts. Fear of what might come from her amazing mind next.

She told them, 'Mummy says she wants to die now.'

Mixed emotions spread through the souls of her family, blended with the unequivocal wonder they had become accustomed to.

They all exchanged looks of despair. Margaret, seeing her statue like daughter lying in the bed, the bed she had been in for over three years, imagined letting her die was the right thing to do, even if it had to be without her daughter's expressed wishes. The fact was, Montana's body was slowly failing, and Margaret hadn't made one single connection with her daughter since leaving the hospital. Although, she couldn't be sure something hadn't happened between Montana and Monty. They all knew enough not to dispel the possibility that Montana had spoken to Monty. They'd all seen too much to doubt it.

Walter gently lifted his granddaughter from the step, placing her on the floor. He bent onto his haunches, bringing himself face-to-face with the sweet girl. She reached out and ran her hand across his face to touch his tears.

Walter's voice threatened to destabilise as he asked his little granddaughter, 'How would you feel if that were to happen my darling?'

She softly wiped away his tears with her tiny thumb. 'Don't cry grandpa, she's going to a special place; a place where she'll be very happy.'

Unable to take her advice not to cry, Walter broke down. So did they all, including the usually unruffled Nurse Heath, whose calming eyes failed to hold back the tears. Little Monty studied the sobbing adults and wondered why they couldn't accept her mother's leaving was something to be happy about.

'Everyone is very sad, Mummy,' she told her mother looking back at her. Monty herself joined the others right then, welling up and openly weeping.

'Oh my God,' Margaret breathed, 'look.'

She was pointing at Montana.

Is she crying too?

Teardrops were slowly emerging from eyes cemented shut; the salty beads clinging momentarily, then releasing and rolling reluctantly down Montana's pale, frozen face.

Monty eased away from her grandfather and went back up onto the stool. She reached out and touched her mother's cheek, intercepting the tears, letting them wet her tiny fingers. The warm fluid swept onto her palm. She stared at the meagre pool that shimmered in the glow of the bedside lamp and thought, *the last living thing - from my mother*. She lifted her hand carefully to her mouth, kissed the tears and said, 'She's going now.'

A sudden squeal from Montana's heart monitor startled them at that very instant; the familiar, thin telltale white line accompanying its message—

. . . Montana Pritchard had finally flat-lined . . .

Ravaged by the prolonged time spent on the

machines, her body had given up; her heart, the first to go.

One by one they all drew close to the bed, surrounding Montana with love and loss; consoling little Monty with cuddles.

'Grandad,' Monty sobbed, attracting his attention and looking up at him with her sad little face. 'Now can we use Mummy's grave?'

Walter's body convulsed, finally releasing an uncontrollable, deep grief.

In the bedroom that had been built in the event Montana ever returned to them, she lay in state for three days, giving everyone time to say goodbye; time to at last see her disconnected from cables and tubes.

Resting in peace.

Half way through the first year in the new house, Walter, Andrew and Nurse Heath fully understood this bedroom would probably be her final resting place. In spite of that, they decided that while it was technically possible to keep her clinically alive, it became mandatory for the sake of Monty and her grandmother.

It was hardly ever mentioned to Margaret that Montana's death was becoming increasingly imminent, and in Monty's case, until recently, she had been too young to understand—or so they thought.

Lying in state, Montana looked more like the girl they remembered.

Walter had brought in an undertaker, another close

friend; a friend he could trust to keep silent about their location. He also made sure Montana's death was registered, but obviously refrained from putting an obituary in the newspapers.

On her last day, Monty's mother appeared to be at peace, and vibrantly beautiful.

Yet, it was time to say goodbye . . .

Outside the house at that very moment, Private Detective, Cameron Josey, dressed in white slacks and an open neck shirt, stepped out of his black Plymouth, wiped his brow and placed on a wide brim panama-hat to combat the summer heat. He looked at the massive house and tried to whistle, but his mouth was too dry to create the sound.

'Nice house, *Fredie*,' he said seemingly to himself. Fredie was Josey's constant companion, a conjured memory of a dead colleague. His friend had died while saving Josey's life in a gun battle, years ago, when they were both rookies. Talking to Fredie wasn't a mental disorder, the disembodied entity was simply a metaphysical companion on constant call; someone he could air his thoughts to. In spite of this highly unusual union he remained a *doubting thomas* of all things supernatural.

The first thing Josey saw as he neared the front porch of the house was the lavish memorial nestled in the deep shade of a broad eucalyptus tree, and a 1958 restored Cadillac parked nearby. He took a moment there to cool off, and admire both.

'The headstone answers the first question, Fredie. We've got the right house.'

There was something about the headstone that didn't sit right though. He studied the clean white stone for some time before it hit him. He smiled, realising his second reason for travelling to the property was already half answered by the epitaph on the grave's headstone.

Approaching the front of the house, he thought about what to say to the Pritchard Family when they opened up; assuming they answered the door. He grabbed the lion's head adorning the ornate knocker and gave it three wraps.

The loud clanging resonated throughout the inside of the house, ascending to Montana's room.

'Has someone forgotten something?' Margaret queried with a start.

The way the sound echoed, Josey could tell the foyer was big. He turned away and walked back down the verandah stairs, taking in the corresponding vastness of the property. As far as the eye could see, mounds of grassy hills randomly swayed in a light breeze.

Quite a place—there's money here.

He moved into the shade of the eucalyptus, next to the grave. The beautifully restored Cadillac sat idly out of the sun nearby, *definitely money*.

He couldn't resist a peek inside the pristine vehicle.

Andrew had moved to the window and was peering down at the parked Plymouth below. He quietly told the others, 'We have a visitor.'

Walter and Margaret joined him and looked down

at the car's mystery owner standing by the Cadillac. The uninvited man moved from the grave and walked back to the front door, going out of sight beneath the awning over the long verandah.

'Patsy,' Walter said softly, 'please come down with me and get rid of him - I'll wait in the kitchen.'

Monty ran to the window to see who they were talking about.

'Sweetheart,' Margaret called urgently as she chased after her, 'come back from the window . . .'

Hearing the latch behind him, Josey turned and removed his hat.

Monty's nurse appeared in the open doorway and gave him a cautious greeting. 'Hello. Can I help you?'

Pretty.

He reached out to take her hand. 'I'm, Cameron Josey. You must be, Patricia Heath.'

She visibly balked when he said her name, and withdrew her hand.

Good start.

Ignoring her discomfort Josey told her, 'I'm a friend of Doctor Borcheck's. I was wondering if I might speak with Doctor Pritchard. Do I have the right house?'

Heath would have said *no* straight out, except for Borcheck's name being mentioned. Josey's client Kristen Poole had warned him not to use *her* name. Claiming to be Borcheck's friend was pure pretense, but sure to work.

Patricia heath looked confused, and overly guarded. 'Let me check with the owner,' she finally answered evasively. 'Can you wait here please?'

'No problem,' Josey agreed.

As she started to leave, he forced a deep breath and exhaled heavily through dry puckered lips. 'I don't suppose I could get some water while I'm waiting?'

She turned and began sizing him up, deciding he was the pushy type. *Good-looking though.*

Josey hardly ever promoted the idea he was a private detective, never pushing the fact unless the information promised to bring a desired reaction. He knew in this case it eventually might, but the announcement could wait until he was sure he had found out what he wanted to know. Generally he had a lot going for him when it came to meeting people for the first time. Primarily it was his instant charm, visually aided by a thick crop of pepper grey hair atop a calm friendly face.

Likable.

It was clear he had put her on the spot asking about the Pritchards, but asking for water was such a reasonable request, she could hardly refuse. 'Of course,' she agreed without opening the door any further, 'I'll bring it to you.'

He heard her footsteps receding across a tiled floor, the duration of which confirmed the size of the room. He heard the distant clink of a glass and a running tap filling it. Gently pushing the door further ajar, he took a sneak peek inside. Perhaps he might see someone standing back waiting for him to leave.

No such luck, the foyer and the spiral staircase that

led upstairs were vacant. There was a small door off to the right where the sound was coming from, presumably leading into a kitchen, or perhaps a laundry. He saw reflected light moving about on the shiny floor just outside the entry; projected there by Nurse Heath—not just her; someone else was in there. The shapes came together, settled, and then moved apart. The faint sound of a child's voice drifted down from upstairs, then abruptly stopped; probably not heard in the kitchen over the sound of the running tap.

Josey smiled.

When the running water stopped, the reflections began to change, indicating someone may be about to exit. Josey ducked back outside and waited as the returning footsteps traversed the tiles back to the front door. Patricia appeared with a glass of water and handed it to him. 'I'm afraid the owner says he doesn't wish to speak with you—sorry.'

Bingo.

Josey had his answer. His method was simple. Starting with mentioning Heath's name along with Doctor Borcheck's, indicated to her that he knew the household had an association with Borcheck. The fact she didn't ask who Borcheck was, even after she returned with the water, and after talking to the home owner, proved the owner was indeed Pritchard, but he already knew all that from the headstone. What he was hoping for was to have Walter Pritchard come out and talk with him.

Never mind, I've got what I need.

He calmly drank some water and removed a card from his pocket and handed it to her.

While he drank, he watched with interest as she read his business card.

'You're a Private Investigator,' she observed with a hint of trepidation.

He finished drinking and handed her the glass. 'Ask the *owner* to give me a call if he changes his mind.'

He gave her the perfect smile, put his hat back on and strode out into the sun. Turning back at the bottom of the stairs, he asked, 'By the way, what did they call the little girl?'—*Montana's baby being a girl, he'd got from Poole*—but it was almost common knowledge in the press anyway. He hoped that asking about the girl might get the nurse to blurt out the baby's name - she didn't . . .

'What little girl?'

Her unconvincing tone, plus having heard the little girl's voice upstairs, was further confirmation that the nurse was being evasive on behalf of the family. He showed some teeth, tipped the brim of his hat and left. She watched him walk to his vehicle and get in.

From inside the car Josey surveyed the many windows of the large house, but saw no telltale movement in any of the shades. One thing was for sure though; Nurse Heath was definitely hiding the presence of Montana's child.

And Montana too . . . if the headstone is anything to go by . . .

After the nurse closed the front door to the house, Josey started the car and drove over and parked beside the grave site. The headstone was right outside the car window. He made out like he was reading the inscription, but in fact was adjusting the side mirror to scan the upstairs windows. He waited long enough to rattle any onlookers that might be watching from inside the house. Then a result; an upstairs blind parted and revealed a small girl looking down.

She's roughly three years old; right age to be Montana's baby.

A woman, too far away to identify in the small mirror, appeared for an instant before the blind closed hastily.

She's more than likely the girl's grandmother. The remaining members of the Pritchard family were doubtlessly in that room as well. Josey had in just two weeks, achieved what his client hadn't been able to in three years; found the Pritchards. The means by which he found the house in the first place was in itself cunning—

A tap on his driver's side window startled him. He looked up into the scowling face of a young man in his early twenties—*Uncle Andrew*—Poole had told him he might find the young surgeon with the family.

'Hi,' Josey said with one of his best beams, yet failing to impress.

'My family and I would like you off our property; right now.' He held his stance giving the detective daggers.

Josey understood the family's adherence to privacy, it was well covered in the press, but he was clearly taken aback by the young man's level of anger. 'I'm sorry,' he told him with genuine sincerity. 'I'm not here to hassle.'

'Right, so take your sorry arse elsewhere – you're not welcome.'

The stabbing comment made Josey feel like the sorry arse he'd been called.

Uncle Andrew wasn't finished. 'I'm guessing you're working for Kristen Poole. I know it's not Borcheck; so fuck off and tell the bitch to leave us alone.'

There was no point in arguing with someone so bent on anger. He was feeling bad enough for even accepting the case, let alone sticking around to take further verbal abuse. He had no way of knowing the young fellow's rage stemmed from having watched his sister die in front of him just minutes ago.

Josey put the car into gear and drove gently away, down the long gravel driveway. He watched the massive house grow small in the rearview mirror, knowing full well the sort of panic his visit had whipped up behind its walls. 'Not liking this one, Fredie, something doesn't feel right.'

As he drove away from the house, he quantified in his mind the direction he had chosen to take. Client or not, his opinion of Kristen Poole hadn't been high from the start. When he first met her, she seemed as readable as a book. This assessment was aided by the dossier on her past misdemeanours with the medical board. People he spoke to painted a dim view of her attitude toward Walter Pritchard and his family, an undeserved affront in most people's minds.

Josey drove back to Sydney that same afternoon. He had done what his client asked for, and now needed to report on what he had found.

Throughout the investigation he had kept his cards close to his chest, not disclosing any of the progress he was making. That decision had become his friend, because now he was able to tell her he'd had no success in finding them. She didn't take it well, because she didn't believe him, and gave him his second serve of abuse for the day, which sealed her fate as far as he was concerned. He told her he was through.

She was particularly put out on account of him being the one who came to her in the first place, asking questions about how he could find the Pritchard family. Josey often took on cases with no client attached at the start; particularly if a case was interesting. Poole took advantage of his interest and offered to pay him for his continued search for the illusive family. But then, talks he'd had with people before he took the case suggested she might be out for revenge. He wished he'd listened. Water under the bridge, he never wanted to see her again.

The altercation with Andrew Pritchard had clearly rattled Detective Josey. When he got back to his office around nine that evening, Max could see just how upset it had made him.

She frowned. 'What're you thinking?'

'I'm thinking I might look deeper.'

'I thought you told Poole to stick the case,' she said, at the same time fully aware he had already been investigating the Pritchard's before he went to see the woman. Max knew him well enough to recognize he was stewing over something. 'All right let's have it, what's up?'

Josey took a deep breath as he remembered. 'I feel bad about going out there. There was a bit of a mis-understanding. I need to go back and apologise.'

Max loved her boss for his deep sense of humanity, but wasn't sure he needed to beat himself up over the infamous Pritchards. 'They're not angels, Cam.' She used his first name when conversations verged on getting serious.

'They're not devils either,' he promised. 'They're just people grieving and trying to get on with their lives.'

His emotions were attempting to surface and she could see he had it bad. 'Tell me what happened.'

He snorted, making out like he was trying to clear dry sinuses. 'It was the headstone. It didn't look right.'

'How?'

'Like she wasn't under it.'

'You mean – like she isn't dead.'

He met her eyes and bounced his eyebrows in confirmation.

She looked at him disagreeably . . . 'That's a

disgusting thought if you don't mind me saying, but to counter that scenario, it wouldn't surprise me if their daughter *has been dead* for the past three years. From what I've heard she was just a shell of a girl when she left the hospital. Anyway, what makes *you* think she's still alive?'

Josey reflected on what he saw. 'I didn't pick up on it straight away, but the year on the epitaph didn't match the age of the stonework, it wasn't only that the stone looked brand new, the soil hadn't been disturbed.'

She didn't appear sold on the idea.

'I'm saying,' he said carefully enunciating, 'until I see a death certificate, I'm not convinced she's buried, *there* or anywhere else. I think you'll find she's still in the house hooked to machines.'

She screwed up her face and groaned, 'Well I don't know if that worries *you*, but it sure as hell worries *me*.'

He didn't respond.

Although he was hired to do a job—to find out if Montana Pritchard was dead or alive—he wasn't convinced he had achieved either outcome and wanted to look further into it. It was the key element in the whole investigation, the very thing that had sent his ex-client on the hunt. Now Josey needed to find out if the death certificate had been held up for some reason, perhaps even lost He pulled in a favour from a close friend at Births Deaths and Marriages, and got a breakthrough; albeit the one he had been half expecting. An application did exist. Not only had it not been lost, it had only just been submitted; lodged on the very day he had visited the Pritchard property. The attending doctor was Pritchard's known ally, Bruno Borcheck, one of the names originally supplied by Poole at the beginning of the investigation, and the ploy he had used to try and gain their trust. The news that Montana Pritchard had passed away, on the very day he had visited the property, explained her brother's anger; all the more reason to go back and apologise.

Three days after discovering the death certificate, Josey drove back out to the house believing he would either see Montana's burial taking place beneath the eucalyptus tree – with the empty grave site having been opened up to receive her remains – or arrive before the burial to see the poor woman lying in state. He figured three days after Montana's death was the right timing. His intention was to set things straight with the family and assure them he was no threat; that he had resigned from the case and that their secret was safe with him.

His timing couldn't have been worse.

As he drove up the long driveway—and even before drawing close to the house—he could see just how off kilter his timing was.

'This's unexpected, Fredie,' he breathed.

He drove right on up to where Montana's memorial had stood, just three days ago. He got out of the car and walked to the edge of the only remaining evidence that the monument had ever been there. Lack of damage caused by the removal of the headstone, and no sign of a hole ever having been dug, confirmed Montana was not buried there. Perhaps that was never the intention. There was no doubt she had died, and recently. This could only mean they had taken the body with them. Something he wouldn't be telling anyone.

What now?

Josey looked up at the house. It was clearly abandoned. Blinds were gone. A few pot plants from the verandah were missing.

Yes, his first visit had definitely given them reason enough to panic. It made him feel bad all over again, but he couldn't have been more pleased that Poole would no longer be disrupting the lives of the evacuees with her vicious vendetta. He wished them all the luck in the world, a world without people like Kristen Poole. A world he wished for himself. Unfortunately, he wasn't to know—as much as he wished for it—he hadn't seen the last of her.

From a concealed position outside the property, Kristen Poole watched Josey drive away. Once he was out of sight, she drove in through the gate and up towards the house, stopping at the site of the missing monument.

CHAPTER SEVEN
The Applebys

In spite of Josey's feelings about Kristen Poole, the annoyingly impervious woman still wanted the PI to carry on locating the Pritchard family. She even offered to double his fee, calling him at his Sydney office to make the offer—less than a week later—as though nothing had happened.

He once again declined, saying he had no further interest in the case.

The next day, a defamatory story appeared on the front page of the Herald;

> An anonymous source claims to have evidence that Doctor Pritchard and his illusive family have engaged in the mistreatment of Montana Pritchard's corpse in their home.

The journalist, Lara Lord, offers a personal opinion by stating that;

> Montana's three year old, the baby who survived in the womb of her clinically dead mother, was being allowed to witness this inappropriate behaviour.

She has to be guessing, Josey thought.

> The reliable source claims to have seen evidence of a fake grave for the doctor's daughter, and believes the family may now be transporting her corpse to a new location.

Bloody Poole has been out to the property, Josey thought. *She's creative, if not deranged.*

> Some people in the community, the source claims, have been aiding and abetting the family under the misguided belief they are doing nothing wrong.
>
> A Sydney based private detective, according to our source, located the Pritchard Family, but refuses to disclose their whereabouts.
>
> The Police are currently seeking to talk with the detective regarding his silence.

Bull-shit!
If Poole intended to disclose his identity she would have gone to the police, not the press. She obviously

already knew the location but made no mention of it.

To continue with the case, which was opposed to what he'd told Pool, Josey had just three names to work with. Meredith Northey, the best friend; Patricia Heath, the private nurse; and Brian Appleby, the young man reported to be the possible father to Montana's child. He thought he would start with Appleby—if he could find him.

It turned out to be easy. Well, it might not have been if young Appleby hadn't still lived with his parents and be blessed with the same Christian name as his father. Only one Brian Appleby appeared in the local phone book. He called believing it might be young Brian himself, but got Brian's father, who seemed keen to talk - *really keen.*

Appleby and Josey came onto the porch at the back of the house, whereupon Brian Senior announced the detective's arrival. The two siblings in the pool stopped what they were doing and gave him a jovial welcome. Their mother didn't even lift her head from the couch she was sprawled along.

'They've had a few,' Appleby explained.

Josey grinned, *Good, loose tongues.*

He introduced his wife as *Bev*, his daughter as *Ash*; and son *Brian*, who they chose to call *Bee* to avoid confusion. In spite of her age, Bev still fitted into a bikini as well as any teenager. When she looked up at him, Josey thought her natural attributes may be invoking a superiority complex, evidenced by her contemptuous expression. He warmed her beyond freezing with one of his smiles. Ash was thirteen and came across as shy. Bee looked the right age at least; he could easily be the little girl's father, as had been suggested.

Josey and Appleby senior got through each other's compendium for the agreed meeting and settled into personal details fairly quickly. Josey expanded on what he had said on the phone, explaining he no longer worked for Kristen Poole, however remained on the case trying to relocate the Pritchard family. He didn't explain why, and they didn't ask. Josey already knew from the phone conversation that Appleby was keen to talk, but didn't quite pick up on his anger until fifteen minutes into the pool-side meeting.

Josey noticed Mrs. Appleby was taking glances at him from beneath her wide brimmed beachside hat;

Concentrate.

'I couldn't be less impressed with Pritchard,' Appleby told Josey, bringing him back into focus, 'his pompous wife rang me out of the blue and wanted to know if my son ever had sex with her daughter. I mean, that's how the bitch put it.'

Without wishing to add salt to the wound, Josey simply asked, '*Has* he?'

That got a sharp look from Mum.

'Bee!' Appleby suddenly yelled to his son. 'Get your butt over here!'

Junior, who was now twenty-something, stopped wrestling with his younger sister and came to heel, immediately making his way out of the water. Looking at the strapping young man launching himself from the pool, it wasn't hard to imagine him falling from grace when he was eighteen. The trim young man scooped up a heaped towel from the deck, wrapped it around his waist and walked over to take up the wicker chair next to his father. His mother was watching her son with a strange sort of anti-pride. Perhaps it was what she was drinking; something that looked like water.

Probably straight Vodka.

She looked away, but was well within earshot.

'Tell Detective Josey what happened,' Dad told his son.

Bee, as he had been called, shuffled on the edge of the chair and clasped his hands. He lumbered into the story like the telling of it was wearing thin. 'We only did it the once,' he revealed sounding surprised. 'To be honest with you, I still can't believe it's that easy.'

Josey caught Mum rolling her eyes. 'A common mistake,' he said to her son.

'Do you know if the kid's mine?'

'I don't. I'm guessing neither do you.'

'I didn't even know she'd had a baby till I heard about the accident.'

'How long after?'

'At least ten months.'

Josey suspected the Applebys may not know the full story. 'Montana conceived two girls in case you hadn't heard, but only one survived.'

'We know that much,' Bev piped up in the background, unimpressed.

'Right,' Josey said sounding slightly chastised.

Beverly wasn't done. 'After her snooty mother finished accusing our son of rape, based on I might add, her self-righteous belief her precious bloody daughter wouldn't have spread her legs willingly, she went *on-and-on* about their little bastard, Monty this - Monty that, like I cared.'

Mum's a piece of work, but at least now I've got the baby's name; *Monty . . . Cute.*

Josey asked Bee, 'Would it worry you if she was yours?'

Bee relaxed into a frown. 'Wouldn't mind seeing her, I guess.'

Bev groaned and sank beneath the rim of her hat.

'Hold your horses right there,' Dad trumpeted at all and sundry. 'We don't know the kid's his yet. And until Pritchard sticks his head up, we'll never get the chance to find out.'

Bee shook his head at his father's lack of tact. 'Yeah okay, Dad.'

Josey wasn't at all disinterested in the boy's plight, but he was primarily concerned with finding out if they knew anything that could help him find the Pritchard's whereabouts.

'So you've had no contact with the family other than that one call from Mrs. Pritchard,' Josey reiterated, looking from father to son—ignoring Mum.

'Nothing,' Dad confirmed in disgust. 'We deserve

to know if our boy is the father or not; don't you think, Detective?'

'No argument, but hopefully once I find them and explain a few things they'll see that point too.'

'I'm not so bloody sure they will. They've got plenty of reason to keep their heads low over that disgraceful business with their dead daughter. Doctors or not, those two blokes should be locked up.'

Poole's cancer spreads.

'Ease up, Dad,' Bee protested with strength enough to shut his father up. His father had completely missed the point. If paternity lay with his son, the Pritchard's *dead daughter* was the mother of Bee's living daughter–*a granddaughter*. It was an ill thought-out comment that could in time come back to bite-him.

This wasn't getting Josey anywhere. He told the kid. 'I make no judgments. I can't say how they'll react when I find them, but I'll do my best to swing them around.'

Josey focused on the father and gave him the facts. 'You need to understand they aren't in any trouble with the police. Don't believe everything you read. If I'm to connect you with them, I want a promise you'll be civil; for your son's sake.'

Brian senior looked at his son and got a *told you so* expression.

'One thing before I head off. Have you had any contact with Montana's friend Meredith?'

'No,' Dad answered, 'not since she called us about

the accident. Don't ask us where she is, we haven't been able to reach her since.'

Josey decided he had all he was going to get from the Appleby's. He wrapped up the meeting and said his goodbyes to the kids and Bev.

As Appleby showed Josey out, he offered the detective a guarantee he would restrain his feelings toward the Pritchards if contact were achieved. 'Bev didn't want to talk to you about all this, but I'm not one to bury my head. I think you get that.'

Josey made no promises about his success in finding the Pritchards, except to say he would be in touch, one way or the other.

Next on the list was Patricia Heath, who he assumed would be almost impossible to find if she was still in Walter's employ.

Her status with the family may have changed; she may or may not still be with them.

Either way, she had disappeared as effectively as the Pritchards. He conducted a search to find out if she showed up among registered nurses, but had no joy.

Meredith Northey was a dead-end too. He found her parents, but they had been instructed not to divulge her whereabouts; a total dead end. He had no further contacts or clues where to look next.

In an intense month of searching through data bases, police-reports, overseas departure records, christenings, hospital admissions; not one piece of information was found. But finding the Pritchards, although forced to the back-burner, definitely wasn't forgotten.

Sitting at his desk in his city office, Josey was still going over the investigation in his mind to make sure he had covered every angle.

Maxine brought him a cup of tea and deliberately placed it on the desk in front of him. 'What's got you so engrossed?'

'The Pritchard case,' he admitted sheepishly.

Max, as he called her, told him she didn't think the case was worth proceeding with. His thirty year old assistant was more of a partner than an office assistant. She spent quite a lot of her time in the field doing reconnaissance and interviews if Josey needed two hands on the job. Her *Glam* Punk look, which was a complete antipode to his casual style, was what he liked about her. He liked her for a lot of reasons; for instance, when not to disturb him; this was one of those times.

She persisted however, as she always did. 'I know you enjoy working for nothing,' she told him with good humoured sarcasm, 'but, for what it's worth, my advice is throw it in the bin with the other hot potatoes.'

A professed Punk, Maxine had once explained to her boss why she liked the crazy outfits. *It makes me feel free*, she told him. He didn't mind her appearance; she was a good worker, and smart. Smart enough not to put tattoos all over her body, or metal pins pierced through various parts of her exposed flesh—he was thankful for that—she added colour to the office. Today she had swept back hair, red in front, blond at the back, pink bra strap showing under a luminescent blue top; tartan short skirt; black net stockings and red lace up boots. The ensemble was topped off with lightning bolt earrings and a thick studded black leather belt.

She released an exasperated breath, again offering her contemptuous attitude toward the Pritchards.

It was a complete waste of time.

Max left him to keep pondering the case. She knew that he wouldn't take her advice, but sensed all the concentration in the world was never going to find the Pritchards.

Little more than a month and a half following his resignation from working for Poole, Josey had to accept the case had gone stone cold.

Although the Pritchard family seemed to have disappeared from the face of the earth, Josey held the faith; believing they would surface when least expected.

He couldn't have been more spot-on, and couldn't have known how long it would be before that finally happened.

CHAPTER EIGHT
Josey

By the time the Pritchard Case again saw the light of day and with any chance of a resurrection, fifteen years had rolled by.

For Cameron Josey, hardly a day was spent not thinking about it. It even remained on his mind during another of those dead end cases, which – in his own idiosyncratic style – he had labeled *The Immortality Connection*. A solution to that case was still pending.

He liked unusual cases, paranormal cases that he would attempt to prove were bunkum. As far as he was aware the Pritchard case was outside the unusual *so far*, and still to be labeled, and still on his mind.

Maxine recognised this wasn't a good time to interrupt him, but it wasn't about to stop her. What she needed to tell him was far too important to wait. The paranormal aspect of the Pritchard case was about to be unearthed.

'Here's a blast from the past that should get your heart pumping,' she announced as she bounced in back from lunch.

Fifteen years hadn't aged his offsider much. Her clothing had toned down to become a little less eye-popping. Josey had developed a little more grey hair, more salt than pepper.

She's got my attention, he thought as she stood in the doorway to his office, *what the hell is she waiting for?*

'You've had a call from *Meredith Northey*,' she told him, emphasising the name as though it belonged to some sort of celebrity. 'She called my mobile while I was out.' Max only ever carried a phone pertaining to the office during working hours.

Josey straightened in his seat like he'd been handed a lost Lotto ticket.

'Ah, that's got you excited,' she observed with a toothy grin. She rattled off the phone number while Josey jotted it down. 'This's good news, Chief.'

'You're dead-right, Maxie.'—He began dialling out.

'Good,' she pinched out in a falsetto voice, looking happy that he was happy. She left him to make his call.

She came on the line.

'Meredith, Cameron Josey here. I've been looking for you on and off, we need to talk.'

'Yes we do,' she agreed, 'and by the sound of it you already know who I am.'

'Indeed I do; Montana Pritchard's best friend, right?'

'Not enough to save her sad to say.' She sounded distressed, even now.

'How did you get onto me? Did you know I was looking for you?'

'I've known for years. I first learnt you were looking for me from Brian Appleby's son.'

Back in touch, Josey imagined.

'I gather you know he's been labeled with paternity,' she said.

'I do.'

'They also told me you were searching for the family back then. Are you still?'

'Please tell me you know where they are?'

'I'm afraid I don't. I'm looking for them myself.'

Josey's excitement waned. 'Go on—I figure you have *something* to tell me.'

He could hear her breathing, *thinking.*

'You know about her daughter, right,' she said in a long breath.

'Montana's daughter, Monty, yes; She'd be about seventeen or eighteen by now wouldn't she?'

Without disputing it she said, 'She's done a runner from the family.'

An unnatural pause followed her information, like she was still thinking. 'I could ask why,' Josey prompted, 'and how you know, but I guess you're about to tell me.'

She let out a breath. 'I warn you, Detective, this is a strange story.'

Josey's excitement recovered. 'I like strange.'

'A little scary too, I need your help, Detective. Can you help me find her?'

'I gave that up once, but when do I start?' He knew she was calling from a Sydney number. 'Give me an address and I'll be there in half an hour.'

She didn't argue.

On the way out of the office to meet Northey, he asked Maxine to defrost the file and get the paperwork started. They were not only back on the case after fifteen long years, but presumably back on the payroll, albeit a different client.

A decade and a half isn't all that long to wait for remuneration he supposed.

The address Meredith gave him turned out to be her home address, a comfortable city apartment on the twenty fifth floor of a harbour-side high-rise overlooking the white sails of the Opera House.

Meredith was now thirty three, the same age Monty's mother would have been. She was one of those girls with character in her face. *A girl* she was to someone Josey's age, now pushing beyond fifty, a girl who either wore no makeup, or used something that made it look like she didn't.

Not that Josey would know, but compared to eighteen years ago she was leaning toward pleasantly plump, making her face look rounder, softer, but still fetching in her own way. Her hair was fashioned into something more conservative in style, and just one colour, essentially her own. Without hindsight, none of how she once looked mattered to Josey, he only saw her in a fresh new light, a person with a refreshing personality.

Her knock-about attire on this particular day consisted of blue-denim shorts and a light green blouse—the exposed tail covering a well-rounded posterior. Opting to get around in bare feet, her thin strapped sandals sat on the floor near a chair where she had slipped them off.

Josey knew from the outset her story would be without an ending, - incomplete.

Otherwise she wouldn't be asking for my help.

His host let out her yarn a little at a time . . .

Her exposé began as they moved through the unit's large living area. Apart from a framed photo montage she'd left resting against the wall on the floor, there were no other pictures or paintings.

She noticed Josey looking at it and explained the montage was of herself with Montana when they were youngsters; growing up together.

'I haven't had time to hang it,' she told him. 'It's interesting you noticed it, because it's part of the story I have to tell you.'

This information brought Josey to more closely study it. Each photo seemed to already be telling stories; simple stories of family.

She furthered her warning to the detective, telling him that what she was about to say, would not compare with the innocence of the childhood photographs.

Her story had a bizarre depth to it, a disturbing hidden visage relating to Montana Pritchard's daughter, Monty. The Monty subject *would have to wait*, she told him, to allow her time to warm up to telling it. 'It's a bit of a long story, why don't we have some lunch first.'

A cliff hanger he thought.

They sat on the deck in the shade and spoke over a light meal designed to impress, and a chilled bottle of chardonnay designed to relax—enough to use first names. Josey requested she call him Cam.

As promised, the Monty story was put aside until lunch was finished and the wine consumed.

'A few weeks ago, in the Mall where I shop, I really thought I'd seen a ghost. A ghost in the identical form of my friend Montana. . . . It wasn't Montana obviously; it was her daughter Monty. Had to be, right? I can't emphasise the word *identical* enough. She looked exactly like I remember Montana, just before her accident. As you rightly guessed, aged around eighteen . . . This - *look-alike*, was with a guy.'

Josey was hooked; this was shaping into his kind of story. He listened, and hoped her account might already be heading toward finding the Pritchards. Instead, he was soon to learn the telling of the story would unequivocally deepen the case; take it well into the realm of the paranormal; just like she'd told him on the phone. 'I was at the mall to buy a coat, but the smell of freshly ground coffee drew me to the closest café . . .'

Meredith weaves her way through the tables looking for a place to sit, and suddenly sees her . . .

'I thought, oh my God, no, it can't be—but there she was – the spitting image of my friend, Montana Pritchard. Dead eighteen years.

The man with her looked like a close friend—a very close friend.'

His hands are clasped over hers and he's smiling.

Bristling.

She's like a purring cat in his grip.

In appearance they are chalk and cheese. She with her clear skin – and he with multiple *tats* devouring his biceps.

Meredith starts towards the table they're seated at, but stops cold - reconsidering her decision to approach.

Bugger-it, I have to know she decides.

She takes six more steps and stands right there beside their table. She wants to say, *Montana, is that you?* But that feels stupid. Instead she simply says *hello.*

The girl looks up, studies Meredith's face; thinks for a moment . . . creases her brow, then, 'I know you,' she says, wiping away the frown. 'Where do I know you from?'

The boyfriend suddenly seems anxious. 'Maybe we should go,' he tells his partner.

'Meredith!' the dead-ringer announces ignoring

her boyfriend's warning to leave. 'Meredith Northey, *right?*'

'Montana?' It's what Meredith wanted to ask from the moment she saw her, even though she knows this can't be the friend who came close to death in a car accident eighteen years ago - a friend who slipped into a coma and . . .

'And that was it,' she told Josey finalising the first part of her story. 'They were gone, just like that. My mentioning Montana's name changed everything. The pair of them shot up from the table and ran from the cafe like hell.'

'So, you feel certain this young woman was Monty, the daughter.'

'It's the only thing that makes any sense. She was much too alike to be anyone else. And why would they run, if not to hide the fact. Not that I understand that either.'

'Good point. But how and why would she recognise someone she's never even met?'

'I have a bit of an answer, but it doesn't come close to explaining why she ran away.'

'Okay,' he said realising there was a lot more to tell. He nestled back and said, 'I'd better let you carry on with the rest of the story. You still haven't told me how you know she was running away from the family.'

She gave a momentary smile that seemed to be hiding some sort of dread. 'This next part is the scary bit.'

Josey looked like an animal frozen in the beam of approaching lights.

'Sorry, Cam; I don't mean to get your hopes up about finding the Pritchards, I just desperately need someone to share this with. I'm still traumatised to tell you the truth.'

Josey leaned across and touched her arm. 'Hey. I'm here to help. Just tell me what happened.'

She took a calming breath and continued. 'I racked my brains trying to figure out how to find her again. I hung around the café. I went to bowling alleys, theatres, bars, you name it; then, I'm walking to work in Paddington, when I see the boyfriend come out of a shop right in front of me and climb onto a motorcycle he'd parked in the curb . . .'

With his back turned, it seems to her that he's taking his time fiddling with his helmet. She wants to walk straight up and talk to him, but hesitates; maybe he's waiting for someone – perhaps he's waiting for her.

Her guesses amount to nothing when he suddenly fits into his helmet and gloves ready to leave.

He's already kick starting the bike – she's craning her neck looking for a way to follow.

An empty cab practically runs her down as she steps off the curb. He's giving her the evil eye until she becomes his passenger, sliding into the back seat.

The bike leaves the curb and does a U-turn in front of them.

'Where're we going today?' The cabbie asks.

'Turn around here!'

He checks his mirror and abides. She's in a bit of a mood he decides, which might explain her lack of concentration.

The bike ahead goes three blocks and makes a right.

'Turn right.'

He twigs. 'Are we following the bike?'

'Yes we are.'

They don't go far before the motorcycle turns into the driveway of a house and goes out of sight.

'Pull up here,' she tells the cabbie.

The driver pulls the cab up in front of the house next door to where the bike went in. He looks to her in the back seat

'I'd like to sit for a while if that's okay.'

His indifferent gesture indicates it is . . .

'So I sat there with the meter running trying to figure out what to do next. Ten minutes later some people arrived at the house and I chickened out. I took the cab back to the apartment.'

Josey had to assume her story was leading up to something that was making her feel uncomfortable; she'd paused again to gather her thoughts.

'That night I couldn't sleep,' she continued. 'I kept thinking will I go back – knock on the door, ask him where I can find the girl. I thought, what's the worst that can happen - have the door slammed in my face? The next day, I decided to bight the bullet.' Meredith hesitated, she appeared really rattled. 'When I got there, I found the door partly open . . .'

Meredith gently pushes on the door, opening it just enough to enter. The way the furniture is shoved all around, indicates there must have been some sort of scuffle. She is about to turn and leave when she notices a man's legs nudging out from behind a lounge; no shoes, long jeans.

She makes it to the door to leave, but on seeing a neighbour coming out of a house across the road, decides to duck back inside and wait. A stain glass panel allows her to look through to the outside. The man exiting the house has met up with a neighbor at the front fence and the two of them look like settling in for a chat.

She looked back at the man on the floor. *I've come this far; might as well use my time to find out if it's him*, she sort of expects it will be; *the guy on the motorbike, the boyfriend.*

Rounding the legs in a cautious arc to see why he's lying there, and then seeing him imbedded in a pool of blood with eyes staring, she's again having second thoughts about staying. Even up close she can't tell if he is dead or alive. *Is it even the biker?*

She suddenly thinks, *what if the killer is still here – or maybe it's not the biker and the biker is the killer.*

It frightens her and the instinct to leave returns. But before she can make her move the victim on the floor releases a desperate groan.

Not dead!

'Help me,' he pleads, his voice muffled into the carpet.

Undecided, she wants to leave, but caves in to a

wave of guilt that forces her to stay.

Without moving *too* close to the critically injured man, she nervously asks, 'Is the person who did this still here?'

He doesn't respond, so she moves around to where she can see his face–to where he can see her for the first time since she came in. His face is so covered in blood she still can't tell if it's him. The tattoos on his arms suggest it probably is – as far as she knows it is his house.

She puts her cell to her ear, but changes her mind and uses the house phone instead. 'I'm calling an ambulance,' she assures him.

He recognises her voice and blinks away blood to bring her into focus. 'It's, you – from, the café.'

His knowing her confirms it's the biker.

'Emergency Service,' a voice crackles in her year, 'what is your address please?'

'Um, I'm afraid I don't live here,' she stutters. 'Sorry, Paddington. Wright Street. Wait.' She leans down close to the almost unrecognisable bleeding biker. 'What number is this place?'

'Are you there Mam?' the female operator asks urgently.

'Yes, I'm trying to get the number from the man who's hurt.'

'Two . . . five . . . Four,' he gargles through the blood.

'Two-five-four,' she repeats.

'What's the nature of,' —

She hangs up, figuring she has maybe ten minutes to

get out. 'I know you're hurt,' she tells the biker, 'The ambulance will be here soon.'

'Monty,' he says through a spurt of blood, 'you have to . . . help her . . . shhhe's, run, run-away . . . in danger . . . s-some, someone, is trying . . . to . . . kill her.'

The biker is close to passing out and he may be her only chance of finding out where the girl is. She doesn't dare touch him, wondering how much forensic evidence she's already left in the place. 'Please – do you know where I can find her?' She feels heartless asking.

'*Boook* . . .' he slurs as he strains to lift his head and point with his eyes.

There's a bookcase in his line of sight, a few feet away, with roughly fifty books to choose from, but one catches her eye even before she makes the move to investigate, *a diary*. On closer inspection she notes its worn cover has Monty's name embossed on it. She picks it up and flicks through the pages, running her hand across the neat, handwritten text.

'This's coming with me!' she tells herself with guilty excitement.

As she is about to leave, a framed photo montage of the Pritchards catches her eye, which includes pictures of herself with Montana when they were kids. Pictures that could lead back to her. She doesn't want to have to explain to police about the crime scene and what she is doing there.

At the risk of disturbing the place any further, she puts the frame under her arm, leaving a telltale patch on the wall where the picture stood.

On her way to the door she pauses near the injured boyfriend. 'I'm sorry, I can't stay,' she apologises. 'Hold on okay. Help's coming.'

A siren can be heard in the distance.

That was fast, time to leave.

A quick glance through the stain glass panel at the front door tells her the chatting neighbours have gone and no one else seems to be about. Safe to move, she opens up and steps out, walking away from the house as casually as she can muster . . .

'Correct me if I'm wrong,' Josey prompted, 'but it sounds like you're describing a murder reported a couple of days ago . . . *Somebody Kelly.*'

'Alan Kelly, yes.'

'Going back to the Pritchard girl for a second, her knowing your name definitely proves she knew you by sight. It's possible she may have seen a recent picture; been told who you were.'

She looked at the photo montage leaning against the wall. 'I've changed a lot in eighteen years. Apart from those few photos, I don't recall any being taken that anyone would have.'

Josey twigged to how she got the pictures. 'That's what you took from the apartment.'

Meredith nodded as she reached into her purse and took out the diary she'd found in the bookcase, 'And this.'—

'So, there are two questions,' Josey summarised, 'How did she know who you were? And what made her run?'

'Read her diary!' she said, handing him the book.

Josey could hardly wait to do just that.

'Maybe you might see something that will answer your questions, I couldn't.'

Monty's personal diary became an invaluable find, one that Meredith had already read; and—as his new client had said—*strange, very strange.*

Monty Pritchard's handwritten diary insofar as getting into the troubled minds of both mother and daughter was bizarre; *And amazingly written.*

There was something very wrong about reading someone else's diary unsolicited, not to mention the illegal act of removing evidence.

In the interests of solving this case, it was imperative he protect her and the Pritchard family from being connected with the biker, Alan Kelly, whose name they got from news reports.

The police didn't need to know just yet that Kelly had died as a result of his association with Doctor Walter Pritchard's granddaughter.

Meredith had become very upset after hearing the young man had died, and she told Josey she planned to distance herself while he took time to read the diary. She was unable to stop thinking about that moment when Monty would learn of her boyfriend's death, and what she would think, or say, if she knew Meredith was the one who called it in. Having already read the diary herself, she was primarily interested in Detective Josey's take on it.

Josey agreed to leave Meredith in peace for a few days and bowed out, taking the diary with him to read in his own time. Over the next few days he gave little time to anything else.

To him, her diary seemed to be a message. Dare he allow himself to believe the message was coming from Monty's mother, Montana? As he read, he had to keep reminding himself that the childlike handwriting was juxtaposed to the content, which did appear to be coming from a much older mind. The first entries in the diary began when Monty was just three years old; around about the time her mother's death was officially certified.

The adult phrasing of her sentences were evident from the very first line.

Diary entry – aged 3

I've been thinking about Mummy. About the things she told me before she died.

The things she told me over the past three years - and, even before that.

Things she told me even before I was born.

My Grandpa and Grandma have heard me say things I aught not to know, things that are very strange to them.

None of it is strange to me.

Everyone thought my Mummy was already dead, in her mind, but I knew she wasn't.

She talked to me all the time.
Taught me stuff I shouldn't know yet –
like, how to write – and read. I don't
understand why . . .

Josey pulled his eyes away from the page, lent back in his chair and recommenced breathing fully. He couldn't believe this very first entry had been written by a three-year-old.

The handwritten letters were indeed childlike. Not a three year old though, more like that of a five year old. He couldn't wait a moment longer to continue reading . . .

I sometimes suddenly remember things
that happened in the past; to my
Mummy. Like it was a dream I'd
forgotten.
Mummy was in a coma when I was born.
I had a twisted bowel.
I came close to dying that day; the first
day of my life . . .

The following pages continued to uncover things she remembered about her own life up to the age of three, and the occasional digression to that of her mother's at that same age. Josey looked at the clock, he'd been reading for an hour.

As truly fascinating as this was, he needed to find something that might help him locate Monty. He flicked forward to when she was five years old . . .

Diary entry – aged 5

Today is my fifth birthday.
I've spent all day thinking about
Mummy.
I can't help seeing her in my mind. I
always see her at the same age as myself.
I see things that she does. I don't know
why it happens . . .

He took a break. Made some coffee and went back
to reading.

CHAPTER NINE
Enlightenment

Jennifer Mackintosh knew her life was in danger. Someone was trying to kill her for God's sake. She had no idea why, but right now in the heat of passion it didn't matter. Her name isn't Jennifer Macintosh of course, except to the hunk on top of her. Her name is Monty Pritchard. She'd changed her name following the murder of her biker boyfriend, Alan Kelly.

That was only a month ago.

The man riding her now had no idea about any of that. He was a need to know part-time boyfriend; a kind of abreaction, a part time feeling of peace.

Sex felt like peace for a while, but then it was over and the real world returned, a world of worry. A worry she couldn't hide in those platonic moments straight after.

'That was great,' *Benjamin Hunk* breathed as he sank back onto his side of the bed.

I didn't climax, she wanted to remind him, but said, 'That's good, Ben.'

He sensed the disquiet; propped up on an elbow to look at her.

'Ben. Get dressed and get out of here.'

He looked at his watch. 'Your right, I need to hit the road.' He sprang from the bed looking relieved to be released. She looked relieved he was going.

But each time that he left she'd instantly revert to feeling lonely.

Her life so far was one big mystery with strange memories that weren't her own. As a kid she had accepted the connection she had with her mother without question, but now she was older and supposedly able to have greater understanding of herself and the world around her. But it had become one upset after another, especially having lost her diary. She couldn't stop wondering who might have it; who might be reading it? *Possibly the police.*

Could they work out who she is from that? Maybe even find out where she is? She couldn't be sure. She hardly ever went out. Once a week she had groceries delivered to the house, never once opening the door to the delivery man. That was something she was used to; living with a family in hiding can do that to you. She thought about them and rode with the swell of guilt. She wished she still had her beloved diary so that she could explain in writing why she had run away.

Thinking back to what happened in Sydney the night Alan was murdered, she couldn't help feeling lucky to be alive. She had been in Alan's house when the intruder let himself in through an open window. In spite of the fact she'd told Alan someone was trying to kill her, he convinced her she'd be safe while he was around. Of course she wasn't, and neither was he as it turned out . . .

Monty awakes to a noise. She is wishing Alan hadn't convinced her to leave the window open.

'Alan,' she whispers, bringing him out of a deep sleep with a shove, 'I think there's someone in the house.'

He's still groggy. 'What?'

'Get something to hit him with,' she pleads, feeling a little foolish suggesting it.

He hears a noise then; throws the covers off and slips into a pair of jeans taken from the arm of a chair beside the bed.

'Stay here!' he urges.

He takes a wrench from a tool box he keeps in a walk-in wardrobe and makes his way into the front room - the room where the open window is. She puts on slacks and *T*-shirt and follows him there. Pausing in the shadows of the adjoining room she watches him as he searches for the intruder in the dark.

Alan doesn't get a chance to use the wrench; a king-hit from a tyre-lever to the back of the head fells him to the floor. There is nothing for Monty to do but hold her breath and hide. Making a move on this lever-wielding-figure dressed in black would be suicidal. She hides in the deep shadows of a wall-unit, pressing herself hard into the corner; as if wishing to melt from sight. The hooded intruder is coming toward her, toward the door that is right beside the somewhat dubious refuge of the unit's shadow. The assailant's hooded jacket—dark with limited peripheral vision—protects Monty from being seen. Once the intruder has gone through the door and into the next room, Monty creeps barefooted, silently, to the front door and leaves the house, away from this horror scene—with no understanding of who is trying to kill her, or even if it's her the killer wants. She remembers getting a fleeting glimpse of his face, enough to see he was clean shaven and white . . .

The mystery was probably a blessing in disguise, for if she had known of her assailant's psychotic state of mind and what happened after she left; it may well have tipped her completely over the edge.

The intruder had crept into the bedroom, and was leaning down to inspect the sheets, Indented both sides.

She's here!

This prompted one more quick-search of the house.

Kelly's still on the floor, and at best certainly unconscious; who cares, he hasn't seen me. Wait! The front door is wide open. I closed that door.

She's gone!—

Don't have to worry about the Police though; she's on the run - from everybody.

I'm making her life a nightmare . . . Good!

She's a strange girl; almost fascinating.

She'll soon be a very dead girl. Just like her boyfriend.

With all reasoning put aside, the assailant raised the tyre-lever and savagely smashed it into the catatonic man's skull three times as he lay on the floor.

She'll probably thank me for it . . .

Monty lay awake and restless at 3am, staring into the darkness of her cabin in the mountains, mulling over the night her boyfriend was murdered.

She still carried the guilt of leaving the house. Fear had prevented her from deciding to contact the authorities, especially when the worst was confirmed; just hours after she'd seen Alan struck down—he was reported dead.

She sobbed herself back to sleep.

Fifty miles away in the city, Cameron Josey was closing her diary. He too was pondering the murder of Alan Kelly. The diary was incredibly detailed, but made no mention of Kelly's murder on the last page.

His new client had come close to witnessing this murder; close to identifying the killer - close to death herself potentially. He still had more than half the book to read. In spite of a strong urge to call Meredith straight away to talk about Monty's adult like descriptions, he decided to give her more res-pite; no more than one more good night's sleep though; that is if she was able to sleep at all. He wondered if he might have the same issue, having now read the strange reflections of this troubled girl. Perhaps sleep could wait a little longer, this case was screaming out to commence.

Speed might be the only thing that saves Monty Pritchard's life, he thought.

Unfortunately, as far as he could muster from the first read, he was unable to find anything in the diary that helped with her whereabouts. He decided to go over the first half again right away. Maybe he would fall asleep doing it. He didn't, he continued on and read the whole hundred pages.

At nine in the morning he showered, dressed and headed for Meredith's apartment; a day earlier than promised.

It was Saturday and Meredith had the day off. Ever the perfect host, she made sure a pot of coffee was ready. Josey was on his third cup. It was needed. The morning sun pouring in from the balcony accentuated the steam climbing from their cups.

'With all of their money,' Josey concluded, 'they weren't a very happy bunch it seems.'

'That's if we can believe Monty's version of events,' Meredith reasoned. 'Like I say, she's a bit, *out there*.'

Josey flicked an eyebrow, 'and fairly unhelpful in telling us where she might be, not to mention the family.'

'Now you see why I need your help.'

'We have to keep reminding ourselves that most of

her diary is written as though she is playing the part of her mother. It's as though it's her mother talking, not her. I can't really see it helping, but I'd like to go over a few things with you; just in case I've missed something.'

'Two heads are better than one,' she said in agreement.

He thumbed through the pages. 'Were you in her school class?'

'I was a year behind, why?'

He reached the diary entry headed *aged 7*. 'I just wondered if you were on this school excursion she writes about here.'

'I wouldn't have been, no . . . Something in it that might help?'

'Nothing specific, but I'm now thinking maybe she's gone back to one of those locations in the pictures.' He was studying the Pritchard family montage that had been absconded from Kelly's place. 'People sometimes return to special places in their childhood - in times of turmoil. I mean, who knows if she's talking about her mother, or herself. Let's keep it real for now, and assume she is making this *mother-memory* thing up.'

'Fair enough,' Meredith said, mulling over the possibilities and sounding less likely to dismiss the weird memories.

Josey massaged his lower lip, thoughtfully reflecting on what he had read.

Meredith cast her mind back too. 'As I recall she doesn't mention the actual place when she writes about the excursion.'

'That's right, but maybe we can read between the lines.'

'Let's give it a go.'

Meredith was in a much better frame of mind following her two day break, which she managed to get in spite of being totally stressed. Josey was beginning to wish he had gotten even a single hour of rest, but then tiredness sometimes helped him concentrate. He read the account allowed, word for word just as Monty had written it, presumably when she was seven years old. And yet, her hand writing looked a good deal more mature than that.

'It's as if she's speaking to the reader,' Josey pointed out. 'Listen . . .'

Meredith came to look over his shoulder, following the words as he spoke . . .

'Diary entry March six; Let me tell you what this day was like for Mummy. Well, for both of us really, because since Mummy died, her memories sometimes become my memories. Perhaps it came to me because I was at school, in the classroom, during a lesson. One minute I was listening to the teacher, the next minute I was somewhere else. I could see my mother and everyone around her. I saw my grandma too, when she was young.'

Monty's descriptions were so strange, yet so vividly written, it was impossible for the reader not to visualise the events as well as if they'd been there. If Monty was making this up, she was doing a damn good job of it. Even Josey's well-honed skepticism struggled as his own imagination was drawn into the pages.

'Monty categorically manages to take the reader back in time,' Josey pointed out as he and Meredith studied the pages. 'Back to when her mother was herself seven years old; getting ready to go on a school excursion . . .

Are you listening my mother asked me.

I know Mummy - don't take my hat off in the sun.

She gave me a cuddle and a kiss.

Then saw I was looking at the dark marks on her face.

Did you and Daddy have a grownup fight I asked her.

She held me close - I could feel her crying.

She turned me to face the door and sent me on my way with a little slap on my bottom.

I stopped at the door and asked if Daddy was coming back home.

I don't know sweetheart - do you want him to.

I didn't answer straight away - then I

said no and left.

Mummy could hear the other children as I climbed into the bus.

When my nine year old brother Andrew came out from his bedroom - he saw her still crying . . .

Josey looked up from the diary to get Meredith's reaction. 'It worries me that she claims to see what her mother and brother are doing without actually witnessing it.'

'Maybe she's just a very talented little writer,' she suggested sounding wishful, 'guessing what is happening based on past experiences, or in this case she hears what happened between her mother and brother before she got on the bus. It doesn't make it any less believable I don't think.'

He turned a few pages.

'It's hard to know. To be truthful I've been think-ing Monty's parents were likely coaching her in what to write, but I accept they'd hardly incriminate themselves to this extent.'

'Do I detect a chink in your armour, Detective?'

He didn't answer.

Something in the diary gained his complete focus. His expression changed, making her think he might have found himself on the verge of a discovery. 'Are we sharing?' she finally asked shifting to the edge of her seat as Josey pointed to what had him so fixated.

She took a turn to read aloud, and as she did the story came back to her from having read it the first time.

> I'm having trouble keeping up with my sore leg.
> Two of the teachers carry me over the big rocks.
> I should be happy here with all my friends walking up in the mountains so far from my home.
> But all I can think about is my father hurting my mother.

> It's lunchtime now. I'm feeling much better.
> The scenery is different to where I live.
> But the mountains are the same ones that I can see in the distance from our house.
> The mountains are funny shapes and sizes.
> Some look like spikes.
> Some are like upside down ice creams with lots of broken rocks on the ground around them.
> I like this place.
> I wish I lived here . . .

'Have I missed something?' Meredith asked Josey, unaware of what had him so fascinated.

He placed the diary on the coffee table and paced over to the photomontage Meredith had placed on the floor against the wall, the framed family photos she had retrieved from the crime scene.

He studied one picture in particular, a unique mountain that resembled a miniature Mount Everest, without the snow. He brought the picture frame over to Meredith and tapped his finger on the glass above the photo. 'Does this ring a bell?'

. . . 'It does look familiar.'

The mountain lay way off in the background, shrouded by the blue veil of distance. In the foreground a group of school students smile at the camera. Among them, a beaming Montana; her plaster cast covered in the graffiti of her school friends.

'Mount Beerwah,' Josey revealed, 'It's part of a group called The Glasshouse in Queensland. I'm guessing this picture was taken on the day the diary describes.'

'Are you sure it's Montana; couldn't it be Monty?'

'Definitely Montana,' he said surprising her with an affirmative tone. 'Look at the age of the bus; I'm guessing it was registered in the eighties.'

Meredith took a closer look at the girl with the plaster cast, and the tropical surrounds of the Glass House Mountains. 'Are you thinking of going up there?'

'It's a long shot I know. I thought you might join me.'

'I can't—I've got to get back to work, but this is a great find. Well done, Cam.'

Josey looked a little disappointed, no more so than

Meredith.

'If *you* think there's a chance of finding her, by all means go. I'll leave it to you,' she reassured him.

Josey wanted to tell her the chances were even less than slim, but he held his tongue. Many times he had solved cases with no more than a gut-feeling. 'How deep do you want me to go into this?' he asked, still a little doleful at losing her spirited company.

'Till you find her.'

'And if I don't?'

'I'm confident it won't be for the want of trying. I sense you want this as much as I do.'

He nodded in agreement. 'You've never asked me why that is?'

'Not my business, I know this much; if you were prepared to find her without pay,' she rubbed her thumb and forefinger together, 'your motivation must now be through the ceiling.'

He grinned and gave her a peck on the cheek.

She blushed, confirming that even as an older man his good looks still carried weight.

His intention was completely platonic, the light flush that rose on his client's cheeks only served to remind him of Rebecca and Molly, his wife and daughter, away from home in a distant part of the world. His grin, although dismissive, assured her there was no need for embarrassment.

She recovered quickly by burying her face into her cup to drain the last remnants of her coffee.

'I'll get started in the morning,' he told her, moving on with business. 'If you need to reach me, go through Maxine. She contacts me every day.' He picked up the diary and gestured for her to take it. 'If I find Monty, my first move will be to tell her you have the diary.'

She hesitated. 'I thought you'd take it with you?'

'Problem is, she won't know me,' he explained. 'Seeing me with the book might freak her into thinking I'm Kelly's killer. Best you keep the diary here. When the time comes, I'll get her to call you to verify my story—or, you could come with me?'

He was still fishing.

'It's impossible right now,' she breathed closing the door on the subject. 'It was hard enough getting away for these last few days.'

Josey relinquished, smiled and handed her the book. 'First things first, let's see if we can find this girl.'

She gave an apologetic shrug and mustered the strength to return his kiss in the chaste manner in which it was given. 'Good luck.'

CHAPTER TEN
Sergeant Brack

This case had a definite element of urgency about it. Monty Pritchard's life may depend on how quickly she could be found.

If, she could be found.

There wasn't a lot to go on, her name being the least likely lead, given she had probably changed it following Alan Kelly's murder.

After leaving Meredith, he went straight to the studio of Art Stapleton, a friend who excelled in portraiture drawing. Josey had met Stapleton during a case in which they were both commissioned to work alongside the police in finding a serial burglar. Stapleton's long unattended to hair and casual clothes, soiled by paint and pencil, made him look the quintessential artist.

On first meeting him, Josey wondered if Art might

be short for *Artist*, but it wasn't. His first name was Arthur.

Showing him Monty in the school photo at age seven, he asked the artist if he could add on eleven years, to make her appear eighteen.

'I know you think I'm good, but a lot changes in eleven years. I can't promise it'll look like your girl now.'

Josey told him it was a moot point and just to do his best.

What he did was a good drawing, but impossible to know if it would match eighteen year old Monty, even if she looked identical to her mother as Meredith had said. Of course Meredith should be able to confirm one way or the other, having seen Monty in the flesh, even though it was only for a few moments. He snapped a shot with his phone and uploaded it to his client. Her answer came straight back, expressing her doubt about the accuracy. Without mentioning the outcome, he shook the artist's bony hand and left with the drawing, lamenting the lack of teenage shots among the pictures in the montage.

Josey took a leisurely 10am flight to Brisbane the next morning and picked up a car from East-Coast; open ended. Until something in the way of a clue showed up, he had no idea how long he would be staying.

Fifty minutes up the Pacific Highway brought him to the tiny town of Beerwah, where he booked into the Beerwah Glass House Motel, just in time for lunch. He didn't feel like eating alone so he called an old mate from the cop-shop to join him.

Josey's travels across Australia and around the world brought him in contact with many people, particularly some extremely helpful members of the police force – they were all friends. People liked his company. He came across as trustworthy.

'I'm in town you old bastard,' he told *Barry Brack* when he answered. 'Can you get your butt to the pub for a bite?'

Brack laughed and gave as good as he got. 'My God, what's this town coming to when riffraff like you get past our defences?' He laughed again and added, 'How are you, buddy?'

'I'm fine, but I'm sure you've guessed I'm on a case.'

'Yeah, right, I'm surprised you bothered with lunch.'

'Can you come over?'

'See you in ten,' his copper mate advised him cheerfully.

'Good on you Baz, see you soon.'

Sergeant Brack came into the Motel Restaurant exactly ten minutes later. It took longer for him to make his way past the staff, chatting about all and sundry. Even a few local patrons wanted to chew the rag with him. He had a jovial face with red fleshy cheeks that looked like he had just come in from an icy wind. Queensland doesn't get many of those. His grey hair, clipped close to the scalp, exposed an almost perfect dome. When he walked he swayed on stocky legs with the surefootedness of a chimp and arms to match, giving his body the appearance of strength - unbreakable.

He got looks from those who didn't know him too; a police uniform will do that; something Josey believed this country cop secretly enjoyed—his own personal popularity parade—hell of a nice guy though - he deserved it.

Finally he made it to Josey's table, beer in hand. He'd had that handed to him by the barman as he swung past the taps. No doubt calculated. Josey was set with a drink, so Brack planted himself and said, 'Cheers. Good to see you again, *ol-mate.*'

As Sergeant Brack tapped his schooner against the detective's raised tumbler of whisky, Josey was sliding Monty's identikit-drawing across the table with his free hand.

The cop over emphasised a deep swallow and cleared his throat. 'I see, straight to business.'

'Seen anyone like this around?'

'Oh yeah, she's waiting for me at home,' he joked.

Josey chortled, but was more interested in a serious answer. 'She's in danger, Baz. I need to find her, and fast.'

'What makes you think she's around here?' Distracted, Baz glanced toward the kitchen.

'Lunch is on its way,' Josey informed him, 'I took the liberty of ordering.'

The sergeant turned back and found Josey had placed Montana's school photo on the table next to the drawing, pointing at the girl with the plaster cast.

'This is her on a school excursion; . . . recognise the location?'

He immediately identified Beerwah Mountain in the background and surmised this was the reason Josey thought the girl's older-self might be in the area.

'You think she's here—based on this picture?'

Josey accepted the skepticism. 'It's a stretch, I know.'

Brack wanted to ask more about the present day girl—the one Josey was looking for right now—the eighteen year old. He slid the school-day shot to the side and took a good hard look at Stapleton's drawing, considering if he had seen anyone like that in Beerwah . . . 'Can't help you with this one,' the cop finally admitted.

Lunch arrived, and Josey held off responding.

'Enjoy,' the young waitress told the town visitor with a welcoming smile.

'Cheers, thank you.'

She had a cheeky glint in her eye for the sergeant as she left.

Brack quickly got back to the business at hand. 'Have you got a name?'

'Officially, Monty Pritchard, but it could be anything by now. '

After absorbing the information for a moment he said, 'Monty's a strange name for a girl.'

'Short for Montana.'

'Fair enough.' He'd just began eating when

something occurred to him. While chewing, he started waving his empty fork at Josey until he was able to speak. '*Montana Pritchard*,' he finally repeated. 'I know that name. Young woman fatally injured in a horror smash with a truck – in Brisbane. If memory serves me there was some controversy with the family.' He tilted his head reflectively. 'Bloody hell, that was twenty years ago.'

Cops don't forget stuff like that.

'Eighteen years—it's her daughter I'm looking for.'

'Obviously no photo,' Brack said reacting to the drawing.

'No.'

Meredith had told Josey the drawing wasn't all that close, so he saw no point in explaining to his friend that mother and daughter were identical to each other.

'Why's she in danger?' Brack inquired.

'Someone is trying to kill her.'

Brack saw the concern on Josey's face. 'And, you know this; how?'

'Her boyfriend was murdered a while back. Before he died he told my client the killer was after the Pritchard girl.'

'Who's your client?'

Josey explained who his client was and how she got the information, finishing with . . . 'would have killed Northey too—if she'd arrived at the scene sooner.'

'Was this murder reported? I can't say I've seen

anything.'

'It was.'

'In Sydney?'

Josey nodded.

'The girl's boyfriend you say.'

'Alan Kelly.'

Josey went back to his meal, his expression verifying an emotional connection to his case. Brack thought to say something about it but decided not to.

Lunch went on for another half hour before Brack had to leave. The upshot was that he was unable to help with Josey's investigation, but he promised to look into the two cases, familiarise himself. Josey deliberately didn't mention the diary, intent on keeping its paranormal content under wraps—for now.

Coppers like facts, and, fact is, so does Josey. Arguably when one window closes, another opens, but so far the detective was metaphorically in a room without windows. *Frustrating* the hell out of him.

Where to start?

He decided the Motel Pool was as good a place as any; probably better than most. After about five laps, poolside spectators who were permanently adhered to their lounges considered he might be some sort of athlete, or fitness junky. Obviously very fit for his age. Fit for any age.

As the cool water cascaded over his skull, his mind was working overtime; joining the dots, making sure no stone was left unturned.

I'll hit on it when least expected, he thought as he was turning at the wall.

What lap am I on – twenty, maybe eighteen? –

Then it hit him, *you're a dummy*, he voiced in his head.

He abandoned his lap half way back along the pool, swam to the edge and catapulted out, drawing attention from several bikini-clad lounge lizards.

He dripped his way into the hotel lobby past the code-of-dress sign; dialed out on the public phone that was there – a pool of water building beneath his feet.

He noticed a master of the house giving him the evil eye, looking like he was about to afford the dripping customer a piece of his mind, but Josey motioned for him to hold off - Brack had just come on the line.

'Baz,' he said a little too loud.

People began staring at him all the more.

'Do me a favour. See if you can get a licence photo of the Pritchard girl when she was aged eighteen, the year of the accident.'

A picture is worth a thousand words, he thought, *even better than a really good drawing*.

Josey was beginning to feel he was on the verge of some well needed progress.

Brack had the licence photo of Montana circulating within twenty four hours. Local police stations, papers, public places all displayed the poster claiming it to be a recent picture of a missing person who could be going by the name, *Monty*. There was no mention of her family name, or any connection made to her mother. The falsification of her true identity was known only to Josey and Brack. Being a licence photo, there was nothing in the picture to date it. Josey was asked to remain in the background of the search, but after only a day of leaving it to Brack, who had only limited time to spend on it, Josey decided not to sit and wait for a response to the poster. He set about doing his own leg work.

He figured business people, who might have seen Monty, would be in and around the kind of places a single woman would go for, say, a hairdo, or a manicure. But he didn't limit his search to just that. *She had to eat - and she probably had a car*.

His first port of call though was to start with the obvious. He went into a salon called *Hair-an-Beauty* in nearby *Landsborough*. It was away from the beaten track and the kind of place she was likely to prefer, especially if trying to change her appearance.

The young girl looked up as Josey approached the counter. 'Can I help you?' Her eyes fell to the poster Josey was holding.

'Hi, I'm helping the local Police in finding this missing woman. Might she have come in here recently?'

'Nice hair,' she responded promptly, 'No, I'd remember if I'd seen *her*. Is she in trouble with the cops or something?'

'She *is* in trouble, but not with police. If you do see her, be sure to contact me or the local cops.' He past her his card and she handed back the poster.

'Keep it. Show it around.'

Josey left the shop empty handed - next stop Aldi in Beerwah. He got to talk with the manager, a pimply face kid not much older than the missing girl.

'Oh yeah, I saw her,' he told the detective. 'Not in here though. I was out having a smoke and she waltzed past. Bit of a snob *but*.'

Josey guessed the young guy's testosterone took ownership of a good situation and ruined his chances as the girl walked by. This was progress though; the young manager's fleeting memory of her proved Josey's hunch was right; *she's in the area*. 'When was this?'

'*Bout* a week ago.'

'And you haven't seen her since?'

'Plenty more where she came from.'

Unlikely, Josey thought. 'Okay, thanks.' He gave the kid his card and left the store.

Outside he noticed a traffic camera mounted on one of the light poles. He placed a call to Brack. 'Who's looking after the street cameras?'

'Rick Dodds,' Baz said sounding unimpressed. 'I gather you're on the case.'

He ignored the observation. 'Where do I find him?'

'The post office, he runs his *shit-box* operation outback in a room not much bigger than a country outhouse. He's completely anal about it, but he'll be able to help. Tell him I said so.'

Josey thanked him and started out for the post

office. Outside Aldi he thought of something he would need and went back in to ask the kid what the girl was wearing.

'Black slacks and a pink top – fair bit showing up top if you know what I mean.'

Josey told him he did to keep him happy and left.

Rick's office was definitely a *shit-box*, like Brack said, two people constituted a crowd. The walls were stuffed with monitors that looked like yesteryear's state of the art. The floor was crawling with dusty cables, among which a small worn patch of carpet allowed for the operator's one and only chair. The room stank of body odour. It could only be coming from one place. Rick's persona was that of a loner, his clothing–consisting of a cap, tatty T-shirt and Jeans with holes that hadn't come off the rack that way–had seldom seen the inside of a washing machine by all reckoning. Completing the ensemble were dry crusty feet graced by worn-out thongs.

Better make this quick.

'What's the pole number?' the guy snapped.

'It's the one opposite Aldi.'

'That doesn't tell me the number,' he grumbled.

'It's that one.'

'What?'

'That one;' Josey was pointing at the monitor that showed the Aldi store on the left of frame. *Who needs a fucking pole number*, he thought, and said, 'How long do you hold the tape?'

'What hole you had your head in?' Mister-personality wanted to know. 'It's all on this,' he pointed out—pushing papers aside and lovingly patting a small black hard-drive on his cluttered desk.

'Perfect.' *Useful after all.* 'Can we run through last week?'

'What day?'

Reasonable question.

'I need to see the whole week if that's possible.'

'Tell you what,' Rick said as he got up from his grimy seat, 'how *bout* I leave you with it. Push this button to play; this one to rewind; this, fast forward.' He pushed an equally grimy button that placed numbers on the screen. 'Time-code window if you need it. Or this button will give you time-of-day if that floats your boat. Okay, I'm off. See you in an hour if you're still here.'

'Right.'

'That's all the time you got,' he concluded as he walked out unceremoniously.

Josey was pleased he was gone, if only he'd taken the smell with him.

After a half hour of studying pedestrians passing the Aldi store, which eventually took him through to Wednesday's recordings, he had forgotten all about the offensive odour.

Five minutes into Thursday, he spotted her outside the shop; just like the young manager had claimed. Black slacks and pink top. There he was, trying his luck as she came within earshot. Josey easily imagined how unsavoury the young bloke's comments must have been. She walked on by without looking at him, *the kid's idea of a snob*.

At last Josey was looking at the image of the present day Monty Pritchard, the subject of his investigation. By all accounts the living image of Montana; her mother, *and quite gorgeous*.

It was a find of sorts. Now he'd have to find her for real.

She was about to exit frame when she turned back, walked past the kid, who she once again ignored, and went into the Chemist shop.

Bingo.

He had established his next port of call. She came out three minutes later carrying a small paper bag; *Medicine?*

While he waited for Rick to come back he ran over the footage several times, looking for any detail that might tell him something about her; something new. She didn't look nervous, although she did walk a little quicker than anyone else on the sidewalk. Dressed in black slacks and a cool-pink pullover with short sleeves and a plunging neckline, she was a definite eye catcher. Under the circumstances it was a sign she wasn't expecting to run into anyone who knew her, or for that matter wanted to hurt her. This actually made Josey feel a little better about her safety, and hoped the poster circulating with her mother's picture on it wouldn't change that, setting her on the run again. He recognised she may well have made a small attempt to disguise herself with sunglasses and an out of character scarf to hide her hair. On the other hand maybe that's the way she always dressed. Bottom line, - she's alive.

In the remote hope she hadn't yet laid eyes on the posters, he rang Brack and asked if he could have his officers remove them, the last thing he wanted was to scare her off.

He didn't wait for Dodds to return, he left the dingy den complete with a smartphone clip and photo of Monty that he had gained from a monitor.

Walking past Aldi on his way to the chemist shop, he wondered if Rick might be watching him from his dingy den.

The chemist looked the right age to have started the shop when the town was first formed. His bent little frame potted around the shelves realigning product that had been shifted out of place by browsing customers. *Still hands on.*

Good hearing too, he turned to the sound of Josey crossing the carpeted floor, his face creasing with a friendly smile. 'Is there something I can help you with today young fella?'

'Hopefully,' Josey told him returning the smile and handing him the poster. He showed his ID and brought up the security camera picture of Monty that he had on his phone.

'Oh, this is about that poor girl,' the chemist said recognising her immediately. 'She came in here a few days ago. Is she all right?'

'Maybe not,' Josey admitted with an extra sense of danger added to his tone.

'I'm sorry to hear that. Is there some way I can help?'

'Some information would definitely help. It's extremely urgent we find her before someone else does. A certain someone who wants to hurt her.'

The chemist had been slowly losing his smile and now looked distressed. He turned and headed in the direction of the counter, effectively inviting his visitor to follow. 'Of course you know I'm not allowed to give out personal information.'

'I understand. Can I ask; did she use the name on the poster—?'

'If you were to ask me about what medication she purchased,' he quickly countered, 'I wouldn't be able to tell you.' The furtive shopkeeper went behind the counter, opened a plain covered register that was sitting in front of him, and then moved away to allow his inquisitive customer to read for himself.

Jennifer Macintosh . . .

It was the last entry on the page, followed by the name of the medication, some sort of syrup for the common cold. He skimmed forward, going straight to the licence details—

Problem!

He immediately recognised the information was invalid – not enough numbers.

He committed the bogus information to his phone anyway. When he looked up from the book he found the old fellow had wandered away, presumably to the back room, out of sight. 'Are you there, Sir,' Josey called . . . no answer.

After a short wait he went to a doorway behind the counter and poked his head around the corner. The missing chemist was sitting at a desk writing something on a slip of paper. Josey let him finish. Once done, the man handed the note to the detective and said, 'Maybe this will help.'

Josey looked at the small piece of paper and saw he had written down a licence-plate number.

'You'll find that's the fellow that was tailing her,' the unassuming gent said with a straight face. 'He was standing outside the store watching her the whole time she was in here. I didn't like the look of him, so I went out onto the street when she left. I watched her get into a car away down the street. He had a car closer to the store, and took off after her real slow like, as if he didn't want her to know he was following.'

'Can you tell me what he looked like?'

'Well, he was a nice looking chap, round about thirty five, dressed up smart like.'

Josey's grin was full of thanks. 'I don't suppose you saw what sort of car the girl was driving?'

He lifted a shoulder. 'Black sedan, best I can tell you. The other fella's car, well, that was one of those tall-as-a-tank things – utility.'

Josey's grin broadened. 'Colour?'

'Dark - green maybe.'

'You're a champ my man,' Josey said earnestly.

The old chemist tore out another page from his note book and wrote down something else. He handed it across and said, 'Find that girl and *you* can be the *champ*.'

Josey showed some teeth when he saw the crafty

old guy had written down Monty's registration plate. He almost shook his hand off.

The helpful chemist had provided him with some exceptional information. He should have felt pretty positive, but with what he now knew, it was clear Monty Pritchard, alias Jennifer Macintosh, was not as safe as he had hoped. The heat was on.

The heat of the day was on too, oppressive, literally. So hot that he decided to return to his motel room and make use of the air conditioning.

He first checked if a car of either description had been stolen. No go.

He called Sergeant Brack and told him what he'd found out from the chemist; that Monty Pritchard was using the name Jennifer Macintosh, and that he'd got the plate numbers for both cars.

Brack smiled knowingly. 'That doesn't surprise me; old Joe doesn't miss a trick.'

Josey puckered his lips and blew out a rush of air. 'He got Monty's number right, but the SUV number doesn't exist.'

'He could have got it wrong,' Brack suggested. 'I'll get it checked.'

Brack had no success finding a matching number plate with the car's make and model on the state data base, but then Josey lucked out with a hunch to give the state of New South Wales a try. Twelve matches were found via the dealers, minus names and addresses due to privacy issues. Brack used his position to break down the impasse, calling state registrations to acquire the missing information. The result muddied Josey's hunch a little, but not so opaquely as to abandon it.

Maxine answered from the phone in Josey's office. 'Boss, what's happening?'

'Progress,' he told her. 'I need you to check out some Sydney addresses I've just sent you.'

She opened her recent emails. 'Right, got it. What's the story?'

'See who's staying at each one. Get owners' names. Knock on every door if you have to, but be careful. In fact, send someone else; call Carl, one of the occupants could be linked to our assailant.'

'You've found who the guy is,' she surmised excitedly.

'Not sure yet, I'll explain later?'

'Cam, come on, at least tell me *something*.'

'Do your best, Max. See what you can figure out, any information will help.'

'Okay . . .'

She'd sounded so disappointed he gave in and told her what he had on the two cars, and that one of them was owned by Monty. He promised to keep her informed on the other.

'What should I tell Meredith?'

'Nothing for now, it's too early.'

'Right you are, Chief.' Her tone was playful, which was usual when she reverted to calling him *Chief*. It's a signal for him to get off the line and let her get on with the job.

'Bye Max,' he chanted, taking the hint.

Armed with the license number of the black sedan and the twelve possible NSW numbers of the SUV vehicle, Sergeant Brack had his men take to the streets, but they found no sign of either. Mobile units were also alerted to be on the look-out. But then around midafternoon, heading home along the north road, Brack was hailed down by one of the patrol cars.

The officer had a breakthrough, reporting that he may have seen the suspects green vehicle pass in the opposite direction, but was unable to follow because he was transporting a felon to the Beerwah cells. He confirmed that the description given matched the green SUV Peugeot that he'd seen; but admitted to not seeing the plate number.

Sergeant Brack rang Josey from his patrol car and informed him. 'I've got six cars on this, which is precious little given the size of the area. At this point in time none of our cars are within *cooee* of the one sighted.'

'And the black sedan?'

'Negative.'

'Do you have a GPS on the Peugeot?'

'Buddy, I can hear the tick-tock of your minuscule gray cells from here. Take some advice—stay out of it.'

'I'm ten miles north of town heading out, Baz. If I'm anywhere near you've got to tell me. Give me a chance to take care of this.'

'I'm not even going to ask what that means,' Brack told him, mentally wiping his hands, but then said,

'He's ahead of you. Give it some gas, you might catch up. But listen to what I'm saying, if you look like getting into trouble do yourself a favour and call me. If you kill someone – we didn't have this conversation.'

'What conversation.'

Brack was off duty and wasn't keen to get involved. He gave Josey his private number and left him to it, his fingers were firmly crossed that his detective friend would at least *try* and stay within the boundaries of the law.

Josey closed a five mile gap before coming within eyesight of the Peugeot. There was still no sign of the black sedan.

He can't find her; good.

Maybe not so good, this meant Josey might not either. Ten minutes later the vehicle slowed and turned into a dirt road. To follow him directly would look suspicious, so Josey sailed on ahead, keeping an eye on the other vehicle's dust plume in the side-mirror. He stopped and did a hook-turn. As he made it back to the dirt road he could still see the dust rising above the tree-line. He followed at a moderate speed to minimise his own dust-trail, travelling a couple of miles before the brown cloud up ahead suddenly ceased. This would be tricky.

At a slower pace he continued watching for sidings where a vehicle might tuck in out of sight. There wasn't a single exit, or fire trail, the tree-line hugged the roadside without interruption. Given the absence of further dust, Josey figured he must have reached the point where the SUV stopped – yet, there was no sign of it.

Where the hell did it go?

As quickly as he had entered the bush, he exited onto a grassy clearing. He brought his car to a smart stop. A hundred yards ahead stood a cabin, a small holiday place by the look of it. The car parked outside wasn't the big Peugeot, it was the black sedan.

She's in there!—Where's the SUV?

Josey slipped his revolver from its holster and kept it in his hand as he got out of the car. Holding the weapon behind his back, he approached the house scanning for any sign of movement. He silently cursed a noisy floorboard when he stepped onto the worn timber porch; froze for a moment. Nothing stirred.

Will the door be unlocked? Is she inside? He recalled Brack's warning about killing someone.

The moment of truth . . .

He put pressure on the handle - it gave, turning a few inches. The latch released, allowing him to push the door inward, creating a small gap that showed him a narrow portrait of the room. It was neat, simple – quiet, *slightly dark.*

Another gentle push, the gap widened, revealing a wider view, which now included a fireplace with a lounge setting facing it . . .

There was still no movement or sound.

He slowly opened the door as far as it would go, wiping on the entire room — and, there she was. She just stood there looking at him. The Pritchard girl, the illusive subject of his investigation in the flesh for the first time, a dead ringer for her mother, and the poster . . . He'd found her—

But something was wrong . . .

Presumably she had no idea who Josey was. He was a complete stranger to her—and yet, she looked unafraid. She didn't ask who he was, or say anything. She held her gaze; staring at him with a nondescript blankness . . . *it's as if* –

His last thought was cut short by an excruciating pain exploding somewhere within the confines of his skull - transporting him instantly to a place he didn't recognise, and minus the memory of how he got to wherever he was.

Maxine and Meredith were looking down at him with worried looks on their faces . . . They were standing beside the bed that he was in; the smell of the room suggesting it was a hospital bed.

'Thank God, you're awake,' Maxine said with a little glimmer of a tear showing.

Those last few moments—before the explosion in his head—were gradually reconnecting him with the blow that came from behind.

'How long have I been here?'

Meredith told him, 'Since yesterday afternoon. You were brought in by ambulance.'

After a moment of realising he'd been hurt, and dealing with his new reality, he looked from one to the other and asked, 'How did you find me?'

'We didn't,' Maxine volunteered, 'your friend,

Barry Brack did. He hadn't heard from you so he went searching.'

He lifted his head. 'I need to—,' the pain sent him straight back onto the pillow.

'You've got concussion,' Meredith warned.

'Which means you're to rest for a few days,' Maxine added wiping her eyes with the back of her hand.

He closed his eyes for a moment.

They waited, holding onto planned-words of support.

'I'm not feeling too good; sorry.'

'Oh, no kidding,' Meredith quipped, 'we would never have known if you hadn't told us.'

He opened his eyes and frowned at her with a slender grin.

'We know you didn't see who did it, at least that's what you told Brack when he found you at the cabin.'

Josey had no recollection of his friend having been there, and his visitor's appeared more confused than he; their blank expressions indicating they may not know about Monty. 'Does he know I found her?'

Maxine and Meredith glanced at each other with no idea what he was talking about.

'I guess that answers my question.'

'You found her?' Maxine said finally registering her surprise.

Meredith then found *her* voice. 'Where – when?'

'She was there, at the cabin, standing right in front of me, looking quite strange really.'

Meredith frowned. 'Strange; how?'

'Not afraid. Not of me–not of anybody.'

Max couldn't believe what she was hearing. 'Are you saying she was okay with whoever hit you?'

'That's exactly what I'm saying. The person behind me was a friend of hers.'

'Oh my God,' Max breathed with concern, 'you don't think she's a party to killing her boyfriend do you?'

Meredith shook her head. 'No way, Brian Kelly warned me she was in danger.'

'She's right,' Josey agreed. He didn't want to mention his hunch until he had more. 'I need to talk to Baz. Find out what he found at the cabin.'

Maxine embarked with fresh fortitude. 'Okay, I know you're not one to be fobbed off easily, so here's what I know. Sergeant Brack *does* have some info apparently, but it'll have to wait–Doctors orders.'

'Max,' he complained with an insistent tone, 'what's he got?'

She took a long slow breath and used the air to tell him; 'Pictures.'

'Of what?'

'No. That's it. I'm not telling you another thing.'

'Max!'

She turned on her heels and headed for the door. 'Bye Chief. I'll see you tomorrow.'

She was gone.

Meredith raised her eyebrows. 'Don't look at me. She hasn't told me either.'

Josey's head ached, big time. He knew Maxine was right, rest was mandatory.

'I'll leave you to get some shut-eye,' Meredith offered. She gripped his hand. 'Congratulations on finding her. I knew you would.'

Congratulations on losing her, he thought as he closed his eyes and obeyed the order to rest.

Three days later, Josey entered Brack's office to look at the photographs Maxine had mentioned. He'd had plenty of time to think about the case laid up in hospital and was ready to put his hunch to the test.

Meredith and Maxine had returned to Sydney once they knew the detective was on the mend, but mostly their departure was due to his unrelenting insistence.

Brack looked up from the photos on his desk as Josey walked in. 'You look all right,' he observed, 'considering, have a seat.' The photos were spread out and rotated toward Josey for his inspection. 'I'm not sure these will help you much, they're not that clear.'

He was right. Josey took his time studying the half dozen shots that were splayed out like playing cards. They weren't taken at the cabin. He didn't expect they would be. Three of the pictures were high angles of the Peugeot, presumably captured on security camera when the stalker returned to town;

Was he a *stalker*, or Monty's *unknown friend*— that was the big question?

The last three shots showed the driver out of the

vehicle. One had been brought up close. He picked up the proof for a closer look.

'Ricky enhanced that especially for you,' Brack told him with a grin.

Good old Rick, Josey thought. He wasn't saying much, it still hurt to speak . . .

The more he studied the man in the picture, the more it dawned on him that his face was hauntingly familiar . . .

'I know this face,' he thought out loud finally.

Then it hit him.

Fifteen years older, but definitely unmistakable; *unbelievable.*

Why act like a stalker outside the chemist shop? This made no sense to him.

The look on Josey's face prompted Brack to say, 'You look like the cat ate your canary, what's up?'

With eyes still on the photo he said, 'Maybe the whack on my head has finally put my brain in gear. This's exactly who I thought it would be.'

Brack could see Josey was pleased with the find. 'I can tell you're itching to explain,' Brack jibed.

'It's her uncle. Uncle Andrew—'

Josey's cell vibrated in his pocket.

'Bloody-hell, are you sure about this?' Brack asked. 'People change in fifteen years.'

Josey saw it was Maxine calling. 'No, this's him alright,' he told him while stabbing a finger at the photo.

Brack was trying to keep up. 'Her uncle is the stalker?'

'No—not the stalker, but he's definitely the one who wacked me over the head.'

Now Brack looked like *he'd* lost a Canary to the cat.

Josey took the call. 'Max, what's happening?'

'Hi Boss, I've got an interesting owner on one of those houses, and don't tell me you know who it is.'

'Okay.'

'My-god, you *do* know.'

'They put the house in the name of Margaret Behl, her grandmother's maiden name. I would have called sooner, but I needed to be sure. Answers have only just fallen into place; including, the guy who hit me over the head is her uncle. Sadly they're both gone missing. Brack has had his entire team out looking for the both of them.'

'Well, you can't win them all.'

Josey thought she sounded a little cagey. 'Max, you've got that tone in your voice.'

'What tone, Boss?'

'The tone that says you know something I don't.'

She laughed and said, 'Monty's at the house right now, with her uncle.'

She couldn't see the smile on his face, but she could hear it in his voice. 'Max, you're a gem.'

'I know.'

Josey ended the call and told Brack, 'I guess the case is shifting back to Sydney. Max has found them, their together at Margaret Pritchard's house.'

'You don't say, saves me the trouble of finding the uncle and charging him.

Josey knew exactly why he wanted to. 'I'm thinking Uncle Andrew might be off the hook.'

Brack wasn't so forgiving. 'You say that, but he should understand he can't go round bashing people over the head.'

'Well, I've got a hard head – no harm done.'

Barry the cop got that his friend needed the uncle to sow ends together on his case. He considered Josey would have to make a complaint before a charge could be laid anyway, and that didn't look like happening.

'Tell you what, old-mate; how *bout* you haul your arse back to Sydney and let me get my life back to normal.'

If Sergeant Brack only knew how empty that wish would become, he would have raced home and told his wife, *we're leaving the country for a year*.

CHAPTER ELEVEN
Missing

The room appeared to be that of a minimal suburban house; drawn blinds subduing the daylight scattering in from outside. Monty was sitting on a three seater sofa, arms folded defiantly. She had been crying. Her uncle paced around in front of her looking frustrated.

'You need to come home, sweetheart,' Andrew told her, 'we have to talk this out; give the family a chance to understand what's happening.'

Monty gave him a solid stare.

He eased off, sat down beside her and whispered, 'You can't do this by yourself. We've all shared this burden you have. Watched you grow with it. Clearly you've seen something that's freaked you out.'

He handed her a handkerchief.

'You know, you used to enjoy the memories. Now

you're older and that's changed. Now they frighten you. We get that.'

Recalcitrant, she dabbed her cheeks and looked at him fiercely, unable to allow herself to be swayed by his pep talk. 'Do you–do you really Uncle? — Have you any idea what I'm going through?'

A moment of silence descended - a chance for her uncle to try and decipher her troubled mind.

He was given little time. She said, 'Maybe you'll understand if I tell you exactly why I left.'

Fear rose in the pit of his stomach, he wasn't a hundred percent sure he wanted to know.

'Okay, tell me,' he prompted bravely.

She pulled free of his comforting grasp to reach for her bag, whereupon she began rummaging through it.

When he laid eyes on what she removed to show him, he felt his heart leap within his chest. It both confused and alarmed him. 'Why are you showing me this?'

He was so shocked, Monty wondered if she was making a mistake, but decided there was no turning back. Teary-eyed, she told him, 'Because this is what my mother saw, the night she was attacked.'

Andrew sank his face into his hands and lent forward with elbows propped against his knees, shaking his head. '*Sweetie*, listen to me,' he said toward the floor–then, removing his hands he met her eyes, adding, 'What you're suggesting is not possible – you just had a bad dream; like Gran says.'

She remained silent—*digesting*.

Again, he shook his head in disbelief, trying to clear his thoughts. 'Do you really understand what you're suggesting?'

She made no comment, as if instantly losing the will to speak. He placed an arm around her shoulders and dropped the subject. Comforted, she curled her legs up onto the couch and snuggled in.

Uncle Andrew didn't really doubt she knew the difference between dreams and mother memories, as everyone had begun calling them, but he hoped this time she was wrong. Her latest claim was too much to bear, or accept.

Her present state of mind had begun the night she disappeared from the Pritchard hideaway in the wee hours of the morning.

Monty had been asleep when she awoke gasping for air.

Her grandmother was the only one who heard the disturbing sounds coming from the room next door. She'd got up, put on a robe and gone into the hall, only to find her granddaughter wandering about in a state of confusion.

Monty did her best to explain what had startled her from sleep, but found she was unable to articulate because of her intense sobbing. She was trembling terribly.

With relentless coaxing, Margaret was eventually able to learn she'd had a terrifying nightmare about Montana, her mother. She had never seen Monty so hysterical before, or heard anything quite as frightening as the dream that was relayed to her. She removed her nightgown and wrapped it round her granddaughter to take her back to her room; finally managing to convince the frightened young girl to return to bed, whereupon she cried herself back to sleep.

Margaret prayed Monty would be all right, but come morning it was realised that wasn't to be – her granddaughter was nowhere to be found . . .

While gathered in the guest room discussing what to do about Monty's disappearance, a deep cloud of despair descends on Margaret as she tells the others what her granddaughter had revealed during the night. 'I didn't see this coming,' she explains, trying not to cry. 'She told me she saw a man trying to *kill* Montana. I've honestly never seen her so frightened.'

Margaret chokes, holding back tears. 'I tried to convince her it was just a dream, even though I knew better, I should have known not to try.'

'This is not your fault, Marg,' Walter assures her.

She persisted with self-degradation. 'I'm not so sure. You didn't see the state she was in. I should have gotten you both out of your beds straight away.'

'Don't blame yourself, Mum,' Andrew tells her.

'And she couldn't see the attacker?' Walter asked.

'No. It was dark, she couldn't see his face.'

'Did she recognise where she was?'

'She acted a bit strange when I asked her that.'

'How do you mean—?'

'Look—we need to concentrate on where she might have gone. Thanks to hiding from the whole damn world, it's doubtful we can involve the police.'

Walter seizes on a chance to calm his wife. 'It might come to that, love. Be damned with hiding if it'll get her back safely.'

They notice their son seems suddenly distant. 'We might not need the police,' Andrew tells them.

Their spirits rise in the faint hope he may have worked out where she is.

'I think we should try the Sydney house.'

Walter brightens, realising he may be right.

Andrew enlarges on his point. 'This is the first time she's mentioned an attack on her mother. If Montana *is* trying to tell her something, I think it would drive her to go someplace where she feels close; somewhere where she'd get a better idea about what she's being shown.'

'I've dreaded this day all my life,' Margaret whispers.

They look at her quizzically.

'Don't you see? She's eighteen, her mother's age when she died. Every other thing she's ever learnt from Montana, she's learnt at the same age. That's why she hasn't seen this before.'

Given what Monty's family have witnessed over the years, all possibilities remain on the table.

'I think you're right, Andrew,' his mother says,

'it's worth a try. Go to Sydney—see if you can find her' . . .

Andrew felt eternally grateful his idea of going to Sydney had led to locating Monty in Beerwah, which was a stroke of luck more than anything.

He had arrived at his mother's house in the belief he would find his niece. He didn't. He was about to turn and go home, but decided to check if any calls had been made. The phone at the house was always kept connected in case accommodation was needed in a hurry, but its main purpose was to disguise the fact the house was primarily unoccupied. Like the house, the phone connection was under the name, Margaret Behl.

Andrew found out about the Beerwah Hotel by using the redial function and then hanging up as soon as they answered. He figured there was no reason for her to go to Beerwah other than it was near where the family lived when he and his sister were kids.

His subsequent trip to the sunshine state paid off— insofar as finding Monty—yet, gave him no clue as to what was really going on in her mind. He'd spent the first couple of days just watching her from a distance. She wasn't aware he was in Beerwah until after he'd seen the posters appearing. He'd then rented the shack so that they could stay out of sight while he was trying to figure out what to do next.

When the detective followed him there, he had no idea who the meddlesome investigator was until after he'd rendered him unconscious, identifying him as the private eye who came out to the house at Trundle.

Andrew had been recalling all this as he made tea, which they then drank in silence while the radio played softly in the background. He felt his niece was looking a lot calmer. He avoided talking about the immediate problem at hand, because he needed the calm as much as she did.

The tranquility came to an abrupt ending with a sudden anvil-like clang from the metallic knocker at the front of the house.

Andrew pushed up from the lounge and paced to a bay window to see who was on the porch.

Monty whispered, 'Who is it?'

The look he presented to his niece transcended disbelief. 'It's Meredith Northey.'

This wasn't received with celebratory streamers. 'Holy shit, how the hell does that bloody woman keep finding me—?'

'Let's find out,' Andrew proposed quickly.

Monty was alarmed her uncle would act so impulsively. 'No,' she demanded sprinting to the window to inspect the unwanted visitor. What she saw made her gasp.

'What?' He was wondering why she appeared so bomb-shelled.

'That book in her hand.'

The book meant nothing to him.

'That's my fucking diary.'

What diary?

Before Andrew could ask the question, Monty bounded toward the door to open it.

'Monty?'

She turned and stopped to face him, wishing she hadn't kept the diary a secret. This wasn't a good time to have to explain it to him.

'Baby, what's wrong?'

'I'll tell you what's wrong,' she said with fire in her eyes. 'The last time I saw that diary, Alan Kelly was lying on his unit floor in a pool of his own blood.'

'Jesus.'

'Exactly.' She opened the door with abandon, revealing Meredith looking quite pensive – and positively hard to read.

Perhaps the cause was the wild expression on Monty's face. 'Where'd you get that?'

Meredith's steadfastness weakened. 'I'm sorry,' she apologised, 'I know you must be wondering, but I'm here to tell you – help you actually.'

'You can help by giving me my diary and leaving before I call the police.'

Meredith knew that wasn't about to happen, but recalled Josey's warning about Monty jumping to conclusions in thinking anyone who had the book must be Alan Kelly's killer. That misconception might still stand, but if Josey had turned up with the book in Beerwah, it almost certainly would have been the greater of two evils.

They thought of not admitting to having the diary until after being reacquainted, but decided that would appear deceitful. Meredith convinced him she could smooth things over before he showed his face.

Andrew slid into view from behind the door.

'Oh, hello,' Meredith chimed. 'Long time no see.'

'Eighteen years.' He brushed past Monty adding, 'Come in. Let's talk about how you're going to help my niece.'

Monty gave him the evil eye, but stepped aside and waved the visitor in with a theatrical sweep of her arm.

As Meredith crossed the threshold, Monty snatched the diary away from her and shut the door, firmly.

'She's been through a lot,' Andrew explained to Meredith, trying not to sound too condescending.

'No, please, my being here must come as a bit of a shock.'

'Can we get past the niceties and get down to why in the hell you *are* here,' Monty protested.

Ten minutes later, Monty had the full story of how Meredith had followed Alan Kelly to the apartment in Paddington in the hope of finding her, only to find her friend dead on the floor. 'When he told me someone was trying to kill you, I just had to find you.'

The way Andrew and Monty looked at each other, saying nothing, it was apparent to Meredith that she had hit some sort of nerve. She decided to leave that subject to Josey.

'I take it that's when you got my book.'

'Yes.'

'And, you've read it?'

'Yes. I thought it might help me find you.'

'I suppose you think it's a load of rubbish.'

Taken momentarily aback, Meredith explained, 'I don't think I'd have gone to so much trouble coming here to tell you that.'

'So why did you - *go to so much trouble?*'

Andrew returned with three drinks clamped together in his palms and placed them on the coffee table. 'Rum and Coke,' he announced.

It was just what she needed. Meredith drank half a glass unashamedly. She could feel the alcohol working its way through her bloodstream, gently settling her nerves. 'You're so much like your mother,' she said with some added *Dutch-courage*.

'So you said last time,' Monty responded with no shortage of sarcasm.

Meredith gazed into the soda bubbles bursting at the surface of her dark cocktail, wondering what she could say to win-over this young girl who looked so strikingly like Montana. 'Your mother was my best friend,' she said lifting her eyes to meet Monty's. 'When I first saw you at the coffee shop, I thought I was seeing a ghost. It was a shock. The day your mother died, a part of me died with her.'

Andrew looked at Monty to gage her reaction.

She appeared to be mellowing; until she said suspiciously, 'You're asking for a damn lot of trust. Maybe you've already been to the police. I hope you don't think I'm the one who killed Alan,' she added with a raised voice.

Meredith was struggling to find the words to respond.

'Monty calm down.' Andrew insisted.

'No, Uncle!' she returned with equal vigour. 'She's read my diary. What does that tell you?'

'Listen to me,' Andrew urged in a calmer voice, 'I've known Meredith most of my life. She was Montana's best friend. I can personally vouch for the distress and grief she suffered when she learnt of the accident. If she says she's here to help, then I believe her. At least hear her out.'

Monty felt compelled to take her uncle's advice, reservedly.

Meredith understood her concerns. 'For what it's worth—I don't think your diary is rubbish.'

Tears welled into Monty's eyes; Meredith's positive comment touched her. 'Thank you for saying that,' she told her mother's friend earnestly, 'for believing.'

'Believing you see your mother's memories,' Meredith quantified. 'It took a while to digest, but some of the things you wrote about, I remember happening. I was there with your mother. That made it easy for me.' Meredith drained her glass and appeared a little unsettled. 'I'll understand if you don't want to answer this, I mean, what's happening to you is truly remarkable, and it gives me faith that there is something, you know, on the other side – I'm just wondering if you can explain what it feels like; when your mother talks to you?'

Monty looked so blank, that her uncle felt the need

to explain for her, to explain how it is for Monty. 'What my niece receives is mostly, sort of hazy. It's like there is a veil over everything. Sometimes she doesn't see anything; she just gets a feeling.'

'Is that what happened the day at the coffee shop?' Meredith asked Monty.

Dismissing the notion, she wobbled her head from side to side. 'I can see why you'd think that, but no, there was nothing extrasensory about it.'

'But you recognised me; knew my name.'

'I knew you from a photograph that was taken of you with my mother. The family kept it beside her bed the whole time she was in a coma.'

Meredith tittered. It was unclear if it was out of disappointment or embarrassment. A frown swept across her face. 'But why did you run when I mentioned your mother?'

She glanced at her uncle knowingly. 'It wasn't from what you said, and I don't want to go too deeply into this, but we ran because Alan got nervous. He didn't know who you were and I had no time to explain it.' She was on the verge of crying . . . 'He, umm, was - very protective of me . . . ,' emotion swept to the surface, preventing her from continuing.

Her uncle stepped in. 'There's more to Alan Kelly than meets the eye. Monty doesn't want to talk about it. But suffice to say, he knew her life was in danger, and basically, he had taken it upon himself to become her bodyguard.'

The colour had drained from Meredith's face. 'Monty love; you must be so terrified.'

'I have my moments,' she sobbed.

Andrew thought about Meredith's promise of help, and with no concept of what that help might be, wondered if she realised what she was getting herself into. But one thing was certain, if ever his niece needed help, it was now.

Meredith reached into her purse and, for a reason that eluded them, retrieved a phone. 'I've got someone you need to reacquaint yourselves with.'

Their dire expressions morphed into panic.

'Who?' Andrew asked.

'It's someone who's helping me.' Her eyes cut to Monty. 'Without him we would never have found you.'

'*Whose we?*' Monty pushed.

Meredith gathered courage and revealed the mystery visitor. 'Cameron Josey. I know you had a run-in with him, but it's time you and your uncle made peace.'

Their inert expressions shed real doubt on the proposed meeting's success.

Once the youngest member of the Pritchard family got past Josey's assurance he wouldn't be pressing charges for Andrew's assault on him in Beerwah, and promised he could protect Monty from her predator, she agreed to speak with him. But first she wanted to understand if he shared Meredith's belief in her gift.

'Have *you* read my diary, Detective?'

'Yes he has,' Meredith elected to confirm with an apologetic tone. 'Sorry.'

Monty shook her head, dismissing the need for penitence. 'If you two hadn't found it I might never have seen it again.'

'Or worse,' Meredith added. 'It could have been found by police at the crime scene.'

A tear rose at the memory of that day.

Josey's glance to his client suggested laying the subject to rest.

Monty recovered and told Josey and Meredith, 'My family truly believes in my gift – or curse, whichever way you want to look at it.' She smiled at Andrew. 'Thank you, Uncle.'

Andrew was only too happy to give his niece his support, now that she had agreed not to mention the specifics of what they had discussed earlier; at least not outside the family circle.

'Uncle Andrew will tell you, at first, tapping into my mother's memories was more like feeling her emotions. I felt there were things Mother didn't want me to know until I was much older. I think she kept those things from me, but each day of my life—as her memories surfaced—I recalled something new of hers; still do.'

Josey thought, *I could really do with something a little less ethereal!*

He asked Monty outright if she knew who was trying to kill her.

She was immediately hesitant, but finally said, 'I didn't really believe it was true until the killer came to Alan's flat. Before that I wasn't convinced it was real. In hindsight I should have been.'

Her answer impressed Josey, because it sounded factual and not so centred around her alleged gift.

'Why do you say *you should have been*?'

'. . . Because Alan told me I was a target.'

Josey frowned. 'Really; how would Alan know a thing like that?'

She looked across at her uncle as though she was about to tell him something he'd never heard before. With eyes back on Josey she said, 'Because he was the one hired to kill me.'

The expected reaction was broad astonishment, especially from her uncle. 'Jesus, Mont; what the hell were you doing with this guy if you knew he was a murderer?'

For Josey though, the disclosure was a light-bulb moment. He held up an open palm to silence further protests. 'Let her finish.'

Andrew was struggling to abide. Josey held him in his gaze, pleading for patience.

Against every one of her uncle's natural instincts he settled, but clearly wanted to say more.

Josey turned back to Monty, 'Are you able to take it from the top?'

'Yes.' Tears flowed again. She forced herself to say, 'Alan just couldn't go through with it . . . He sort of fell for me, you know, and wanted to protect me.' She became deeply introspective, suggesting to Josey she may have been in love with Alan Kelly.

'He was no bloody angel,' she said with rising anger. 'He had connections with some biker-gang. That's what he told me anyway. I never met them. I asked who they were, but he wouldn't tell me. He said he *couldn't* tell me who it was that hired him because of the way they set the thing up. He kept calling it *the hit*. I asked him to stop calling it that. The man who sent him to kill me was what he called a, go between. It was all done over the phone apparently. He never met the guy . . . Alan was planning to take me somewhere he said they'd never find us.' She panned around the faces to see if they understood.

'Monty,' Josey asked drawing her back to him, testing. 'Does your mother know what's happening to you right now?'

'I'm sure you believe that's not possible. I'm not even sure myself. Like most people, you probably think that whatever memories I have of hers was given before she died. That's the only thing that makes any sense, right.'

Josey guessed that the Pritchard family believed messages were being sent to this day, and the claim didn't surprise him; he felt that they may have been feeding information to Monty for years.

'Why are you asking me about my mother anyway, I thought you were here to figure out who Alan's killer is?'

'And that's exactly what I'm doing; I'm just trying to see if this has a connection to what happened to your mother; and, I'll go so far as to say I think you're trying to work that out too.'

She shrugged her shoulders despondently.

He continued with a reassuring smile . . . 'So, in

your memories, you see the bad things that happened to her?'

'Yes, some really bad things. The imagery is vague. It's a feeling of complete dread, a feeling of her being violated. It's hard to explain.'

Josey's eyes speared onto her uncle. There was apprehension there; perhaps a bit of fear as well.

'You used the word *violated*,' he said to Monty. 'Am I to understand your mother told you she was raped?'

'Ease up, Detective,' Andrew protested.

'I know she was,' Monty said courageously.

Uncle and niece locked eyes.

Josey suddenly felt he was being insensitive to her ordeal. He wanted to move on to the next phase; to find out what she could be suppressing in relation to her mother being raped. He believed someone had actually told her this. There was one way to find out, but he wasn't sure how she would react to it. She seemed relaxed at the moment, so he decided to put the idea to the test. 'Monty, can I ask how you would feel about being hypnotised?'

Monty glanced at her uncle. This was Josey's third inkling that something was being held back between them. 'If I'm to help you, I need you to trust your instincts. Hypnotism will help bring that out in you.'

She was still looking at Andrew as if she needed him to give his approval.

If *she* saw an answer in his expression it escaped Josey's powers of detection, but he did have some theories.

'If it's okay with you, Uncle, then it's okay with me.'

Her answer sounded like a warning. In other words, *if I say something you don't want me to say, don't come crying to me later*.

'Can I take that as a yes?' Josey asked him.

He shrugged. There was not much else he could do.

Her eyes welled a little, but she forced herself to recover.

'I'll take you to meet Anthony Steel,' Josey told her. 'He's a friend, and a very good hypnotist. You'll like him. After that, I'll get reacquainted with your grandparents, tell them what I know.' Josey noted that look of foreboding again in Uncle Andrew. 'Is there a problem?'

Monty's eyes were fixed on her uncle as well, who seemed set to have a coronary. He appeared trapped. Finally she told Josey, 'Things, you know, their sort of a bit strained between me and the family at the moment, probably my fault.'

'I'm sorry,' Josey said to them both, 'something I should know about?'

'No.' Andrew's answer sounded final, so Josey left it there. He was guessing they knew the answer to the question, which he would follow up on later.

Trepidation remained on Monty's face as she said, 'I hope I'm not going to regret this.'

'You'll be fine,' Josey assured her – *hopefully*.

She looked to Meredith for support, and was told. 'It's your decision, sweetie.'

Monty's eyes welled, but she quickly recovered, convincing Josey she had the strength to do whatever was necessary to find some peace in her life.

CHAPTER TWELVE
Anthony Steel

The following day.

'My name is Montana.'
'How old are you, Montana?'
'Three.'
'Do you know where you are?'
'Yes.'
'Can you tell me; where you are?'
'I'm at home.'
'Do you know where your home is?'
'Yes.'
'Tell me where your home is.'
'It's in the country.'
'What's it like where your home is?'
'There is grass, and trees, and big mountains in the

distance.'

'It sounds very beautiful.'

'Yes. It is. It's very beautiful.'

'Do you feel happy?'

'Yes, of course. Why wouldn't I be?'

I'm glad you're happy. It's just that someone told me you aren't always happy. Is there something that makes you unhappy sometimes?'

'Yes.'

'Can you tell me about it?'

'It's when I'm not allowed to ride my Pony.'

'That makes you unhappy?'

'Yes, but it's not his fault. I'm not allowed to ride him when he is sick.'

'I see. Does he get sick a lot?'

'Not anymore.'

'No? Did someone make him better?'

'No. He died. That made me very sad.'

'I'm so sorry to hear that, Montana. Did your parents buy you another pony?'

'No. I didn't want one.'

'Do you have any other pets?'

'I don't like pets.'

'Wasn't your Pony your pet?'

'No. Peppy was my friend. He wasn't a pet.'

'I understand.'—

'Do you want to know a secret?' Montana asked the hypnotist.

'Oh—you have a secret?'

'Yes. Would you like to know what it is?'

'Well, yes, if it's okay for you to tell me.'

'It's my secret. I can tell you if I want.'

'Go ahead. Tell me your secret.'

'I'm not really three years old.' She whispered.

'You're not?'

'No. That's only from when I was born.'

'Doesn't that make you three?'

'No, silly, I was in Mummy's tummy for nine months.'

'I am silly aren't I; you're actually three years and nine months old, right?'

'Yes.'

'Montana?'

'Yes.'

'I'm a little confused.'

'Why?'

'Well, I don't know if I'm talking to you or your mother. Her name is Montana too, isn't it?'

No immediate answer.

'I don't understand. My mother's name is Margaret. My name is Montana. Some of my best friends call me Monty.'

'Oh, I see. Tell me; do you mind if I keep calling you by your full name - Montana?'

'That's all right, because you're not one of my best friends.'

'True, but I hope I can be. Montana, can I ask what year you were born?'

'I told you—three years ago.'

'Do you mean in the year two thousand?'

A pause.

'No.'

'Why not?'

'Because Mummy told me I was born in 1984.'

'1984, okay. And Mummy's name is Margaret.'

'Yes.'

'Let's go back to before that; just before you were born; back to that time. Would you like to?'

'Yes. I love being there.'

'*There*. Where do you mean?'

'In Mummy's tummy. It feels nice.'

The memory makes her laugh

'Is something funny?'

'I'm floating.'

'Can you tell me what it feels like—floating in Mummy's tummy?'

She releases another sweet giggle.

'It feels wet.'

'That must be nice. Can you see or hear anything?'

'Yes. I can see light. Oh, now it's dark again.'

'That's interesting. And what can you hear?'

'It sounds like a drum.'

'There is a drum in Mummy's tummy?'

'No, it's not really a drum. Mummy told me it is her heart.'

'She talks to you?'

'No. I hear her thoughts.'

'Is she thinking anything right now?'

Pause . . . A fearful frown appears, raising concern in the hypnotist's usually calm persona.

'Monty. Is your mother all right?'

'No. She is thinking bad thoughts.'

'Can you tell me about them?'

Stress

'Monty, listen to my voice. Are you feeling afraid?'

'Yes. So is Mummy. Someone is trying to hurt her.'

Sobbing

'I'm sorry. Would you like to stop now, Monty?'

'Yes. I want to *stop* . . .'

Monty has good reason; she is entering the dream from the night she ran away.

Dear God . . . this is real;

Inside her induced hypnotic world she is reliving the nightmare of being entombed in the manifestation of her mother; wrapped in the smell of leather and oil, soaked in the stale stench of the prolonged presence of sweat.

I didn't ask for this . . .

Steel's distant promise is telling her she is safe. That couldn't be further from the truth, she is on her own. No one outside can see or hear what is happening – not even the calming voice can aid her escape from the beast pervading her soul. All on the outside are blind to *see*, or *feel* the sheer brutality and unimaginable strength of the monster within . . .

Dear Jesus, I sense all that is happening inside the mind of my poor mother, terror, helplessness, and—hate.

Creatures abound, assisting, surrounding the frenzied violence, forcing things against her willpower.

She screams . . .

Monty's piercing cry permeates both worlds, a sudden siren that rocks the emotional foundation of those observing the hypnotism.

'Get her out of it!' Andrew demanded . . .

Monty doesn't hear her uncle's stress; pleas from Steel are fading—dropping into a deep, dark well.

She hears only her mother, ascending from its depths, crying.

At the rim, her lifeless form rises into view, impaled on the bloodstained tooth of *a rust encrusted anchor*.

Black oil, piebald with blood, slithers from the gross entanglement like syrup, returning to the hell-hole from whence it came . . .

Andrew knew better than to interfere, but he couldn't stop himself. He shoved Anthony Steel aside and began shaking his niece violently. 'Monty; wake up . . . *Wake up!*'

She doesn't hear or see the panic that is besetting the hypnotist and the others.

The assertions of beasts consume all others, chanting their messages in unison as one evil

choir—
No one can hear you; you're powerless . . .
Stop this . . . No . . . you're powerless . . .
I'm not . . . You are . . . you're powerless . . .
No . . . you're powerless—
Strength conquers!
Irrational guilt devours her.
Please don't kill me . . . .
But then, adrenalin explodes in her veins; mustering the will to *break free—*

Away from her hypnotic world, Monty bolted upright, eyes wide in sheer terror . . .

The beasts of hell *screech* in failure as she *lashes out—*

'Get the hell off me. . !'
Heard by all, her plea is a brutal awareness of her veiled struggle.
Her body was trembling, fighting . . . the abhorrent smell of sweat and oil still lingering—like poison.
Wrestling to contain Monty's wild thrashing, Steel's disconcerting panic confirms all control of his subject has been lost. 'While you can hear my voice!' he repeats, 'you are perfectly safe! Nothing bad can happen to you!'
The perplexed audience watched on helplessly, Josey in particular swamped by trauma, this was his idea.
Meredith wasn't about to let him forget it. 'I knew

this was a mistake.'

'Monty!' Steel was shouting now, 'Wake up; your safe!'

She freed her arm from his grip and brought it around in a wide powerful arc that connected with his temple.

Steel took the hit intended for *the assailant in her mind.*

Stumbling to the side, he lost his footing and fell; freeing her to head straight for her shoulder bag. No one moved. When she turned and faced them, the revolver in her hand assured the playing cards were firmly in her favour. Her eyes blazed with wild immoderation. In her flurry the bag had fallen to the floor, splaying its contents at her feet. 'Don't try and stop me,' she warned as she bent and forced the disarray back into the bag. 'I will shoot anyone who tries.' Her eyes blazed with wild intemperance.

The mishap was clearly stressing her beyond that of the hypnotic induced psychosis.

Something's missing from her bag.

'Stop this Monty!' The demand came from her uncle.

She pulled the trigger – no hesitation – very little thought – nil preparation in her aim.

Andrew got lucky, if you can call getting shot *lucky*, collecting a non-lethal through-and through to the deltoid muscle of the right arm. 'Ssshit! Jesus!' he swore through clenched teeth.

She continued rummaging in her bag, panicking over something she couldn't find. She gave up;

stood—and without a shred of empathy fired another shot—it smacked into a wall somewhere; *wasted;* she was waving the gun about randomly, inevitably clearing a clear path to the doorway, whereupon she stopped to train the pistol on Josey.

He managed not to flinch, not to respond in any way, letting her vet the enraged force that was driving her.

'Monty,' Andrew pleaded, 'the detective is not your enemy.'

Backing away with her eyes purposively fixed on Josey, she portrayed no eagerness to listen.

Steel, distraught, wasn't sure if they were dealing with Monty, or her mother.

Josey realised Monty was seriously unbalanced in this moment.

Enough to kill for? Clearly the answer was yes.

It was also clear her present state of mind couldn't entirely be attributed to the hypnotism; Steele had simply unearthed some preexisting mindsets. Josey needed to understand what those mindsets were. He needed to know what she believes she saw while under hypnosis. Does she somehow know what he has discovered about her mother's death? Or is it something else? Dare he tell her what he has found? Will the revelation unbalance her even further? It was practically a moot point; he had to do something, because she looked ready to shoot.

They were *all* about to learn what Josey had discovered. He shouted at her with the urgency of a man on death row's eleventh hour. 'I know your mother's death was no accident—!'

His brash statement rocked her to the core, not because it was a revelation, but because *it wasn't*.

Her trembling intensified, she was wondering how the detective could possibly know . . .

Josey noted that the expression on Andrew's face was one of utter surprise like everyone else, but his silence was way off kilter.

While Meredith couldn't have appeared *more* surprised, Steel remained blank, apparently still dealing with his failure to control his patient.

All that could wait; Monty was on the ropes and needed to be kept there long enough to defuse her anger, *be clear, fast and calm Josey decided* . . .

'I've found your mother's car!' he told her in the hope she might calm down and listen.

'Is this some sort of trick?' she responded sounding reasonable and rational.

'It's not a trick, what I discovered shows that someone deliberately wanted your mother to die in her car. Or be seriously injured. The brakes had been tampered with. If not for the truck running a red light she may never have been hurt, but I promise you, her death was no outright accident.'

For Meredith, his finding Montana's car was enough of a surprise, but finding proof she was murdered was beyond belief. 'When were you going to tell *me*,' she asked with an undisguised hint of annoyance.

Is he telling the truth, or is this a clever ploy to snap Montana back to reality?

Suspiciously, Monty scanned all the faces that were fixed on her in anticipation of a response. She'd make her own decisions about what people knew and didn't know, and wasn't about to be railroaded.

Josey felt he was reaching her. 'If you put the gun down I can explain.'

It was impossible to read her intentions . . . He hoped her silence meant she was processing the information about her mother's car, and that she was about to hand over the gun. If that's what she was thinking it would never be known, because she reacted with pure instinct when Andrew made a move to approach her. She fired the gun at him and bolted out into the corridor. Her departure was so sudden that she'd missed knowing Andrew had taken the bullet.

Josey got to the door in time to see her enter the stairwell. He checked over his shoulder and saw Meredith was going to Andrew's aid as he limped in pain toward a chair. Blood was already pumping through his trouser leg below the left knee.

'I'm going after her!' Josey shouted out to them.

They looked up in response, but he was already gone.

Andrew raised the trouser-leg to inspect the damage. 'Damn, its hit the bloody tibia,' he said as though impartially making a medical assessment on an injured patient. He had no reason to doubt his self-diagnosis. Shaking his head in disbelief he told Meredith, 'I can't believe she's done this.'

'Did anyone know she had a gun?' The question came from Steele, who was peeling himself off the floor, rubbing the red blotches left by Monty's backhand.

'She's a desperate girl,' Meredith offered.

Andrew flinched; – 'And dangerous it seems.'

'She is now,' Meredith added.

Andrew's disapproving eyes met Steel's.

He looked a beaten man as he announced, 'Wish the detective luck people, your niece needs to be found—and quickly.'

Josey came onto the street as the bus Monty had boarded was pulling away on the other side of the street. He saw her moving down the aisle, contrary to the forward movement of the vehicle.

The gun had been a complete surprise, the hypnotism a complete disaster. For the first time since starting this case, Detective Josey wasn't feeling confident it would end well.

You don't notice how fast a missed-bus moves until you need to chase one.

He broke into a sprint to keep up, ducking and weaving between disgruntled city strollers. A layer of sweat was beginning to latch onto his shirt. 'I'm getting too old for this shit, Fredie,' he said unconsciously glancing to the heavens.

A woman passing considered him a bit of a *weirdo*.

Half a block ahead the bus came to a stop and passengers began their exit. He quickened his pace, peering between traffic and milling pedestrians like a footballer darting left and right to reach the other side of the street, and the stairs that led to the subway. He caught a glimpse of her amongst the crowd that had vacated the bus to transfer to trains, but by the time he reached the entrance she was out of sight.

This's all my fault.

The stairwell was laden with weary travellers picking their way to the surface; still no sign of her.

Please don't do anything stupid.

Josey leapfrogged down multiple steps, deftly avoiding the human cluster.

He reached the platform to see her boarding a waiting train, three carriages ahead of his position. Stragglers were facing their last minute chance to get aboard, and with a bit of luck acquire a seat. Josey squeezed through the doors as they shut.

The train began its exit from the platform with ever increasing speed, leaving behind a splattering of latecomers watching it recede into the tunnel with envy.

Josey apologetically made his way through the plethora of passengers toward Monty's chosen carriage.

'What's you're hurry, buddy?' one disgruntled guy grumbled.

Josey avoided engagement and kept moving.

Once he reached her carriage he proceeded with added caution, careful not to draw attention, covertly scrutinising the sea of human cargo. He quickly spotted her. She had a seat facing him, but was looking out the window.

She has a gun, he reminded himself. *How do I approach in a way that won't encourage her to use it?*

He pushed away pent up tension on a lengthy breath.

How the hell did I allow this to happen? She's gone from victim to perpetrator in one short afternoon.

He was thinking this when her eyes fell on him. Her hand didn't sink into her shoulder bag and come out with the gun as he feared it might; instead she crabbed her way past seated passengers to reach the swaying sea of bodies blocking the isle. Josey guessed she would be making her way toward the exit at the far end of the carriage in preparation to leave at the next stop, which wasn't far off.

He followed suit, pushing his way through the hairy sea of swaying heads, hoping she wouldn't suddenly appear in front of him and start firing point blank.

Unbeknown to him, she was singling out a large tattooed man who was sandwiched amongst those standing. Ironically he looked like a biker; like Alan Kelly, someone she thought might intimidate on her behalf, her heart pounded as she approached him.

The rough looking character was already scaring her and she hadn't even made eye contact yet. If she was going to, she needed to do it now. 'Excuse me,' she said as she brushed up against him. 'There's a man on the train trying to kill me.'

Her warning was overheard by people close, raising a murmur of panic. Caught off-guard by her attractiveness and her alarming claim, instinct drove him to buy into getting involved.

'He's at the back of the carriage coming this way,' she told him.

Josey could see people milling about up ahead. Something was going on. He got a line of sight as Monty and the big guy emerged from the ruckus and locked eyes with him. Josey gathered why she might be talking with him. There was no mistake; Monty's disturbed mind was still capable of cunning.

The train is pulling in, he noted, *I can see how this goes . . .*

Tattoo-man approaches, says; lady back there tells me you're threatening her.

Then I say; that's because she's got a gun in her purse and I'm just trying to prevent bloodshed.

The *hulk-of-a-man* reached him and happened to notice the holstered gun under Josey's coat. He said, 'The girl's getting off – you're not!'

Josey watched her go. She stepped onto the platform and made her getaway without looking back. As the train moved on, Josey flashed his credentials at the clueless Samaritan and told him, 'Guess I'm back to square one; enjoy your day, big guy.'

***

'I did warn you,' Meredith told Josey after he had

returned from his failed pursuit. It seemed he was to bear the full brunt of blame for Monty's psychosis and her unexpected departure - and, for subsequently losing her.

Josey didn't turn from the window.

Outside, the high-rise buildings surrounding Anthony Steel's apartment stood like sentinels, hiding Monty Pritchard from view somewhere within their dark concrete fingers.

Doing her best to sweep over what had happened, Meredith shifted to the edge of her arm chair, wondering what was going through the detective's mind. 'Cameron?'

When he faced her, she could see he was rattled.

This's a first.

'You can't tell me that you're still skeptical after all this,' she mulled.

'Never completely skeptical, Meredith,' Josey corrected her as he turned back to the cityscape. 'Fact is I'm suspicious of skepticism, even though I lean ninety percent that way. I prefer to think I'm open-minded.' His mood was sullen and not entirely convincing. He felt bad enough without getting a lecture from his client.

Meredith reddened as her annoyance faded. She shifted some of the blame back toward herself. 'I should have told you not to do this.'

'Actually open-mindedness is the best approach right now,' Steel told Meredith. 'Hypnotism can only disclose what a person believes to be true.'

Meredith glared at him, *don't you start.*

'I'm not saying her memories aren't real, I'm saying they don't have to be.' He turned to Josey and added, 'If I were you though, I wouldn't dismiss them too quickly. I know of three cases where children claimed to have received messages from their mothers while still in the womb.'

'Just three of many,' Josey agreed as he turned away from the window. He rattled off what he knew of the subject. 'Scores of kids interviewed, all report feeling submerged – wet. Some saw light, just as Monty said she did. Some said it was always dark. There have been metaphysical studies of structure in the brain and all that. The subject abounds on the internet, most of it I take with a grain of salt. I just need to find our girl and keep her safe.'

End of lecture, now get off my back.

'I see you've done your research,' Steel said oblivious to his hurt.

'Always, but none of that closes my mind to a practical solution.'

'Ninety percent skepticism alive and well,' Meredith observed, but at the same time recognising he was already blaming himself and didn't need any extra help. She dropped the blame game and asked about the brakes. 'Was that part real?'

Josey crossed the room to where Monty had dropped the contents of her bag and began scanning the floor. 'Very much so.'

Meredith glanced at Steel to see if he had any understanding of what Josey was doing. He shook his head.

'I wouldn't mind hearing how you figured it out,' Meredith pushed.

He continued searching the floor as he answered. 'I asked Sergeant Brack where Montana's car might have been taken after the accident.'

He lent into the lounge and lifted a cushion – placed it down and turned on his heels with eyes cast down.

'Brack told me the city police had some property out of town where they store vehicles at life's end; most of the time they get snapped up by anyone who thought they can make a buck out of the parts.'

He lifted his eyes to meet Meredith's gaze, seemingly abandoning whatever he was looking for.

'Following a hunch, Brack came with me to the yard and we found Montana's wreck hidden away in a back corner.'

He began treading a wide arc around Meredith, forcing her to rotate in her chair to keep him in view.

'The *Vin* matched, so I poked around and found the hydraulic lines had been deliberately sabotaged. I sort of understand why this fact hadn't been discovered by investigators back-in-the-day. The way the perpetrator had damaged the brake-lines was almost undetectable. Missing it was entirely probable – especially given the lines were severely damaged in the accident.'

'You do realise,' Meredith pointed out, 'although you didn't even make-mention of the brakes, you say Monty knew her mother had been murdered.'

'Here's the thing, apparently Montana's father was

advised—by investigators—that the brakes had failed to stop her vehicle. The sabotage was missed, no one knew about that. Walter passed on what he *did* know to his wife and son. It's conceivable Margaret might have transferred her version of the story to her granddaughter when she was old enough to understand.

'It's clear the family knew about the brake failure, including Monty eventually. The *whys* and *wherefores* are hypothetical, but one thing is certain, someone deliberately hoped to murder Montana Pritchard—in her car—on the night of her eighteenth birthday. And that's a fact.'

Steel put his bid in. 'And someone is still out there trying to kill the daughter, the big question is why.'

Josey acknowledged his friend's point, why would anyone want to kill both mother *and daughter?*

Meredith wanted to clarify a point. 'How'd you know Pritchard knew about the brake failure?'

Josey commenced a second lap of the room. 'I located a witness to the accident, a guy who apparently tried to help Montana before the rescue teams arrived. He told me that in a brief moment of consciousness, Montana claimed the brake pedal had gone straight to the floor. The witness also said he had no doubt that was true, because Montana's car made no attempt to stop.'

Meredith was looking a little despondent. 'What are we going to do about this?'

Josey reappeared in her peripheral, heading once again to where Monty had dropped her bag. 'You, nothing, but *I'm* heading over to the hospital to have a little chat with Uncle Andrew.'

'If it's all the same to you I'd like to tag along.'

Josey crouched down and began peering under a couch. 'No disrespect, Meredith, but I need to do this alone. I need her uncle to loosen up about what's going on with the family. You're a little too close.'

She had to accept his point, but suspected there was more to his decision than met the eye.

What's he doing?

'You're already onto something!' she guessed. *Why else would you be looking under every piece of furniture?* 'What the hell are you looking for?'

His search didn't falter. 'Let's put it this way, I don't think Uncle Andrew is telling us all he knows.'

'And that prompts you to start looking under the furniture?'

'Indeed it does,' he told her distantly.

She might have been wrong, but it looked like he found what he was looking for, a small object that he took from beneath the couch and put in his pocket without mention.

CHAPTER THIRTEEN
The Necklace

Andrew had elected to go to the Sydney arm of Carmel-Care hospital, which only required a quick call to his father's friend, Bruno. He didn't need to check in; a colleague took care of the surgery and kept the operation off the books. Later he was taken to a private room where he wouldn't be noticed by other inmates. A trusted nurse saw to his needs.

He lifted his head from the pillow as Detective Cameron Josey entered the room. 'Have you found her?'

Josey was a little surprised to see him in traction, wired to the bed like a trapped marionette. He walked in without answering, slipped off his coat and placed it over the back of a chair by the bedside. 'More than a flesh-wound,' he observed as he sat.

Andrew knew it wasn't his leg or arm the detective had come to talk about.

Josey thought the news he had for the laid up patient was all bad, and wasn't in a hurry to give it to him. Finally he bunched up his brow and answered Andrew's question about his niece. 'I'm afraid not.'

Andrew let his head drop back onto the pillow. 'Then why are you here?'

'Doing my job.'

'One could argue you've done enough.'

'One could argue you haven't.'

His head shot off the pillow to meet Josey's eyes. 'You've got a nerve.'

'I'm not here to make friends with you, Andrew. I'm here to find out why you're withholding information.'

Trying to assess how much the detective knew he asked, 'What's this about?'

'It's about you not being straight with me.'

'Is that so?'

Josey stood, walked around the bed and to the other side of the room with his back turned.

Andrew followed him with his eyes and met his gaze when he turned.

'Are you sure there's nothing you want to tell me?' Josey asked as if the answer was already clear to him.

The answer had a defensive tone to it. 'About what?'

'About why Monty ran away.'

'You know *why* as well as I do.'

'Meaning, what she told you about her dream.'

'Exactly.'

The detective strode back to his coat and took something from an inside pocket, holding it hidden in his closed fist. He relaxed his hand, allowing a tiny tarnished necklace to fall free and undulate at the bottom of an equally tarnished chain. 'Tell me about this.'

The only thing the necklace had going for it was its uniqueness, fashioned in the form of a ship's anchor.

Andrew looked like a kid caught-out, but mustered enough defiance to say, 'Where'd you get that?'

'First things first,' he told his captivated listener. He swayed the chain left and right, causing the schlock trinket to swing like a pendulum. 'Let's go back to the first time I laid eyes on it . . .'

Fifteen years younger, dressed in white slacks and open neck shirt, Josey steps out from his Plymouth, wipes his brow and places a wide brim hat on to combat the summer heat. He looks at the massive house and tries to whistle.

'Nice house, Fredie,' he says to himself.

Nearing the front porch he sees Montana's lavish memorial nestled in the shade of a broad eucalyptus tree, and parked nearby, Pritchard's 1958 restored Cadillac. He takes a moment there to cool off, studying the epitaph on the grave's headstone.

After knocking on the door of the house he moves

back into the shade of the tree next to the grave. The beautifully restored Cadillac sits idly out of the sun, beckoning for an irresistible peek inside.

He pans over the lush green leather of the seats, the plastic-free dashboard, and the wraparound windscreen. The whole interior is pristine, except for an old worn-out necklace dangling beneath the rearview mirror. The trinket strikes him as being at odds with the rest of the car. Why would such a rich eminent doctor allow such a cheap item of jewelry inside a restored 58 Cadillac? . . .

With the nondescript necklace swinging in the grip of his hand Josey said, 'I see this now has your attention; as it got mine – and Monty's it seems.'

Andrew huffed. 'This doesn't mean what you think it does.'

'No?—believe me, I get that he's your father, but there are limits.'

'You're barking up the wrong tree, Detective.'

'I guess I shouldn't jump to conclusions. But, what I will do is talk to your father to see what *he* has to say about it. Ask him why his granddaughter suspects he raped her mother, his own daughter. Am I on the right track?'

It wasn't discomfort that Josey saw; his reaction was closer to *objection*.

'She's wrong'—

'Oh I see. She's right when you want her to be, and wrong when you don't.'

Andrew stewed over his new understanding of the detective's resolve to get to the bottom of what was going on. 'You haven't told me how you got hold of that.'

'When Monty dropped her bag, the necklace slid under the couch. She knew it wasn't among the items she could see, and it panicked her.'

'Well, maybe so, but not for the reason you think.'

Josey paced around the bed studying the trinket. 'Your father raped your sister,' he said without making eye contact, 'in the Caddy.'

'Good luck proving that.'

Josey returned to the bedside. 'I don't need to prove anything. Whether or not your niece is right or wrong is of no immediate interest to me. My job is to find her—and keep her safe. I should think that's what you would want too, am I wrong again?'

He had to concede. 'No, you're not wrong, about that I mean—but I promise you, my father did not rape my sister.'

Josey wasn't about to argue the point. He waited.

Andrew finally responded with sarcasm. 'You've got a good bloody memory, I'll give you that.'

'It wasn't just this,' he explained, juggling the bunched trinket in his palm. 'I could see you and your niece were hiding something; something to do with your father.'

'Very clever, but all that aside, how does any of this help you find my niece?'

'I'll know that after I speak with your father.' Josey picked up his coat to leave.

'A piece of advice, Detective; be ready for all hell to break loose when you accuse my father of raping his daughter. He's already set to tear your balls off over your little hypnotism stunt.'

Josey grinned. 'Let's wait and see shall we.'

Two minutes later, Josey missed his chance to speak with Walter Pritchard, he passed the doctor and his wife near the ground floor elevators without either party seeing each other.

CHAPTER FOURTEEN
Into her own Hands

Following her encounter with the detective on the train, Monty Pritchard walked north along *Pitt Street*, a one way street that ran to the south, ensuring anyone following would need to be on foot. She used shop-front reflections to watch out for suspicious characters behind her. If there was anyone, they were doing a pretty good job of staying out of sight.

Her mind was curiously clear now, compared to the state she was in immediately after the hypnotism. With the clarity came guilt associated with shooting her uncle. However, she had no choice but to move forward. A plan of action was already fostering. A plan that would prevail until her mother finally got justice. She didn't have to worry about the detective right away; she'd seen him continue on the train in the company of the biker. To make doubly sure no one was following, she stopped at a coffee shop and sat at a pavement table, affording her a wide view up-and-down the street. She stayed there for half an hour, nervously scanning for furtive observers.

Those men and women who *did* turn their heads in her direction were clearly doing so on account of her being especially easy on the eyes.

'Can I get you something else?'

The voice startled her. She looked at her watch; 11.45 - almost lunch. The tables would be needed for workers grabbing a quick bite. 'Thank you no, I was just leaving.'

'See you next time,' the young waiter said as invitingly as possible

She managed a smile and left.

Making her way to Hyde Park she sat on the grass in the sun, along with all the other grazers, people and pigeons alike. She wasn't in the least bit hungry. Her moment of clarity was once again eluding her; the hypnosis had unsettled her more than she thought. The indelible nightmare ebbed its way back into her mind, but anyone watching her would never suspect she was dealing with an identity crisis, quite literally. It wasn't that she saw herself as Montana—her dead mother—but rather her mother's memories were devouring her own, swamping her thoughts. Driving her on - *to make the call, or not make the call*?

For an hour, she wrestled with that question. Events and places poured through her mind like snapshots in time.

She reached into her bag and took out her cell phone. Seeing the gun reminded her of the shooting. It made her stomach turn. The missing necklace flashed through her mind. She recalled the spilt contents on the floor, and wondered if the troubling trinket had been found. Panic set in once more. She wanted it back.

How the hell do I handle this?

She made her decision.

She punched a number into her cell and waited.

'Hello, this's Patricia. Can I help you?'

It was good to hear a friendly voice. It brought her back to herself; back to being Monty. 'Patty, it's me.'

Nurse Heath knew the voice immediately. 'Monty, thank God. Baby, are you all right?'

'No. I'm in a lot of trouble,' she breathed.

'I've heard. But you're not helping yourself by running.'

Taken aback, Monty needed to quickly move beyond a lecture. 'Pat, listen to me; there was a man my mother knew, who everyone thought might be my father. Do you know who I'm talking about?'

Heath knew enough not to play dumb with Monty, not with her talent for knowing things about her mother's past. 'Brian Appleby. Why do you ask?'

'I need his number.'

'Why?'

She ignored the question. 'You'll find it amongst mum's contacts; a little green book in my side-table draw. Do it quickly.'

'Sweetheart, you're frightening me.'

'Join the club. Just do it. Please.'

'Okay, I'm going,' Heath grumbled as she made her way to the bedroom.

Laid up in his hospital bed with restrictive rods inserted into his leg, Andrew wasn't getting much rest. His condition did little to restrain his parents anger over what had happened. His father in particular wasn't one to mince words, or consider that eavesdroppers might have little interest, or patience, for things that aught not to concern them. He spoke loudly, as if no one else mattered but himself. Dirty-looks directed his way usually ran off him like water off a ducks back. Thankfully there weren't many people within earshot, thanks to the privacy of the room, but his voice still filtered into the hallway.

'What the hell did you say to make her shoot you?' he demanded.

'Okay, so now everyone in the hospital knows I've been shot. Thanks, Dad.'

'How could you let this happen,' Margaret weighed in.

I told you,' he reiterated in a whisper, 'she was psychotic.'

'It obviously wasn't safe for her to be hypnotised.'

'She gave the okay. What was I supposed to do?'

'Tell her no!' Walter bellowed.

'Dad, keep your voice down.'

He did, but not by much. 'I'll tell you this; if anything happens to her it'll be on your head.'

'That's rich,' Andrew told him defiantly.

'What's that supposed to mean?' His anger was regrowing.

'All right you two,' Margaret ground out through clenched teeth, 'stop.'

The battle subsided momentarily, but Andrew had a little of his own anger brewing. 'Maybe Dad, you might consider taking a little of the blame yourself. Firstly, your womanising didn't sit well with her.'

Walter looked ready to explode.

'Not now,' Margaret told Andrew urging him to be quiet.

'Let him talk,' Walter said waving his arm in the air.

She went to respond, but Andrew cut her off. 'We all know how he treated *you*,' he reminded his mother.

'I said not now.'

'No Mum, this needs to be said.' He kept his voice low, what he was about to say was a whole lot more than other people should hear.

Walter too decided it may be prudent to keep their conversation between themselves. 'Son, get it off your chest.'

His parents seemed suddenly uneasy, especially his mother.

What will this information do to them? Will they react with more anger, or sink into complete despair? Will my father deny everything?

'She saw more than your affair, Dad.'

Walter waited and wondered what was about to come from his son's mouth. His relationship with his son and granddaughter had irrevocably eroded since his regrettable indiscretion with the other woman; an affair that lasted no more than three months—undisclosed for more than two—yet, suspected by Margaret from the first night that he decided not to come home. When she discovered it was one of the nurses from the hospital, the wound cut even deeper. To make matters worse she knew the girl to talk to, a wildly attractive young red head. At least her stunning looks weren't an affront to her own. Walter's keen eye was often testament to his wife's good looks, albeit sliding toward advancing years.

'I only found this out a couple of days ago,' Andrew continued, 'I got her to open up; tried to talk her into coming home. She flatly refused. She broke down and told me what had her so upset. Not straight out. She was obviously having trouble talking about it.' He straightened himself in the bed and winced. 'Actually, I'm having trouble myself.'

'Get on with it,' Walter demanded with his usual impatience.

It was time to get to the point and he knew he wouldn't like it, *this was supposed to be the bloody detective's job.* Denying the truth was no longer an option – *not anymore*. 'All right, Dad - she thinks you raped Montana when she was seventeen.'

It was extremely clear that Walter had not been expecting this, his shock was genuine, his apparent disgust beyond description.

Good acting?

'This is a sick joke, right?' he finally asked with a sudden dry mouth.

Margaret was looking at him the way she did the day she confronted him about the Nurse Cook affair; *no*, this look was far worse than that.

'Your own damn daughter?' she breathed with restricted air.

Walter swung on her, eyes fiercely defensive. 'Margaret, don't listen to this. There's no way—'

She turned on Andrew. 'You're saying she *saw* this?'

The simple, reluctant nod he gave his parents sank into their souls. They, better than anyone, knew if Monty says she saw it, then, *she saw it*.

Walter launched into defence mode. 'There has to be some sort of mistake. Son, tell me exactly what she said to you.'

'It's not what she said; it's what she showed me.'

'Showed you?'

Margaret mustered her own impatience. 'What on-earth are you talking about?'

His gaze was fixed on Walter. 'Something that placed the rape of Montana in the Caddy; the necklace that Dad had hanging on the mirror, she took it the day she ran away.'

This information evoked deep misunderstanding in both his parents. Walter elected to voice the confusion. 'I don't get it. What in the-hell has the necklace got to do with anything?'

'It's what she saw in the dream about Montana's rape. She said her mother saw herself in the rearview mirror during the assault, along with the hanging necklace; it points to Montana being raped in *your* car. I mean, what else was she supposed to think?'

Finally understanding why their son was looking at them with such disdain, they inexplicably joined forces. It was Margaret who changed the course of the conversation. 'Where's the necklace now?'

Andrew couldn't fathom why she was asking. 'The detective has it.'

'*The detective*,' she repeated with annoyance, 'You're father and I have already discussed this; we want him out.'

He looked at his father. 'Even with what we now know—'

'What *do* we know, Andrew?' she snapped. 'What Monty saw was as a result of a really bad nightmare, she thought so herself, I was there.'

Andrew might have expected this rationalisation from his father, but not from his mother, *she's protecting him*.

'Your mother makes sense—'

'Shut up Walter,' she demanded, eyeballing the both of them. 'None of this gets repeated outside this family, and that includes not talking about Monty's gift . . . Do I make myself clear?'

Crystal clear.

Margaret had taken charge.

'Get that thing back, Andrew. Tell the detective he's not wanted. That man is off the case. I'll be telling Meredith Northey that myself—after I call the police.'

Walter was just as surprised as Andrew; her threat to call police came as a complete surprise, evidenced by their gob smacked expressions.

Although armed with Brian Appleby's phone number, Monty found she was unable to make the call. She had no real handle on whether or not it would work. It's just that he was a close friend of her mothers. She wasn't even sure why she was so positive about that, unless she'd been influenced by Meredith–before the shooting–or maybe it was the bedside photograph that she'd mentioned to Nurse Heath. In actual fact, she felt confused about everything. Especially about firing the gun at her uncle – she *loved* her uncle.

Needing time to clear her mind, Monty left the park and booked into a nearby hotel.

She stared at Brian's number half the night, afraid that if she dialed it into her phone the handset might explode in her hand.

Following lunch at the hotel the next day she finally worked up the courage to make the call.

'Who's this?' come a blunt response from a man in her ear.

On hearing the voice of Brian Appleby, she hesitated; then stammered into the phone, 'It, it's, Montana Pritchard.' Monty had no idea why she chose to use her mother's name. In spite of the fact things had mostly returned to normal—or so she believed—she was still slightly addled.

After several seconds of silence the voice said, 'Is this a joke?'

'I wish–and no–it's not a joke.'

More silence, then a light turns on. 'Oh, Monty. Montana Pritchard's daughter?'

She had no idea how he knew of the name Monty, but let it slide. Obviously on hearing the name Montana, he hadn't immediately connected to her daughter, but he had been a lot quicker than expected in working it out.

'Yes,' she admitted with a waver to her voice.

'You sound scared. Are you all right?'

She sobbed. 'No. I need your help. Someone is trying to kill me.'

At the other end of the line, Brian—now thirty seven—stood in the hallway of his unit trying to make sense of the strange call. He cast his mind back to Cameron Josey's equally strange visit, recalling how his father had reacted in telling the detective how Montana's mother had professed his paternal responsibility.

He finally said, 'Tell me where you are.'

He listened while she told him, all the while dealing with the possibility he may be about to meet his illegitimate daughter. 'Stay put,' he told her, 'I'll see you soon.'

He tore the page out of the notebook he'd written on and pocketed it; grabbed a bum-bag and headed out the door.

Josey made it out of the city to the beginning of the freeway heading west, which would take him across the mountains toward the Pritchard's second hideaway. He had been openly given the new address by Andrew before the session with Anthony Steel; before the calamitous hypnotism. It was a couple of hour's drive, so he figured it had better be worth it. He had no interest in denigrating Pritchard about what he did-or-didn't do with his daughter, as disgusting as it was. He was more concerned with what he'd do when confronted.

Is he the would-be killer as well as a rapist?

Earlier, Josey had decided announcing his arrival might scare him off, but on giving it some thought, decided it would automatically implicate him without the need to make the trip. This was never about physical confrontations. That's not how Josey worked.

He made the call.

'Who's calling please?' come a flat response.

He knew it was Nurse Heath the moment she spoke, *she still sounds evasive*.

He deliberately lifted his spirits. 'Patricia, you may remember me; I came to the family's previous abode just after Montana passed away. It's a bit of a long story as to why I'm—'

She cut in with, 'Detective Josey, I had a feeling you'd call.'

'Really?'

'Sorry, I had to be sure it wasn't the Pritchard's. I've had a call from Monty.'

He brought the Plymouth onto the shoulder and screeched to a halt.

She's worried about the Pritchards. I can almost guess why.

'Did she say where she was?'

'Not exactly, but I think I might know where you can start looking.'

'Please,' *I knew I liked Heath for a reason.*

'The call was about, Brian Appleby. She wanted his phone number, which she told me was here in her mother's bedroom.'

Appleby, the boy thought to be Monty's biological father.

'Were you able to give her the number?'

'Detective, can I talk candidly to you about this.'

'It's vital you do.'

'Margaret is fuming. She asked that I not talk to you.'

That explains the evasive tone, 'What reason did she give?'

'Have you seen the news?'

Where's she going with this? 'I've been on the road. What's happened?'

'Margaret's got the police involved.'

You're kidding.

Josey's Blue-tooth alerted him to an incoming call. 'Patricia, can you hold a moment?'

'Sure.'

'Max. What's up?'

'You and the Pritchard girl are all over the news; did you know?'

'Just about to find that out it seems.'

'The Pritchard woman is telling them you're responsible for her disappearance.'

'Nice. Listen, I've got Patricia Heath on the line. Stand by; I'll need your help to deal with this.'

'Right you are, Boss.'

'Patricia?'

'Yes.'

'My partner just filled me in.'

'Right; you apparently stirred things up at the hospital.'

That was the idea, Josey thought, *but not by involving the police.*

'Monty isn't too keen on talking to you either,' Patricia volunteered, 'but I figure you might be her best chance of staying out of trouble.'

'I gather you know her state of mind.'

'I do, and it leads me to think Appleby might be in her firing line. I'm told she has a gun.'

'Correct.' It had already occurred to Josey that Appleby may have come to the surface during Monty's hypnosis. Finding him before she did was now critical.

Patricia didn't hesitate about giving Appleby's number out when he asked for it, and he thanked her once again for her help.

He swung the car through the turning bay, laying rubber toward the city. Returning wasn't going to be routine. Two things were a priority; finding out more about the status of the police involvement, and getting rid of the Plymouth, they were bound to be looking for it. If he was to have any chance of finding Monty, he needed to stay clear of the law - for now.

Twenty minutes later he pulled into a stopover on the highway and placed a call to Maxine from a pay-phone. 'Hi, can I speak with Detective Josey please?' he feigned.

She knew it was him of course, but didn't say his name, or mention the trouble he was in. She knew not to, because the police had already called by the office asking for his whereabouts. She told the officers that—as far as she knew—he was on the south road travelling to Eden. It wasn't necessary to relay this to Josey, but she did anyway, concluding with, 'Can I get him to call you?'

'No that's fine,' Josey said, speaking code, 'Just let him know next week's function is on. We've decided on the Hydro.'

Maxine had no trouble understanding this instruction, The Hydro-Majestic—a refurbished retrospective-hotel on the western side of the Blue Mountains—was on his route back to Sydney, a popular meeting place for travellers, and in Josey's case, private detectives on the run. 'Cool, I will,' she confirmed without further conversation.

An hour later, Maxine pulled into the designated car-park in Josey's other car, an old white Corolla—a particularly common car—which he had registered in his wife's name. A smart cop might work out the connection without much trouble, but locating it would take longer than finding the Plymouth. Maxine parked several cars away from where Josey sat waiting behind the wheel. She casually walked over to give him the keys, plus a new throw away mobile. She knew instinctively that if her boss needed to swap cars, he most likely wanted to swap phones for the same reason.

'Thanks, Max.'

She beamed and said, 'That's all right, *James*.'

'*Money Penny*,' he responded, humouring her.

She grinned playfully, handed him the items through the window and walked into the hotel and sat where she could still see the Plymouth. After a minute or two she saw Josey get out and walk to the Corolla, get in and drive away. She knew the keys to the Plymouth would be sitting in the ignition waiting for her to take the target vehicle back to town, which she would do after a couple of light beers, during which she got more than a few looks from other patrons. Her Punk appearance still aroused a certain fascination, but not so much as it used to; older demographics testament to the gradual acceptance.

As she sipped through her beers, Josey's abandoned-phone rang hot. She kept it on silent, ignoring all calls, other than to take note of names to later relay to her boss. The Police rang twice, along with Meredith, Andrew, and a half dozen others whose numbers meant nothing. The biggest surprise was Kristen Poole, who Maxine could almost see rubbing her hands together in delight at the other end of the line. Trouble for Josey always managed to make the dragon lady ecstatic. Maxine had no idea why the impervious woman would bother calling; it obviously wasn't her that made the story go public this time. But then, maybe she was calling for some other reason entirely. She couldn't imagine it was to simply pass the time of day.

Bitch.

Maxine almost took the call from Prague. Josey's wife and daughter were there on a working holiday and somehow had heard their usually law-abiding man was on the run from the Australian cops.

Sorry, Mrs. Josey, you will have to wait with the others.

Not answering was protocol when the Chief wanted to stay out of sight, no matter who the caller was.

Traversing the freeway, Josey carefully poured over the case in his mind, oblivious to the noises and idiosyncrasies of his aging transportation.

What have I learnt so far—?

Montana was apparently raped in her father's Cadillac. Although this information had been derived from a large degree of speculation and wasn't any sort of proof, he didn't mind subscribing to it, that's why he gave the uncle such a hard time about his father. The real-lead was Monty's call to Brian Appleby.

Presumably the two will meet.

Why else would she need the number?

He thought to have Maxine try calling Appleby,

but decided not to. It wasn't clear if Appleby was a target or a potential perpetrator. For that matter, there was no proof that he was either. Plus his family may have already heard from the police.

Walter Pritchard on the face of it might need to remain on the suspect list - on both counts - but his assumed involvement in calling the police kind of circumvented either.

Maybe, Doctor Pritchard, you're smart enough to cover up your guilt by involving yourself in trying to help the Police. I guess the jury's still out on whether or not you raped your own daughter.

Josey shook his head, clearing the clutter. He had to keep reminding himself, hypnotism or not, these so called facts were at best loosely tenable.

He also figured the idea that the rape took place in the doctor's car, didn't automatically make his father the rapist. That assumption wasn't even close to water tight. Anyone could have been in that car that day, even Uncle Andrew.

There's a thought.

What he didn't know, was that the pristine car was off limits to anyone other than the doctor. He knew it might be a possibility, but hadn't had a chance to ask the question.

Josey thought about the share farmer, no one had said much about him; least of all Monty. Josey hadn't been told the guys name, only that he lived and worked on a few acres three kilometres from the Pritchard house in Trundle. All Josey had been told was, Bruno Borcheck had introduced the farmer to

Walter as a man who could be trusted to keep their location a secret. He was the one who brought the food in twice a week. The Pritchards never had to leave the property. As the story goes, Walter and Andrew kept their sanity by helping the share-farmer with his daily chores, producing vegetables for a local market. Margaret spent all her time with Monty. They professed to have had plenty to do looking after the big house.

Apparently, in their spare time Margaret and Monty would chat for hours, probing into the young girl's memories of her mother. Josey felt there was a strong possibility Monty's present insights came directly from *Grandma Pritchard* back-in-the-day. He was also beginning to get a gut feeling the malefactor was someone, as yet, unknown.

Josey had picked up most of the family info from Doctor Borcheck during a chat with him at his private hospital following the shooting at Steel's unit. The shooting of course had only threatened to bring the family out of the cold, whereas calling in the police had nailed them firmly into the public arena. They were obviously desperate to find their daughter. For the moment, that was in everybody's favour, if it served to bring Monty out of hiding.

Pushing all this aside, Josey shifted his focus further into the case, beyond what he might learn from the Applebys, toward what else he could unearth in relation to the tampering of Montana's brakes.

Who had the opportunity?

By the time he was halfway to the city, Maxine's text came in, listing all his unanswered calls. First he rang Sergeant Barry Brack to hopefully solicit some inside help.

'Bill Hendley's heading up the case,' Brack told him without hesitation. 'I know the guy, but he's somewhat unreachable. I'll do my best to find out what I can.'

Next, Josey called Meredith. She didn't know who it was until he spoke, his replacement phone presented no-caller ID.

'This is going well I don't think,' she quipped.

'My first instinct too, but it's not that bad really. The publicity might be just the help we need. At least the Pritchards have pulled their heads out of the sand. As for Monty, her seeing this could be a good thing; it might be enough to bring her home.'

'The publicity won't help *you*, I wouldn't think.'

'Under control; trust me.'

He refrained from telling her of his plan to visit the Applebys, finding their son's whereabouts might well be a longshot, and he didn't want to get her hopes up too soon. The fact young Appleby would now be somewhere in his thirties meant there was a very good chance he had already left the nest. Or, if he was still living with his parents there was no guarantee they hadn't moved from their original address.

At the end of the conversation Meredith reverted to positive thinking, telling him he had her complete trust and that she would sit tight and wait for further developments.

Josey decided not to return Andrew's call; he was probably involved with the police as much as his parents.

As for Poole, s*he can piss in the wind.*

Josey pulled into the street of Brian Junior's family home and parked a hundred yards from the house to check for the presence of surveillance police. If he was caught-snooping the game would be up and he'd have no choice but to go quietly and claim he had no idea the police were looking for him. The issue wouldn't be *snooping*, that's what private investigators do.

He waited in the car, forced to assume the Appleby's could well be at home, and most likely would have seen the news; he needed to tread softly in case they were of a mind to turn him in. Their number was in his alternate phone, Maxine always made sure she uploaded all his numbers. He called and got the answer machine.

Old man Appleby announced himself, his wife and his son. Perfect, the young man still lives with his parents. Josey hung up.

CHAPTER FIFTEEN
Closing In

A neighbour was mowing his grass in the front yard of the house next door. *Even more perfect.* After deciding all was normal, Josey slipped on a cap and sunglasses; drove down and parked in front of the house. He stood outside the car for a moment. No one approached, so he crossed the street, walked up to the front door and was about to knock.

'Hey!—'

He swung toward lawn-mower man.

'. . . The Applebys aren't home,' the helpful neighbour announced.

Josey wasn't interested in leaving a message so he launched into finding out if the man knew where they were. 'Do you know where I can find Brian right now?'

'Which one?'

'Either.'

'Is everything okay?'

Josey expected the question, 'nothing to worry about.'

'Right, well, if it's young Brian you want he has his own apartment at Darling Harbour.'

Must be an old message on the answer-machine.

'You might find his parents at Cockle Bay, but you better hurry, their heading off across *the ditch* for three months–on their yacht.' He'd mentioned the yacht with a slight toss of the head, like it was a bone of contention. 'The young bloke goes with them sometimes.'

Josey imagined their *young bloke*—now in his thirties—would probably prefer to be doing his own thing. He didn't buy into any further conversation. Taking his informant's advice, he got the address of Bee's apartment, thanked the man and hurried back to his car. At least now he had some sort of lead.

Ten minutes later he parked in King Street near where he was told the yacht would be moored, and made a quick dash to the wharf. He figured with embarkation looming it was best to find out if the neighbour was perhaps right about the son being with them, and conceivably with Monty as a passenger—voluntarily or otherwise.

What a way to get away.

Three yachts sat in wait. The *Sealavie* was the only one that had people fussing about on the deck; a man and a woman. Josey found an outdoor table at a cafe facing the water. It took only moments to determine that the man and woman he had seen at a distance tweaking the boat were in fact Brian's parents. Now, it was sit tight-and-wait to see if anyone else showed up for the ride.

The idea of sailing out to sea for three months made him think of his wife and daughter enjoying their holiday on the other side of the world. He hoped they hadn't gotten wind of what was happening in Australia.

He placed a call.

'I know not to think the worst,' Rebecca told him as clearly as she could. 'But you'll understand our concern. Care to enlighten?'

'I'm not in police custody—not yet anyway.'

'Oh, that sounds reassuring.'

In her mind's eye she saw him smirk. 'Do we need to come home?'

'No. I'm not in any danger. It's a straightforward case, a misunderstanding by police. It'll all be straightened out in a couple of days. Is Molly there with you?'

'Nice. Change the subject. She's in the shower. We were getting ready to go to the consulate to find out what's happening to you.'

'Not a good idea. Don't let the authorities know where you are. So long as you use this number I can keep you up to date and out of the firing line.'

He could hear his wife breathing at the other end of the line, *thinking*. Then, 'All right. Be careful?'

'Always, give my love to *Mol*. Tell her not to worry.'

'Okay,' she breathed. 'Love you.'

'Ditto, talk soon.'

'Bye.'

As Josey was hanging up he overheard Doctor Prichard's name being mentioned. A woman with a rather shrill voice, who sat with a group of friends three tables away, was responding to something on the screen of her smart phone.

She excitedly told her girlfriends. 'He's been questioned by police about what happened with his daughter.'

'Who's Doctor Pritchard?' one girl asked.

'Doctor Pritchard. You know, the doctor who abducted his comatose daughter from hospital, ages ago.'

Even after eighteen years, with the public's original interest in the Pritchard story, it wasn't hard to understand why it was again finding its way into the new media.

Josey suspected Kristen Poole might be relishing Pritchard's past being regurgitated - brought back into the limelight. Apart from his own personal experience with Poole, Meredith had filled him in on how much the two medicos hated each other. Bad press was inevitable anyway, right from the moment the doctor exposed himself to media scrutiny. Josey completely understood why he had. Here was a man desperately hoping his daughter might contact him. Josey doubted she would, even though her grandfather's actions were increasingly suggesting total innocence of the attack on her mother. Plus, logic demanded, if Monty's alto ego still truly believed her grandfather was the rapist, she would almost certainly have contacted the police herself by now. That hadn't happened, so Josey was even more convinced now that it was someone else she was looking for, someone she had identified under hypnosis.

I'll cross that bridge when I come to it.

He thought about the connotations of that scenario and rejected any suggestion her dead mother had anything to do with her new direction. Fact or fiction, Detective Josey was determined to circumvent the possibility she may be planning revenge against someone she believes attacked her mother, an act that would ruin her life, a life already prone to flights of fantasy.

Time was of the essence; his own identity was becoming quickly well known, thanks to an excellent picture of himself that the media had gotten their hands on somehow. During his call to Brack, the Sergeant had warned. 'You'd better get a good makeup artist.'

Josey considered Brack was exaggerating, but he didn't ignore his advice. Although his stubble was hardly approaching a beard, his newly acquired country-bumpkin clothes and sunglasses created a new and different person to the one in the picture.

On the yacht, Appleby regained his attention, waving at someone on the pier. It was *Bee*, older but easily recognized. He had emerged from a crowd on the boardwalk and was making his way toward the boat. He was alone, which at the moment could mean one of several possibilities.

One, he hasn't hooked up with Monty.

Two, she's back at his apartment.

Three, she's already on the boat.

. . . The alternative doesn't bare thinking about.

The possibility Brian junior might be Monty's target, or vice-versa, hadn't as yet escaped Josey's consideration either. If one were to believe the Intel, that back-in-the-day he was suspected of being her paternal father, in *her* mind that might automatically make him her mother's rapist. If he *was,* Josey surmised, unless he was somehow aware of Monty's fictional gift he wouldn't be expecting she knows about it, or much less believe she wants to kill him for it. Actually being the rapist could make him all the more interested in meeting her. Of course if the coitus wasn't rape, then it was reasonable to expect that even an innocent affair with Montana would furnish him with an emotional connection enough to prompt a meeting. It's a meeting that would be bound to create some awkwardness, given Montana's identical resemblance to her mother. But then, Bee's interest in Monty may be as simple as a thirty-six-year-old-man enjoying the magic of revisiting his youth, albeit with his illegitimate daughter.

Too deep; this is all hypothetical, first things first. But it did raise a question, one that couldn't be answered right now; does Monty believe she is the result of the rape?

Josey focused back on the yacht, he needed to see

if Brian would go with his parents.

Maybe get a glimpse of Monty before that happens.

However, fifteen minutes later Bee was leaving. The trio looked to be having a really heavy conversation. His father handed him something that was small enough to fit inside a fist; possibly a key, *to the boat?*

No. As Brian walked away, his parents were already releasing the ropes in preparation to set off, leaving their son on the pier.

No sign of Monty.

Josey's only option now was to follow Junior.

After leaving the boardwalk, Bee continued on foot into the city. In York Street—using the key his father had given him—he let himself into a parked Beamer that was waiting in the curb, *presumably Dad's.*

Josey made a dash for his own car, which was just around the corner in King Street, *a lucky break.*

He pulled away with little more than a quick glance in the rear view mirror, raising the wrath of an advancing van driver, his objection expressed with a resounding horn-blast.

Rounding the corner into York, Josey saw the silver BMW turning toward the harbour. He tailed the car across the famous *coat-hanger*, over the harbour and into Milsons Point. He was still wondering if Monty might be on board the yacht. It even crossed his mind she may have been harmed by Brian in self-defense, if in fact she had decided to use her gun on him, and now because of it; were the parents helping their son escape.

He followed for another two blocks, down to the water front. The *Beamer* slowed outside an apartment block and nosed onto the apron of the drive, waiting for the street level car-park door to glide open.

Josey drove on by, negotiated a three point turn in the tiny street, parked and waited with the motor running in the belief Bee's car might soon exit and go back toward the harbour bridge, possibly with a passenger.

Hopefully in the land of the living.

In no more than five minutes the silver sedan drove out of the car-park with Brian at the wheel, now dressed in fresh clothes with the addition of a cap, maybe suggesting a boat trip. Josey hoped Monty would be waiting on the parent's yacht and not taking a nap in Bee's boot.

The traffic was heavy enough to disguise Josey's pursuit. They traversed ten miles of the Pacific goat-track, then onto the freeway north. Forty five minutes later the BMW pulled off into the tiny town of Brooklyn, nestled beneath steep cliffs on the banks of the Hawkesbury River. As they were the only two cars that had made the exit it became a little harder to follow undetected. Josey had been to the town a couple of times in the past and knew there was only one road in and out, culminating in a Marina on the banks of the river. He parked to the side of the road and let Bee's car continue on out of sight. After a short spell, Josey continued on until Brooklyn Road became Dangar Road, leading onto the Marina.

Driving in, he saw Bee had pulled to the side near the mouth of one of about ten jetties lined with luxury boats. He'd walked to the end of one and now relaxed in wait, a *boat trip*?

Josey parked his car at the furthest pier and walked to the water's edge. Lifting his binoculars he panned in the direction of the river's mouth, which was just out of sight behind the steep banks. A couple of craft slid into view, having just made their way in. Too far off to make out, but he was betting one of them was the *Sealavie* coming to pick up their son.

Is she on the boat?

Maybe this has nothing to do with Monty at all.

Maybe Brian is just delivering the car for his parents to use while they're in Brooklyn.

Josey wasn't about to risk not being able to follow in the event his target boarded a boat, so he walked to a nearby shed to investigate hiring transportation.

A guy working on a hull in dry-dock lifted his head as the detective entered displaying his credentials. 'Morning,' Josey announced, 'how quick can you help a working man in need?'

The guy gave Josey a quick glance and lowered his eyes to the ID, which was held close enough to read. A friendly looking fellow, solid build with arms like pistons; dressed in shorts, T-shirt, no socks and sand-shoes, he returned to working on the hull and said, 'Pretty quick, how far and how fast, Detective

Josey?'

'Fast, not sure how far.'

The *boatie* faced him and then pointed to a speedy looking yacht resting in the water against the dock. 'That one can whip you out in about ten minutes from now. That fast enough?'

'Hopefully.'

'Cost you three hundred an hour,' he warned, 'Including skipper. That's me, name's Hank.'

'Not a problem, Hank.' Josey went to shake his hand, but the skipper was couth enough to suggest he think twice by displaying his oil covered palm.

'Done,' Josey said relaxing the gesture. 'Call me Cam.'

'Know where you're headed, Boss?'

Josey left the question open, immediately clinching the deal with three hundred cash in advance. He glanced to the approaching yachts; a focal point not missed by his seafaring chaperone. Josey saw that he noticed. 'I may need to leave as soon as I get back, if that works.'

Hank grinned in understanding.

After leaving the boatshed, Josey walked across to the Hawkesbury River Marina and bought himself a beer, which he enjoyed on a sunny balcony overlooking the jetty. With the binoculars strung around his neck, he looked every bit the relaxed tourist. He lifted the glasses and examined up and down the river. Mostly down-river in the direction of the sea, his only real interest was in any craft that might appear to be approaching the pier to pick up

Bee. Nothing came.

He casually finished his beer and wandered back down to the boatshed to make sure his rental was being prepared. He needn't have worried; the skipper was already at the wheelhouse with the screw gurgling in the water.

'Climb aboard,' he invited, 'make yourself comfortable, clocks on hold.'

Comfortable was an understatement, this gleaming machine had all the comforts of home.

Three hundred is cheap.

Josey sat at the stern and made no attempt to give Hank any instructions.

'I'm guessing we're not in a hurry,' the skipper said with his back turned. Getting no response he checked over his shoulder to find his passenger preoccupied at the back of the boat glued to binoculars. The detective's line of sight confirmed the distraction was the guy standing on the pier in front of the Marina.

'I think we might be in business,' Josey told the skipper.

Hank figured his passenger had captured the runabout that seemed set on a course for the jetty. 'That's Billy Bateup's boat. He's come round from Patonga if that's of any interest.'

'Depends on where he's headed when he leaves.'

'That'll be Patonga, it's the only trip Billy ever does.'

Josey panned the binoculars, tracking with the runabout till it reached the pier. Billy Bateup was indeed Bee's ferry provider. When he pulled alongside the pier there was a short mandatory greeting, then straight to business. As Bee stepped aboard the ferryman's *Tinny*, which according to Hank only ever returned to base, Josey said, 'I guess we're off to Patonga.'

'Patonga it is, Boss,' Hank responded leaning on the throttle.

At least he's not calling me, Chief. 'I need to follow without them knowing.'

Hank smiled to himself. The big launch churned up a wake and powered away into a sweeping curve. 'I'll go wide, wait and see where they go.'

They hadn't gone far before Billy's mandatory trajectory was confirmed. The runabout had pulled away from the pier and was turning in the predicted direction.

With the pursuer in the lead, the two craft proceeded down river approaching Juno Point, whereupon they would get a clear view of the open sea.

Rounding the point, Josey panned his binoculars seaward. A couple of sailing craft were making their way in. Too far off to make out, but he was becoming sure by the minute that one of them was the yacht that left Sydney with the Pritchards onboard.

Timing's about right for a boat that size.

The same anomalies kept repeating, it was still anyone's guess as to what was going on.

The only thing that possibly made sense at this

point was choosing Brooklyn over Patonga to bring the car in, avoiding the round trip through Umina.

Hank was bringing his boat further around Juno Point. 'If I keep going around the point she'll be out of sight!' Hank warned referring to Bateup's boat a few clicks back. 'I can go straight out to sea and keep her in sight, but there's a bit of a swell up if you're good with that.'

Josey lowered the glasses and turned to the craft following.

Hank was right about the swell; it was becoming difficult to maintain footing. 'Go ahead, Skipper,' he agreed while taking a call on his cell.

Hank's grin confirmed working with a private detective was considered above his usual station as a tour guide for rubbernecks. When Josey's call connected, Hank turned away and kept his eye on the open sea ahead.

'Meredith. I may have some good news,' Josey announced into his cell.

'Please tell me you've found her,' she responded excitedly.

'Not exactly.'

'What does *not exactly* mean?'

'It means I might have. I'm about to find out.'

'Where are you?'

'Brooklyn, on the Hawkesbury – well, almost.'

Hank was keeping busy, but clearly hearing the detective's side of the conversation.

Josey became guarded, still gambling the skipper didn't watch much television. He could have held off telling Meredith exactly what he was up to at this point, but felt the time was as good as any to bring her up to speed. 'Do you remember the nurse at the house?' He avoided mentioning the Pritchard name.

'Of course, Patricia Heath.'

'Right. Well I spoke with her. She gave me a heads up on a call our subject made asking for Brian-you-know-who's phone number, which she was able to pass on to both of us.'

'Sounds weird, why do you think Heath felt okay entrusting you with that?'

'The call was the day the family went public. Our subject told the nurse the family's story about me wasn't true. Anyway, the thing is, I think, for better or worse she wants to meet with him.'

'With Brian, why?'

'That's the sixty four thousand dollar question.'

'Okay, so what's with the Hawkesbury?'

'There's a possibility Brian's family are helping them hide aboard their yacht. That's assuming their together. I don't know that yet.'

'Really,' Meredith chimed with surprise. 'And if they are, what are you planning to do?'

'I'll make contact. See what happens.'

Josey was only able to sustain talking with Meredith for a short while longer, his stomach dictating the need to take his leave. Looking back toward Patonga Beach, he could see Billy Bateup's boat enjoying much calmer waters behind the ever diminishing waves.

'Okay,' Josey told his client finally, '*Gotta* go,

shows on.'

She was a little bemused by the sudden urgency. 'Right, good luck—stay safe.'

He hung up quickly for fear of regurgitating into the phone.

Hank noticed his passenger was done with the open sea. 'Back to the beach?'

Josey's response was immediate. 'Please.'

Once Hank had nursed the launch to a discrete distance off Patonga beach, Josey's stomach began to settle. A jetty stretching a hundred yards off the centre of the small strip of sand was where young Bee once again patiently waited, presumably for another aquatic journey.

What exactly are the Appleby's up to?

Whatever it was, the longer it went on the more Josey was convince he was on the right track to finding Monty.

When the two yachts entering the river's mouth separated and came close, he was able to identify the Sealavie heading straight for Patonga. When she finally nestled alongside the jetty with the sheets away, Josey noted that Bee's father didn't bother tying off, opting to throw a rope loosely over a pylon to assist in keeping the craft abreast. Bee's mother, Bev, remained at the helm with the on-board motor running, while her husband made his way to the bow to give his son a helping hand aboard.

Still no sign of Monty—maybe I've jumped the gun talking to Meredith.

An occasional glance was all Josey needed in order to watch what was happening aboard the Sealavie.

With Bee onboard, the two men disappeared below for a few minutes. When they came back on top, Bee took over the helm, replacing his mother, who then joined her husband, stepping onto the jetty.

Is Monty waiting below? Why not just pick Bee up at Brooklyn?

The answer came as a young female fitted with a backpack ran onto the jetty, presumably having left the cover of a small seaside cafe. Josey sank low, resting the binoculars on the side-rail. And - there she was, his extremely evasive person-of-interest, all thoughts of her being dead, thankfully discredited.

Dad removed the temporary restraint from the pylon as Bee took command of the vessel. Monty preparedly accepted Appleby's hand as she stepped onto the boat, signifying there was no coercion involved in her joining them. Once she was seated, Bee lent on the throttle and the yacht churned away toward Juno Point, or out to sea.

Josey was looking chuffed. 'Okay, I've finally got my girl.'

'Game on.' Hank speculated.

Remaining low to avoid detection from the jetty, Josey gestured to wait. 'Let's see which way she's headed.' He tapped the face of his watch. 'If she goes seaward we might be out of business.'

Hank checked Sealavie's course. 'They're not putting up sheets,' he told his passenger. 'Means she's headed up river.'

Josey was more than a little impressed with his skipper. So much so that he felt obliged to impart at least something of what was going on. 'You can ask questions you know, Hank.'

Hank eyed him.

'Within reason,' Josey added.

'That's okay, Boss. You seem a decent type. If I thought otherwise I'd have had you off this tub . . . Besides, I already know who you are, and who she is.' He'd tossed his head in the direction of Appleby's yacht. 'I figure since the Pritchard girl isn't here on this boat, your obviously not the bad guy their making out.'

Josey approved of Hank's logic with a hearty laugh – then countered, 'Maybe I just haven't abducted her *yet*.'

The skipper grinned.

'I'm in good hands then.'

'Good as your mother's, so long as you don't try shooting me or anyone else.'

Josey noticed his jacket had opened, exposing his holstered pistol.

Hank's permanent grin suggested he might be really enjoying himself, *guns and private detectives, outside his usual ferry job*.

'Deal,' Josey promised, closing his coat.

'He's rounding Juno Point.' Hank advised.

This meant the Sealavie's heading was indeed upriver, and not back out to sea as Josey feared it might be.

Hank eased the launch forward, careful not to draw

any undue interest from the shore. He noted the detective's other two persons of interest—still standing on the Jetty—were taking a good look at the gleaming white boat, but that was normal for a magnificent craft like this. Hank was familiar with the reverential glances he got from people.

If the Sealavie had turned toward the mouth of the river, it would already be game-over. Equally, if they motored too far up river, Josey might still run out of time. The Hawkesbury was no small waterway, running all the way to the Blue Mountains, nearly a hundred miles away as the river winds.

Hank took a glance back to Patonga beach. 'Your other friends just got picked up by Billy.'

Josey turned and saw the runabout leaving the jetty. 'My guess is they're heading back to their car at Brooklyn.'

Hank took his launch out through the heads to allow the two boats to get some distance between them, and to allow Billy Bateup to pass and get well ahead.

The onboard phone blurted above the sound of the boat, he snapped up the hand piece and answered, 'Roz?'

A female voice responded over the PA. 'You've got another customer, a flash looking gent.'

'How long can he wait?'

'He says he can't.'

Hank turned to Josey to see what he thought about him taking the job.

'I need a couple of hours, but an hour's fine if you need to go.'

'Rozie, tell him two hours at the very least, if he can't wait; tough.'

'Okay, *Darlin*, see you when I see you.'

He hung up. 'Can't stand dick-heads,' he told Josey as they began to renegotiate a swell.

Josey wasn't even certain two hours would be enough.

The skipper saw his passenger was looking a little pale again. 'Keep your head low, Boss, I'll pour on the power and take the lead; save some time and make sure you don't throw up over my shiny deck.' While he took the big launch up river at full bore, Josey spread out on the bench-seat and closed his eyes.

Brooklyn, with its cluster of buildings nestled tightly between steep bushy cliffs, and splatters of massive boulders, formed a backdrop for Billy's runabout as it made its way in. Ahead of Hank's position, Bee's yacht was passing beneath the shadow of the expressway.

By the time Hank and Josey reached the bridge, the Sealavie was rounding a sweeping twist in the river to the south. Near fifteen minutes had passed since leaving Patonga.

Josey's stomach was settling down the further they reached into calmer waters. The wake was now stretching back to the distant road bridge at Brooklyn. Juno Point, Patonga and the open sea could no longer be seen.

The journey had brought them to the first major bend in the river, and near to a small island whose only inhabitants were dead people. It couldn't be seen from water level, but Josey was familiar with the fact there was a very old, abandoned cemetery at its crest. As they were about to skim past, Josey noticed Bee's yacht was pulling in about a kilometre ahead.

'Swing in here, Hank!' he suggested.

'I can get closer without them noticing if you want.'

'No, this will be just fine, a good vantage point for the time being.'

'Right you are.' He turned the launch three sixty to port and slid in next to a refurbished floating jetty that adjoined a path to the top of the deserted island.

'Two minutes up, two minutes back,' Josey promised as he leapt from the boat.

'Go for it, Boss. I'll give you a blast if I need to split.'

'I'll be quick.'

Josey ran from view up the bush track, arriving among a small array of toppled tombstones just in time to look down and see someone tying off Bee's boat at the jetty. He took a closer look with his field glasses resting atop a gravestone, confirming it was indeed young Bee that was moving about the deck.

Monty must be below while Bee deals with the tie off, looks like they're staying.

Bee leaped onto the timber jetty and disappeared into a bush track just beyond where the jetty joined the shore. Panning across the tree tops he was eventually afforded a mosaic glimpse of a shack, barely visible beneath the bush canopy, which Bee went into.

He panned back to the yacht.

No movement.

Back to the track - there was bee again, returning to the yacht. He stepped aboard and stood at the galley door looking into the bowels of the boat. A moment later Monty slipped into view from below. The two of them made their way off the boat, across the jetty and followed the same trodden path that Bee had just used, disappearing beneath the treetops momentarily before reaching the shack.

Josey scurried back down to the boat and asked Hank to set off toward where the Pritchard's yacht had berthed—'Not too close.'

'There's a secluded beach adjacent, below the cliff. I'll put in there.'

Josey liked the way Hank played along. If he was curious about what was to happen next he didn't show it.

Josey had been set down on a small secluded beach from where he gave the skipper his leave. 'I can't say how long I'll be,' he admitted. 'Any chance you ferry after dark?'

Hank's expression indicated *not usually*, but said, 'Call me.'

They exchanged numbers and Hank powered away toward Brooklyn.

From the beach—looking up the face of the rocky

incline—Josey could see part of the eastern side of the shack. To his left, poking out from the bush-line, he could see the tip of the jetty where Bee's yacht lay at rest. If by chance, Monty and Bee instantly reappeared to leave again, and with no way of following, Josey would be forced to confront them before they set off. In spite of the fact Monty had held a gun on him, and presumably still had the weapon, Josey decided her demeanour now seemed somewhat more relaxed than the last time he saw her. As for Bee—given he and the girl appeared to be at ease with each other—there was no reason to believe he was involved in any sort of felonious behaviour.

Josey clambered up the cliff face, negotiating the boulders that had sat like motionless sculptures for centuries. His ascension brought him to the edge of the bush track that Bee had used to reach the small holiday dwelling. From here he could clearly see the shack to his right and the jetty and yacht to his left. He waited, and listened. A window opened and a light from inside stabbed out into the failing light of dusk. Josey silently advanced to the open window and cautiously peered inside. They were moving about the tiny living area in silence, shifting chairs and other paraphernalia. In a small cupboard, Monty found coffee and a percolator.

Josey couldn't help feeling a little voyeuristic at this point, and hoped things weren't about to get weird between them.

Aboard the launch, Hank had pushed whatever

events were about to take place at the holiday shack completely from his mind. If someone hadn't been urgently waiting for him, he would be pulling in for the night. His wife often alerted him on the radio if passengers were in special need of a speedy journey, even at night if the money was right, which is why he was expecting to procure an immediate assignment as he nursed the launch into port, unless of course Roz had managed to scare the would-be client away with the price. She hadn't, he was still waiting, but not necessarily abound with patience

'I'm a bit pressed for time,' the intended passenger called from the wharf, anxiously eyeing his gold watch. Lifting his eyes to the wheelhouse he added, 'Your wife said it'd be all right if we go straight away?'

Hank studied the man while urging the hull into a gentle caress with the dock, like Roz told him; he looked pretty sharp, black suit and shiny boots, *obviously not looking for a joy ride*.

'Right, no worries, where're you off to?'

Without further invitation, the agile man jumped aboard with the grace of an athlete.

'I was hoping you could tell me,' he confessed with a slanted grin.

Good on his feet - been around boats.

'Say again,' Hank queried.

'I'm with the detective you took out.'

Hank considered his claim suspiciously, failing to hide a slight hesitancy. 'You don't say.'

The guy continued to move slowly toward the base

of the ladder leading up to where Hank stood at the controls.

'Can you get me out to where he is? I was supposed to be with him, got here a little late.'

Although the would-be passenger's explanation sounded reasonable, there was something about his demeanour that didn't sit right.

'I'll let him know you're here,' Hank told him as he swept up his cell and began dialling.

'Don't,' the man demanded.

'What?'

The *athlete* bounded up to the wheelhouse like a monkey, and with his back turned to the wharf, pulled a silenced gun from under his jacket. 'Take me to him, or I'll drop you where you stand – Don't think I can't drive this bucket without you.'

Hank's immediate thought was, *everybody's got guns today*.

Under the cover of night, Josey surreptitiously watched through the open window, eavesdropping on Bee and Monty's conversation, a dialogue that had taken several minutes to get started. It wasn't an exaggeration to say the exchange was unexpectedly arctic. He thought to knock on the door and hopefully be invited in. That plan got muddier the more he thought about it. Given Monty had already pointed a gun in his direction; he decided he might learn more if he stayed outside and stayed alive.

Inside the dimly lit room he could see her agitatedly pacing around. They hadn't spoken for five minutes. Bee sat propped on his elbows at a table looking decidedly frustrated.

'Don't get me wrong,' she was suddenly saying to him, 'what your family has done for me; it's appreciated believe me.'

Bee lent back in his chair and said doubtfully, 'But?'

'*But,*' she emphasised with heightened stress in her voice and wavering confidence. 'I've changed my mind. I've got too much other *stuff* happening in my life.'

Her tears welled so easily that it shocked him. 'Why are you crying?' he asked with gained concern.

She couldn't speak.

The atmosphere in the room sank into awkward silence once more. Josey could see Bee was giving her a moment to recover, and possibly time to broach the subject further, perhaps delicately, but finally he was unable to skirt around the problem he had. 'You'd already done the DNA test before we met,' he went on to say. 'So why wait till now to tell me?'

She kept eye contact, but gave no answer.

'I wouldn't have minded you know—if you were my daughter—I did love your mother in case you're wondering.'

She recognised Bee was harbouring some hurt of his own. 'I'm sorry,' she apologised. 'Please forgive me; I'm under a lot of stress.'

That much was clear. He waited.

'Although I knew you weren't my father I was aware you could have been.'

'I should be the one apologising,' he offered with complete sobriety. 'It wasn't my intention to bring you out here for an interrogation.'

His empathy tugged at her heartstrings. 'I know,' she told him.

Glancing over at the percolator he suggested they take a break.

She clearly welcomed the diversion from her internal war.

He had a war of his own brewing. 'My parents are completely stifling,' he admitted as he moved to the kitchen bench. 'They can be utter control freaks at times.'

Behind his back she tilted her head in agreement.

'I mean, they don't understand how uncomfortable this is for me.'

And me, she thought.

'I have to be honest, when you came to us for help my first instinct was to turn a blind eye, pretend it wasn't important that I could be your father, but when I saw you, your incredible resemblance to your mother - I just had to help—'

He arrived with their coffees and sat opposite her at the table. 'All these conditions are my parent's doing. I know it's not what you asked for—'

'My decision has nothing to do with them, or the reputation of their pretty little future daughter-in-law.' She immediately realised she'd snapped at him unfairly, but right at that moment couldn't think of a way to mend the damage.

They drank in silence, entombed in their personal thoughts.

Josey suddenly realised it was all about saving face, *the Appleby's want Monty out of their son's life because he's getting married.* The hair stood upright on the back of his neck, this was turning into a huge waste of time. But, at least he had established they were not a threat to each other. He wasn't to know what was coming, and how it would change everything.

Monty finally reached across and touched his hand. 'I'm sorry for what I said about your fiancé. I was out of line.'

'There's no need to apologise.'

'Well maybe there is, my using paternity to gain leverage worked on your parents as surely as if I'd pointed a gun at them.' The thought of shooting her uncle gave her a chill.

Looking at this vibrant young woman sitting opposite, a girl half his age, he found himself drifting back to the warmth and charm of her mother, so identical. He recalled the nights they'd spent in each other's arms hanging out together, quite secretly; innocently.

This beautiful recollection engendered in him a need to remember that this beautiful young woman in front of him was not Montana, his lost love, a woman with whom he had only once consummated their love, a love lost suddenly at the hand of a drunken truck driver, or so he believed.

'None of this matters anymore,' he reasoned. 'Once they find out I'm not your father they'll back off. Any hold they had on you is gone.'

'Which also means they've got no more need to help me,' she said pointing out the irony. 'I realise I don't deserve their help after the trouble I've caused.'

'I'm not my parents, Monty. I'll see to it you're safe. You deserve that. I owe it to your mother.'

Seemingly true to her state of mind, panic turned to a measure of frustration. 'When we get back to Brooklyn I'll be leaving. I don't want to see your parents. Please tell them I can't leave Australia; and anyway, it's not right to be taking money from them. And, it's not right to be wrecking your marriage.'

Bee watched her shrink inwardly, presumably filtering memories that were extremely troublesome and probably way beyond anything he could possibly imagine.

She had deliberately omitted telling Bee and his family about her mother's rape. If she had, it might have annulled the suggestion Brian was her father. That almost certainly would have stymied her original appeal for help from the Applebys. But as he'd said, it was in the past.

Even though she could only claim to have sensed her mother's rape in her nightmare – and again under hypnosis; she adhered to the belief the necklace in the Cadillac proved her mother was indeed raped in her grandfather's car - which, on top of the DNA, exonerated Brian completely. She did however mention her mother's murder to Bee—without going into any detail—and that she believed the same person was trying to kill her. Hence the reason she needed to go into hiding. She made no mention of the brakes, because then she would have had to bring Detective Josey into the conversation.

Monty's claim her mother was murdered in her own car and the circumstances surrounding it, made Bee wonder why she hadn't just gone to the police. She'd done her best to explain why she couldn't, but it was difficult for him to understand. She also told him about the shooting and what led up to it, which explained why she appeared so screwed up when she first made contact.

Although she didn't want to, she was cornered into mentioning Josey and his cohort Northey.

She was beginning to wish she'd stayed at home where she had the perfect place to completely vanish. She'd managed to do so for close to eighteen years without too much turmoil. Now that her parents had brought the police into it she could no longer go back to the family; or so she believed.

*

It was clear to Josey that Bee was drawn to facilitate his parents' wishes in respect to Monty's desire for help. Yet, principally it was the rich, intimate relationship he'd had with her mother— amplified by the exacting physical similarities the daughter possessed—that really drew him in.

In spite of this willingness to help her, it was very apparent Bee's prevailing parents were pulling the strings; hell-bent on making sure Monty disappears from their son's life. Undoubtedly this action for them was imperative if Bee was to have a normal future with his bride-to-be. His dubious history with Montana—and his recent connection with her troubled daughter, a woman wanted for questioning by police—would irrevocably scare off their future daughter-in-law; and her family. Not to mention, following the arrogant way Margaret Pritchard broached the subject of intimacy between Montana and Bee–there was no love-loss between the Pritchards and the Applebys.

Whatever the fine detail of the agreement was, between Monty and the Applebys, it was now being abhorred by her, none of which helped Josey. There was still only one fact in the case; and that is, someone had tampered with Montana's car the day she died. As for Montana's rape, there was real evidence in the form of Monty's absconded out-of-place Cadillac Jewelry.

As grubby and confusing as all this was, the scenario was about to become a whole lot more damnable, beginning with a long, loud horn-blast from a vessel close to shore.

Hank?

CHAPTER SIXTEEN
An unexpected Death

The alto tone resounded from the river walls in a constant boom, demanding attention.

From his vantage point outside the shack, Josey had a clear line of sight to the stretch of water adjacent to the beach at the bottom of the cliff, and to the source of the warning sound. He could see it was coming from Hank's launch. The skipper wasn't alone. The distant figures were at odds, fighting. It was hard to see the detail, but it had to be Hank leaning on the horn. It had to be the unwelcome passenger dressed in black that was trying to stop him. Then, one figure, presumably Hank, staggered across the deck and fell overboard. The aggressor took control of the vessel, advancing it out of sight behind trees, toward the beach. Inside, Bee was getting up from the table to investigate the sound.

Josey drew away from the window and put his back up against the wall, just as Bee reached the window. He heard him say to Monty, 'I can't see anything.'

'It's probably nothing.'

'Probably.' He left the window and returned to the table.

Josey had two problems, one, he needed to let them know of his presence, and two, quickly convince them he was no threat. Deciding there was no time to waste he burst in unannounced, startling the already frightened occupants to their feet. Bee's chair got launched across the room. Monty grappled with her shoulder-bag, drawing her pistol onto the detective for the second time. 'How the hell did you find me here?'

Even though it had been fifteen years since laying eyes on Josey at Bee's parent's house, he recognized him immediately. 'Far out,' was all he could think to say, and although the penny had dropped, Bee was baffled as to how the damn guy somehow managed to show up after so much time. 'I think you should leave, Detective,' he told him bravely, 'you're not needed here.'

'You should listen,' Monty advised Josey, 'if I can shoot my Uncle I sure as hell can shoot you.'

'Shoot first and talk later if you've a mind to,' Josey hastened, 'but I suggest you save your bullets for what's about to happen. I promise you Monty, there's nowhere to run this time.'

'Try me.'

'You're suspicious, I get that.' He was pleading

for understanding. 'I'm asking you to trust me. I know you believe someone is out to kill you, and I believe that too, and right now, even more so. You're would-be killer may be about to try again. I haven't got time to explain, but I'm going back outside to try and stop him, just keep that gun ready and don't let anyone in but me.' He glanced to Bee. 'And turn off the lights.'

Josey turned his back on the shaking gun and left, trusting Monty wouldn't pull the trigger.

She maintained her aim on the closed door. Bee did his best to snap her out of it, but she was too frightened to break her stance. He left-her-be and took charge, locking up and turning off the lights.

Josey made his way down the rocky incline as fast and silently as he could; gun out of its holster; half expecting to be ambushed, coming face to face with the felon.

He stopped twice, listened . . . no sound of movement.

Is he still on the beach or in the bush coming toward me?

Two minutes later he reached where the bush gave way to the sand and hid inside the tree-line, surveying the area.

Hank's boat was held fast by its anchor.

No sign of the suspect.

There was a splash.

Believing it might be the skipper battling in the water; Josey broke his cover, sprinting across the beach in the direction of the sound, wondering if he would hear a shot, or just feel the bullet that took him down. He made it to the water's edge without incident. In the dim light he saw Hank struggling to keep his head above water, only ten feet from shore. Josey waded in until his feet left the sand, leaving him to *swim* the last yard to reach the embattled skipper. Treading water he took hold and swam underarm, dragging the sizable man into the shallows. With feet on the bottom he gained further purchase, enough to haul him up onto solid sand. He saw why Hank had been having so much trouble in the water, blood was pouring liberally from under his left arm.

'The bastard shot me,' he said sounding disgusted with himself. The bullet had hit somewhere near the upper ribcage. 'Thanks Boss,' he spluttered. 'Normally I'm an okay swimmer.'

Josey looked over his shoulder, surveying the beach and the incline leading up to the shack, looking for any sign of the gunman. Hank could see he was concerned the shooter might already have made it to the top. 'You'd better get on up. This guy means business.'

He was right, *no sound of a gunshot meant he was using a silencer—a professional.*

Wanting to be sure the skipper didn't bleed-out on the beach, Josey told him, 'Put your hand over the wound and squeeze your arm in tight; you're losing a heap of blood.'

He did as asked and again encouraged Josey to go and take care of business, which he did without further hesitation.

It was deathly quiet beyond the solid cabin walls, barricades serving not only to protect, but also to screen against ungovernable imaginings—

Sudden pounding on the door froze Brian as stiff as a store-mannequin.

On impulse Monty swung her pistol to the sound and jerked the trigger.

Josey felt the wind of the through-and-through bullet the instant it splintered a hole into the locked door. 'Don't shoot; it's me – open up!'

They hesitated.

'Hurry,' Josey warned breathlessly!

Bee made the move. Josey pushed in through the partly open door, slamming and latching it after him.

'What the hell is going on?' Bee demanded. They could see the blood on his clothing.

Josey was battling to recover from his rapid ascent from the beach. 'There's someone here,' he breathed to Monty. 'I don't know if he's the one who killed your boyfriend, but he's here with a gun, and he's already shot a man.'

They glared at him in stunned silence.

Josey forced air into his lungs. 'The skipper; that brought me here,' *another breath,* 'he's on the beach; badly hurt.'

'So where's this guy with the gun now?' Bee asked anxiously.

Monty was beyond frightened, gripping her gun so tightly Josey was concerned she might panic and fire it again. 'Please, put the gun down till you need it,' he cautioned.

Bee was the only one in the room without a gun at this point. 'What do we do?' he asked in the hope the detective had some sort of experience with crazed gunmen.

'Have you got any weapons here?'

'Not likely. I've never even held a gun.'

Monty snapped out of her immobilisation and asked Josey, 'Did you see him?'

'Only at a distance,' Josey said still gasping for air; *she's wondering if the man is her stalker. Is there any doubt*?

Josey almost hoped it *was*, because if it wasn't, none of this was making a whole lot of sense. Another hunch began to grow in his mind. It didn't weaken his first; instead it gave him two major suspects on equal par. He was nowhere near ready to mention either one in front of present company.

Not yet.

The room took on a *glow*. It was coming from light hitting the laced curtains. Shadows traversed the floor and folded over furniture and walls as the source of the illumination apparently elevated.

'What is it?' Monty asked puzzled by the strange light.

Josey was already at the flimsy shades to try and answer that question. Monty cowered further into the room; afraid a bullet would pierce through the glass and kill the detective, leaving her and her *gunphobic* friend to deal with whoever was outside.

'It's a flare,' Josey informed them.

The lingering fire-work was lighting the ground outside as broadly as sustained lightning, showing the gunman wasn't anywhere near.

Josey guessed it was Hank who had fired the flare. *No mean feat in his present condition.* He would have had to swim back out to the boat with strength rapidly flagging. '*The Skipper's calling for help,*' he mulled aloud.

Waiting to see what their adversary might do was getting them nowhere; laying low created time for the perpetrator to hatch a plan that could end in their demise. Whatever the case, the threat needed to be faced. Josey hoped the flare would stick-around long enough to hold the gunman at bay. There was no telling how long the transient light would last.

'Stay put,' he told the others as he once again left them to close up.

As he made his way beyond the tree-line bordering the shack, the light overhead was already fading, creating deepening shadows in which to hide from view. He didn't get time to ponder this mutual advantage, because he heard the cabin door open behind him. Unbelievably, when he turned, he saw Bee and Monty standing outside on the porch—

The man dressed in black appeared out of the shadows and jostled them inside, slamming the door closed behind him.

Josey ran, his worst fears surfacing like the paws of a predator. He felt powerless—

The window shades lit up as a shot rang out inside - *loud and clear*. This gave him renewed hope. On reaching the porch he smashed the door in with one aggressive kick. The scene that spread-out before him was exactly what he'd expected; the perpetrator on the floor and Monty clutching the gun that shot him; shaking wildly.

'Monty!' he shouted, 'it's over.'

Instinct drove her to swing the gun onto him. He darted out of the firing line, ending spread-eagled on the floor. The weapon in her hand became a mere token of protection. Seemingly unaware of her kneejerk reaction, she made no attempt to realign her aim. Undoubtedly, shock was setting in.

For Josey, the sound of her gun-blast had been the best thing he could have hoped for. It told him she had gotten her shot away before the attacker had a chance to fire his silenced-weapon.

Josey now needed to get Monty's gun away from her. Moving easy-like, he judiciously prized the weapon from her hand and handed it to Bee, who held the butt clenched between his fingertips as though it might bite.

Monty remained impuissant; unable to tear her eyes from the perpetrator lying motionless in a growing pool of blood, afraid he might suddenly reanimate and use the gun still clenched in his hand. Josey moved to the body to put her mind at rest. He checked for a pulse. There was none. He nodded at Monty, confirming the man was dead. She didn't take the news too positively. Prizing the fingers apart he relieved the assassin of the daunting weapon and held it up for Monty to see the man was no longer a threat. He could see she was viewing it as a bitter-sweet result; yes the danger was removed, but she had just *killed* a man. He went to her and she immediately wrapped her arms around him, sobbing into his shoulder, welcoming the embrace of a man who presented no threat.

'You're okay,' he whispered against her hair, 'it was self defence. You're not in any trouble. We'll talk to the police and sort this out.'

She pulled away sharply. 'No! I don't want the police!'

Her reaction startled him. 'Honey, we have to—'

'It's not him,' she blurted.

Josey's mind raced, piecing together her meaning; recalling what he knew of her troubled story.

She must have seen the man who killed Kelly. That's the only way she could know this is not the same man.

It also meant Josey's hunch was gaining credence.

How many stalkers are there?

Josey concluded that all these anomalies fitted neatly into what he believed was really going on. 'There's no one else here,' he told her, 'you're safe.' He pulled her back in and held her tight.

She lifted her head to gaze up into his calming face. Wiping away tears with the back of her hand she asked. 'How can you be sure—?'

'*Help*' . . . The plea was an almost inarticulate groan from behind. They spun and saw Brian clutching his chest. His hand edged from under his jacket as he lowered his eyes knowingly, his palm was covered in blood; *his* blood.

Monty shook violently. 'No, no, no, no; please–not Brian—'

He collapsed onto his knees and sank back onto his heels—stunned—life was leaving.

Josey prized away from Monty's grip and bent onto his haunches beside Bee, easing him gently onto his back. The young man's eyes were already becoming increasingly distant.

Josey had seen shots to the chest before. It was almost always fatal, *no less this time*.

Monty knelt; guilt devouring her; clearly feeling responsible. 'I'm so sorry,' she said, unable to hold back tears. *I've killed him*. She could see his end was near.

He struggled with the apprehension of death, until mercifully his failing mind saw the beautiful Montana looking down at him, her crying smile beckoning . . . he reached up and wiped her tears away–and went to her willingly . . .

. . . His arm fell to his side and an unspoken avowal died with his final breath . . .

Organs shut down; eyes vanished behind a milky white veil—

Those left behind saw nothing of where he went.

Josey had seen death up close like this many times, but Monty never had . . .

She hadn't even seen Alan Kelly that way. 'I don't understand,' she pleaded, looking to Josey for support.

He recognised her stress was more than just feeling

responsible for bringing Brian here to meet his untimely death.

She's thinking it was her bullet that killed him. 'Listen to me. You didn't shoot Brian, okay.'

He drew her attention toward the silenced gun in his hand and told her. 'Brian was shot with the shooter's gun. After he came in you only fired your gun once.'

Understanding crossed her face as gently and surely as clouds releasing a warming sun; palpable relief.

Josey carefully urged her away from Appleby's corpse, and walked her to the other side of the room. 'I'm here for you,' he said battling emotions of his own.

She allowed herself to sink back into his arms.

Monty was about the same age as Josey's daughter, Molly. Their names were similar. It once again made him think of his family on the other side of the world. The promise to his wife that he was safe was losing cogency, fast—

Josey's phone rang! It was, Brack.

He sat Monty at the table and told her. 'I need to take this. It's someone who can help.'

But Josey was about to have that little breeze-of-hope taken from his sails as soon as Brack came on the line.

'Buddy, are you sure you've been telling me everything?'

Josey was taken aback by his friend's blunt tone. 'Something wrong, Baz?'

'Not unless being implicated in the murder of Alan Kelly there isn't.'

'You're kidding.'

'I kid you not. The whole state of New South Wales is looking for you right now. Only a matter of time before this goes national.'

'You do realise I didn't—'

'Hey!' Brack bellowed into the phone. 'This's *me* you're talking to. If you'd topped Kelly you'd hardly have mentioned his name to me.'

Josey calmed and said, 'Right.'

'So; who hates you enough to dump-you-in-the-shiter?'

Josey was already pondering the same question, but Brack couldn't be told what Josey suspected at this point, because friend or no friend, as a police officer he would be required to pass forward the information - or even be forced to act on it.

Josey thought of Maxine. The police would be tackling every avenue that might lead to his whereabouts. She once again would have been first on the list of contacts. He dare not call her, not even on the alternate line. All he could do is wait for her call when deemed absolutely safe, which obviously wasn't yet.

What a mess.

On impulse, he used a handkerchief to begin wiping fingerprints from the silenced gun. They were all his. The gunman wore gloves.

'You there, Buddy?' Brack prodded.

'Sorry. I'm just trying to sort out how to handle

this.'

'You could turn yourself in, clear your name, how's that for an idea.'

Ignoring the sarcasm, Josey looked at the two bodies lying on the floor and said, 'There's something else.'

'Figures, what is it?'

Josey considered his friend was being a little flippant about the whole thing. He looked over to Monty, cradling her head and weeping, too upset to look at the carnage. Josey lowered his voice into the phone. 'I've found the girl,' he told Brack. 'I'm with her now. Believe it or not, she's just survived an assassination attempt; managed to kill the hit man.'

After forty years in the force, nothing ever surprised Brack, especially when it came to people, but this time he'd had some preliminary assistance in understanding Josey's predicament. 'Like I said, I had it figured; your friend the charter-guy raised the alarm back at Brooklyn.'

Excellent—Hanks alive.

'You could have started with that.'

'Wanted to hear what you had to say.'

There was something else Brack needed to hear. 'Yeah well, my girl is pretty damn upset about the shooting.'

'Why? Her stalker is dead. That's *got-ta* be good.'

'According to her it's not him—'

'Wait, back up,' Brack demanded with frustration in his voice. 'I thought you said she didn't know who the guy is.'

'I'm guessing she got a glimpse the night Kelly was killed. I've yet to talk to her about it.'

Josey filled Brack in about the shooting of her uncle and tried to explain the reason. The upshot was that there was nothing in the system about it, which indicated the Pritchards hadn't reported it. That's as Josey expected, and thankfully one less thing to worry about. Killing the hit-man was enough.

'Right, well, tell her to get over it, she's no doubt killed some other scum-bag.'

'Problem is, the scum-bag has killed Appleby; he's the son—'

'I know who he is,' Brack interrupted. 'Okay look, that's unfortunate, but it changes nothing. His parents have been with police in Brooklyn spilling their guts for the last two hours. I'm telling you buddy; hold your butt there till the police arrive.'

'And say what?'

'Explain the situation; convince your girl she's got no choice but to get involved; let her explain the runaround she's given you; that you've been trying to find her. Bring your client into it. The young girl's wanted for questioning too now, and if they're to believe your friend Hank, the police will believe you're no threat—'

'Can you weigh into this?'

'Might not be a good idea me poking around. Could do more harm than good.'

In spite of Brack's ultimatum, Josey trusted his cop-mate to have some sort of escape plan if a meeting with police were to go badly, but there was another problem. He moved out of earshot from Monty and told Brack, 'Talking to the cops might not be that simple.'

'Why?'

'Because there's a chance Appleby's parents might be the ones who hired the hit-man.'

Mentioning to Brack that the Applebys were suspect murderers was of little consequence in keeping this part of Josey's hunch alive, but he dare not mention the rest because it could seriously affect a successful outcome.

Brack considered Josey's claim and remained silent for a moment, then said, 'Listen to me, Cam, his parents are on their way out to you as we speak. When they find out their son is dead—and if, as-you-say they're involved in the attack, which inadvertently puts them behind their son's death—they might be of a mind to lay this on you and the girl. I don't know - you know them better than I do. This one's yours I'm afraid. It's your call. *Leave* and they're bound to use it to save their skins. *Stay* and you'll be tied up answering questions for months. Maybe that's not a problem, but if it is—'

Josey knew Brack was right, and that a decision would need to be made soon. Monty was an absolute certainty to want to high tail it away from the police, she would never be happy until the man allegedly responsible for the rape and subsequent death of her mother was brought to some sort of justice. That might not end well either, she had demonstrated she was capable of shooting at the enemy, which might even turn out to be an innocent person . . . and another thing; *was her gun registered?* Forensics would be looking closely at the bullet buried inside the assailant. Without witnesses to say who fired the gun, both she and Josey would become joint suspects, yet again. That didn't mean Josey was prepared to interfere with the crime scene any more than he already had.

The question remained; *why would the Appleby's go to such extremes to protect their son's future?- given they don't yet know Monty is about to flatly refused their offer of money, or refuse to leave Australia . . . perhaps murder was their goal from the start.*

But, either way, Josey believed Bee had no idea they might be prepared to kill on his behalf. And, even if they were killers, they almost certainly wouldn't have been planning to kill their own son, because their overall plan was to protect him, albeit a cocked-up plan.

With Bee's parents on their way to the holiday shack there was precious little time to ponder the situation, but Monty was in a very fragile state and would need a degree of counseling, or so he thought. When he explained the Pritchards were on their way she wanted out and practically led the way.

It was time to take Brack's advice and leave.

The course of action was clear, the means, not so clear.

CHAPTER SEVENTEEN
The Borchecks

Bruno Borcheck's Ambulance travelled south with its two fugitives. It had taken a lot of tricky setting up; they were wanted for questioning over not just one murder now, but two, and possibly three once the police scrutinised the crime scene at the shack. They wouldn't find Monty's gun, but its absence wouldn't provide her with immunity – they'd have the bullet. Josey didn't know Borcheck well enough to ask for his help in whisking them away in a hospital vehicle, that task had been yielded to Walter Pritchard.

*

As predicted, it had been hard to convince Monty that contacting her family was the only way forward if they were to be given time to find answers. Contacting her family was the last thing on her list of priorities, but more than anything though; she needed people around her who cared for her welfare. She now seemed comfortable including Josey as one of those people. Frankly he could have done with having his own family around to keep things grounded, but by the same token he was intransigent in his resolve to keep them out of it. Rebecca and Molly would remain oblivious to his predicament until the full blown affair ultimately advanced into the clutches of the police and the press.

After the conversation with Brack, Josey's plan had hatched quickly. He knew it wouldn't be long before the news of the bodies in the shack made it into the media. It was a story that would inevitably bring a spotlight onto the Pritchards as well as themselves - a fact that needed to be explained to Molly's family.

The shooting prompted an immediate need for Monty and Josey to get away from the scene of the crime, as it would no doubt be labeled by the police. It was a simple enough task to walk through bush to a road that clung to the hilltop above the Appleby's holiday home.

Once on the road, acting as father and daughter, they persuaded a passing motorist to believe they had become disoriented in the bush and lost their way. Their ploy managed to procure a lift to the nearest garage, and a public phone.

Josey decided the safest call Monty could make

was to contact Andrew at Carmel Care's sister hospital in Sydney, where he was recuperating from his gunshot wound. He hoped the police would not be permitted to monitor the hospital's phones.

Apprehensively, she made the call, launching into a heartfelt apology for shooting her uncle, expressing genuine relief that his leg was mending well.

Andrew graciously told her not to worry, and that no real harm had been done to her relationship with the family, or to his leg.

Between bouts of crying she explained everything that had happened since leaving steel's office. Josey gave her plenty of leeway to air her emotions.

'I love you Uncle,' she told Andrew toward the end of their conversation.

Believing her uncle would most likely contact her grandparents without being told to, Josey decided to enforce the initiative by suggesting she advise Andrew to speak with them in person, and to emphasise the dire situation their granddaughter was in. Not to mention solicit their help in finding a way to keep Molly from the clutches of the police, not only her, but themselves.

As it turned out, Monty's grandparents had remained in Sydney. Borcheck and his wife flew down from their Brisbane hospital to be with the family; to best assist in whatever the next step demanded. His hospital had once again become the Pritchards home. Requests to visit the city police in Surry Hills were so frequently made, the Pritchards decided it would be prudent to stay around the southern metropolis to avoid the constant travel from the far west. Reporters hung around the hospital like flies at a city dump, but it wasn't hard for Borcheck to enforce the condition they stay outside and well away from any contact with his guests. If it became necessary for them to make a quick getaway, he had plenty of ways for the Pritchards to leave the building without being seen.

It took only a couple of minutes waiting beside the phone box for Monty's grandfather to call her back. She immediately dealt with his concerns about her safety, and pleaded with him to trust she was safe with the detective. 'Let me talk to him,' Doctor Pritchard demanded.

Following a short conversation in which Pritchard was satisfied his granddaughter's chaperone could be trusted, and having received an apology for the accusation of rape, he amiably agreed to help, unreservedly. It suited him knowing she was with the detective voluntarily, rather than with the police *involuntarily*. And it pleased him to know Josey had found her and protected her against a killer. He also agreed to play along because he wanted to find out what else the detective had discovered.

Borcheck was already on board without question, Walter and he had a bond to be envied. Bruno came on the line and conveyed his plan to Josey, telling him to stay put near the public phone and wait for a confidant out of Newcastle, who would pick them up in a hire car and take them to a small airstrip nearby. From there the doctor would have them brought via air-ambulance to meet with everyone at the Hospital. No one would ever know they were there.

Andrew stood on the rooftop as the chopper set down on the pad. From the window, his niece looked down and spotted him leaning into the gale of the rotors with the aid of a crutch. Guilt gripped her heart as she gave an uncertain wave. His beaming smile went a long way to easing her mind; he at least seemed happy to see her returning.

Pleased to have been able to bring the family together finally, Josey trusted the reunion would serve to settle everybody down. For himself, he needed to delve deeper into Monty's beliefs, find out exactly what she thinks she saw during her hypnosis. Although she hadn't spoken of it, he suspected she may believe she is harbouring the identity of her mother's attacker. He also suspected she would be wrong. Most of all, he needed more time with her to prove he was right about that. There was another motive behind wanting to be in her presence; so long as they remained together he could protect her from potentially making a very big mistake.

Monty definitely wasn't out of the woods, but now in the arms of her family, he felt that part of his job—which was completely outside the commitment to his client—was done.

As always, the Borchecks couldn't have been happier to have everyone join them for lunch in their private penthouse adjacent to the helipad. They had gathered for a meeting of the minds and to discuss what to do next. Monty's position was extremely delicate. One dead body was hard enough to explain, but two or three was going to be a real challenge. Josey would certainly vouch for what happened at the shack if asked, but it would only be his word, and substantiated only by her, the shooter.

The fact remained she had actually killed a man, albeit in self defence. A lengthy court case would ensue, which could go either way. Walter was already talking about Lawyer friends he would solicit to act on her behalf. Of course that couldn't happen without first presenting Monty to the police. He cancelled that idea himself.

Before the meeting, Josey had pulled Walter aside and revealed he had a strong hunch about who the killer was, but would need the families help to prove it. He also told him they would have to move fast or they would fail in that goal. Walter agreed to work with him and to do whatever it takes to make that happen.

'This may sound a little strange, ' Josey told him, 'but the solution lies in Beerwah, your old home town; and I need to get the whole family up there, with Monty, as soon as possible. I'll also need a few hours with your granddaughter, alone, before making any announcements to the family; including yourself, because I have to make sure I've got this absolutely right. Even what I'm telling you now should be kept from the others for the time being.'

'I'm afraid I don't understand.'

'Trust me; it's for Monty's sake.'

Anything that was intended for Monty's ultimate benefit was a good enough guarantee for Walter. He forthwith agreed to Josey's terms.

Keeping the family together wasn't to be so easy though. Walter and Margaret had a problem with going to Queensland, because they were required to visit Police Headquarters in Sydney in the morning, and again every week for the foreseeable future.

'I understand,' Josey said, 'but we should be able to work around that.'

'What do you have in mind?'

'Doctor Borcheck has property on the outskirts of Brisbane that I've checked out, which would make a perfect place to set everyone up, and a good hideaway.'

'Well, yes, a very good idea,' he agreed. 'It's clearly remote. I'm guessing you know that.'

Josey's expression confirmed he did.

'Bruno will be happy to help, but as I said we can't go up there until after our meeting with the police.

In order to reach an agreement from Borcheck to allow the use of his property, it became mandatory to spell out Josey's plan. He jumped at the chance to help, as expected.

Bruno would take the detective and Monty ahead in the air ambulance while her parents attended their meeting with police. The following day Walter and Margaret would accompany Andrew in the chopper to be with Monty by midmorning. This would give the grandparents another week in the northern state before they had to return to Sydney to show their faces at the police station. Josey told Walter and Bruno that he hoped to have the case closed by then. They couldn't hide how impressed they were. Josey's standing had improved beyond all expectation.

At the meeting with the rest of the family, Monty sat quietly listing to everyone's opinion on what she should do, but in fact had already made up her mind she wanted to give Josey a chance to help her find the perpetrator. Margaret didn't take her eyes off Monty the whole time, worried the conversation might be dragging her back into the depths of depression. Josey had concerns about that too, but this was an opportunity not to be missed. Talking with the family while they were all gathered in one place allowed him to give his thoughts on dealing with the police. He wanted to make sure everyone was on the same page.

He told them, 'Keeping the police out of the picture is only a temporary measure. I have to warn you, we're getting very close to having to involve them.'

Acting as Josey's secret confident, Walter asked, 'When do you see that happening?'

Josey told them, 'If we drag this out we'll get in far too deep to redeem ourselves, so, no more than a couple of days.'

Monty pushed her plate away and stood from the table. She looked rattled. 'Forget the bloody police,' she told them, 'I'll do this by myself if I have to.'

Stunned by the sudden outburst, no one had an

immediate response. Josey had seen this before and was half expecting it. Her demeanour was part of why he wanted to monitor her alone.

She was shaking. 'I need to get to the bottom of what happened to my mother,' she pleaded. 'I don't trust the police can help me do that . . . not in a week—not ever.'

Margaret went to her side in an attempt to console her, but was rejected; pushed aside. The distressed young girl left via the sliding glass doors that led out to the rooftop, near to where the air ambulance sat at rest, six stories above the ground. So long as she remained in sight, they were satisfied to leave her by herself for a while.

It was time to ease Margaret into the arranged plan. Walter launched into another segue for Josey, saying, 'Our granddaughter's not ready.'

'Not ready for what?' Margaret snapped, familiar with her husband's impetuous decisions that sometimes ended badly.

He ignored her and stayed on the detective. 'I'll understand if you refuse, but I need someone to hide our granddaughter until she can get herself sorted.' Once again Walter was secretly adding fuel to Josey's endeavour.

'Walter,' Margaret protested, insisting on his attention.

He ignored her again. 'Will you do it?' he asked Josey.

Refusing to help Monty had never crossed Josey's mind, as Walter well knew, and this led to the clincher to get Monty and the whole family near to Beerwah. He gave Walter the nod. 'Of course, I'll do whatever you ask.'

It went without saying, encouraging Monty to proceed on her present path was necessary, but it was also very dangerous, which was the whole reason Margaret wouldn't be fully informed about what was happening until she was in the air flying to Beerwah tomorrow morning. Now with Walter replacing his concerns with the need to proceed, his resolve to offer support was making as much sense as it ever would. Fantasy or otherwise, Josey had to remind himself of the probability her mother was raped in her grandfather's car and murdered in her own. That had been explained in part. The Pritchard family all knew the brakes had failed.

The fact was, Monty couldn't be trusted to talk with the police without revealing her claims in front of them. Explaining her ethereal experiences to police would be difficult for them to grasp, or believe. Even though Josey could substantiate her claims the brakes on the car were tampered with, it would undeniably result in a bogged down investigation. The police would undoubtedly ask what led him to look for evidence in the first place. That didn't worry him; his answer would be based on the evidence given by the witness who was at the scene of the accident. It was just the time it would take to round up the witness and get the story across to police, because loss of time at this point would seriously stifle his endeavor to quickly corner the killer. Revealing the detail of his hunch right now could be detrimental to his case; and definitely UN-conducive to Monty's state of mind if the truth were leaked back to her.

Except for Margaret—who still wanted to involve the police—the family were all feeling that nothing about their plans had changed. There was still the matter of finding Monty's would-be killer, and making a link to whoever killed her mother, which most likely wouldn't happen if everyone was in custody. At least this way Josey would get time to get answers to some much unanswered questions. Not the least being; what story were the Applebys currently telling the police about their son's death?

Are the police believing their story?

Putting Bee's parent's intensions aside, there was a probable chance the Appleby's were completely innocent of wanting to harm Monty. They at least did not fit into Josey's hunch about who killed Monty's mother, *Montana.*

CHAPTER EIGHTEEN
Monty's Mindset

Within the hour Josey and Monty were heading interstate aboard the air ambulance, piloted by Borcheck himself. Borcheck took advantage of their midair confinement, asking to hear Monty's side of the story following her sudden departure from home. She didn't seem to mind him asking. Josey knew a lot of it already and wondered if she would mention the suspicions about her grandfather. She made no mention of that, or the rape. It was possible of course that Borcheck had been told these things by Walter.

The story she relayed to Bruno began with the hypnosis, telling of how she didn't know what to do after wounding her uncle, and how utterly confused she was. She confirmed Brian Appleby's name had been raised many times while living with her grandparents, but only after she herself had one day brought it up. When she insisted on having first learnt of Appleby from her mother, Borcheck didn't blink an eyelid, suggesting to Josey that Borcheck indeed already knew of her proclaimed gift.

Except for the fact Josey had pieced together aspects of the case—that would now take it in a practical direction—he could have been forgiven for accepting her fanciful claims of a special gift, preferring the probability her knowledge of Appleby had been somehow gained from the family. In respect to her tracking down Brian Appleby, the facts remained the same; desperate for help, she had conjured the belief Brian was someone who might sympathise with her plight. Given that she had learnt he was a close friend of her mother's; not just close - but intimate,

Josey concluded her belief was reasonably well thought out. Josey couldn't deny though, Appleby had never been one of her suspects.

To enhance her chances of soliciting Appleby's help, she admitted to taking the reckless step of suggesting Brian was her father. Then, after getting the attention she needed, admitting to having already had a DNA test that proved he had no paternal connection. In spite of this deception, he continued to help her. His enthusiasm hadn't mystified her, she was aware her mirror image likeness to her mother had undeniably drawn him in. She expressed remorse over what his involvement ultimately led to, forcing her to excuse herself from telling the story.

'The big problem for Beverly Appleby,' Josey surmised while Monty spent a moment recovering, 'was that her son was engaged to be married, and any talk of paternity, true or false, in her mind was potentially damaging. Her plan to protect her son, and his future wife, arose as soon as she found out Monty had surfaced with her accusation, which of course was an accusation they had been dealing with since the death of Monty's mother. This was the last straw for her.' Josey had a question for Monty on that score. 'How did she convince you to hold-up at the shack?'

Monty realised the detective was trying to build his case. 'She told me they wanted to protect me from the police, not to mention my would-be killer.'

Josey sensed she hadn't been totally convinced. 'But, her real motive was to encourage you to take her Money and agree to disappear, right?'

Josey knew Monty had no idea how long he had been outside the shack listening in on her conversation with Brian, and he used this moment to let her know.

She didn't want to grill him about it, because if he hadn't been there, who knows what would have happened.

The Applebys were drawing closer by the day to no longer being serious suspects, certain facts in their case were making Josey's second hunch seem more likely. Facts like, the hit man having a silenced gun, *you don't have a silenced gun unless you plan to use it*. If the Applebys had been behind the use of a gun at all, the plan most likely would have been *not* to use it, which doesn't tie in with opting for the one gun that premeditates shooting to kill. Monty's refusal to accept money to disappear could well have meant the plan was to simply arrive in the middle of the night and abduct her; *force* her to go someplace, which could easily be blamed on whoever was trying to get to Monty in the first place. Josey reasoned, the situation with the Appleby's didn't exist before Monty's sudden appearance in their lives, separating the attack at the Hawkesbury from previous attacks; but this only applied if his original belief were true - that is; Bee's parents had hired the hit-man. Josey no longer believed that. He was now convinced the Hawkesbury attack was totally unconnected to the Appleby's, leading to the conclusion all the attacks on Monty were instigated by just one person, Josey believed he knew who that was. Once he proved it, that's when he would finally involve the police. Having already spoken to his trusted friend Barry Brack didn't count of course.

Eight hundred and twenty two kilometres later the air ambulance flew over the city of Tweed Heads, crossing over the border into Queensland, the journey ending twenty minutes later, ten miles out of the adjacent twin-town of Coolangatta, where Borcheck had his remote holiday home. This was to be the Pritchards latest hideaway and Detective Josey's too. Given he had less than twenty four hours alone with Monty, he would have to work fast to get inside her head. He had two things to clear up, things that so far he hadn't been able to talk to her about. He needed to understand if Monty thought she had either identified her mother's attacker—or her own—while under hypnosis, something that Josey refused to subscribe to.

Once the family arrived the task of solidifying his hunch would escalate tenfold, along with his job to clear Monty's muddled mind once and for all.

Needing to get straight back to his hospital in Sydney, Borcheck got down to settling them into two rooms of his otherwise vacated ten bedroom house. 'There's a car in the garage out back if you should need it,' he told Josey. 'It's gassed up, and the keys are in the kitchen pantry.' He only stayed ten minutes before leaving in the chopper, lifting off from a one acre paddock at the front of the property.

The generous abode was equipped with food in the freezer, clean linen, and most importantly, a landline that couldn't be traced to its fugitive guests; not unless they were to mention their names and be overheard by the authorities via a phone tap. For that to happen, every single phone in the country would need to be tapped into, because Borcheck had bought the house around the time he was doing battle with Kristen Poole, and so that she would never find him he listed the owner as his mother, using her maiden name.

Monty told Josey she needed a light nap to recover from the long flight, so they separated into their allotted bedrooms.

Using Borcheck's land-line, Josey placed a call to Maxine at the office and asked for *himself*.

'I'm sorry, he's out of reach right now,' she said fully aware of the ruse.

'That's all right; please ask him to call me on this number.'

'Will do.'

'Right, thanks.' Josey hung up in the knowledge Max would immediately head out to make contact with Meredith Northey, as had been arranged when the time was right to bring his client up to speed with what was happening. Undoubtedly she would be watching the news and wondering what she should do to contact him. Max knew to act dumb if Meredith jumped the gun and called the office, which she had already done – twice. The code-calls, set up just after the shooting at the shack, necessitated that Max take a trip to meet secretly with Northey and tell her how to safely make contact with the detective. Meredith's call came in from a public phone box an hour later.

'I'm so sorry I got you into this, Cam,' she told him right up front.

'Forget it; this is what you pay me for.'

Apart from being able to give his client information about the progress on the case, having Meredith on the line was a perfect time for her to have a talk with Monty. Josey felt the talk would be a win-win. The girls were on the phone for an hour talking mainly about Meredith's teenage friend, Montana, and comparing what they each knew about her history and the fatal accident.

He let them have their heart-to-heart, moving off to the kitchen to prepare an evening meal.

Following dinner, he made it clear to Monty they needed to make good use of their time while waiting for the others to arrive in the morning. *To leave no stone unturned.* He wanted nothing more than to announce his breakthrough when her family came through the front door.

The dishes were left unwashed; he wanted to get down to work.

'I have something that belongs to you,' he told her as they faced each other from their respective armchairs. She wasn't able to fathom what it could be until he removed the necklace from his pocket.

Wonderment left her face as she said, 'Oh, that; you found it.'

Josey wanted her to have it because he thought it might be conducive to delving into her mindset. But she had clearly decided the trinket had served its purpose and was of no further use. For the time being he rested it on the arm of the chair.

Earlier, Josey had found out from Monty that the unattractive piece of jewelry belonged to Walter's father, who was a merchant seaman and the original owner of the Cadillac. Her grandfather had decided to keep the worthless trinket in the restored car as a memento.

'How are you feeling about our talk,' he asked, 'ready to start?'

Her eyes were on the necklace. 'Ready as I'll ever

be.'

He suggested she open her mind to her own personal memories, and not to leave the smallest detail out. 'Don't worry, I'm no hypnotist,' he assured her. 'We're just having a chat.'

'I'm all right, Detective. I know you're trying to help. Go ahead.'

Right up front he asked her not to use up energy trying to convince him of her clairvoyance. 'Just deal with the facts,' he told her. 'I only want to know *what* you know. Not how you know it. Do you understand?'

She shrugged despondently. 'Whatever. But I don't know what else I can tell you. You've read my diary. I've told you everything.'

This was going to be tougher than Josey thought. 'Please tell me again; if that's okay.'

Her eyes were on the tiny anchor again . . . *She's battling* . . . He placed his hand over it. 'Would you like me to put this away?'

She shook her head and stared at the floor . . .

'Monty, listen to me. You're being far too controlled by the belief everything has to come from your mother.'

She looked up at him; a film of tears had surfaced.

Josey couldn't allow anything to influence his approach. 'I'm sorry to tell you this, but your mind is completely closed. It's something that happens to people under deep stress.'

Josey was no more a psychologist than he was a hypnotist, but he did believe himself to be a good detective, a detective needing to deal in hard cold facts.

'Let me start by saying, you and I both know, that somewhere out there – there is a killer.'

'Of course,' she told him, totally agreeing.

'You have to allow me in, so that together, we can expose this person.'

She blinked away the tears and nodded. 'If you think you can.'

Josey was sticking his neck out further than he had ever done on any other case, but he understood she needed his help. What he couldn't understand was why she ever thought she could find the killer by herself. He doubted she knew who it was, otherwise why wouldn't she have come right out and told someone. She'd had plenty of opportunity.

She needed a shot of confidence, so he gave her something positive to latch onto, 'I know I can.'

She smiled and wiped her wet eyes with the back of her hand.

CHAPTER NINETEEN
Mindset

Over the next four hours Josey coaxed her through her minefield of memories, more than once bluntly stopping her from referring to her mother as though she was somehow feeding her information. As usual, her psychic beliefs were putting him off. Particularly since he knew she doubted some of them herself. He recalled her saying; *the insights had to have been implanted before my mother died.* Josey didn't really believe in her insights one way or the other.

Considering Monty had to deal with sticking to Josey's rules of engagement, she did fairly well in answering the questions, but she did have one mini meltdown as a result of his reprimands.

'Look, I'm completely fucking stressed out in case you haven't noticed! Can you please get off my bloody back about my mother' . . . Her voice trailed away to a whisper.

He needed to calm her, *compromise*. 'Truce, okay? If you feel the need to refer to your mother's memories, just pretend they're yours, how's that?'

She eventually gave a sort of shy grin. 'I've got no problem with that.'

Her stories following the meltdown still required Josey to be quick in deciphering whose memory she was actually referring to, hers or her mother's.

She recounted her grandparent's problems in a way that was largely creative, sounding more like it was her mother telling the story - telling of difficulties that had been long standing; arguments that had manifested when her mother was the child in the story. It wasn't as if she were in a trance while telling these stories, not like when she had been under hypnosis - this time, she seemed in complete control. She was in a good place finally – like she must have been back when she was writing her diary.

But, just like the diary, when she reverted to telling the story from a third party point of view, it became truly bizarre once more.

'My mother heard yelling one night. She got out of bed and went downstairs and found my grandparents having a ding-dong argument—

'She's yelling at him, *how could you do this to your children?*'

Monty had taken on a voice, role-playing to demonstrate the conversation in the story. All the more weird given she wasn't even there at the time.

'He says, *leave the bloody kids out of it, this has nothing to do with them!*

'My grandmother broke down and cried her eyes out. So, next thing, he tries rationalising what he'd done; *it was nothing more than a fling, Margaret.*

'Gran got really angry . . . *I don't care what you call it. You were having sex with that woman while I was at home cooking your bloody meals, washing your stinking clothes. I could smell her on your underwear!'*

Josey was taken aback by the exacting language Monty was using, the make believe tone of the voices. Was she making this up? Or was she somehow recalling what someone has told her - word for word. He tested her on it. 'Monty, would you mind dropping the theatrics? They're a little disconcerting.'

She became very serious as she considered the detective's request . . . finally she said, 'You don't believe all this shit about my gift do you?'

No point in hiding it. He shook his head and hoped she wouldn't spin out. 'Even if I did, I'd still need to conduct my investigation in a practical way. Remember what I said, I don't need to know how you know, only what you know. Do you think you can help me with that?'

She gave him a quizzical grin, but didn't agree or disagree to his terms, but she did do exactly as he asked.

'One night, Granddad punched Grandmother in the

face during an argument and she fell and injured her back. He left, and my mother and Gran never saw him again until Mum was ten; that's when Granddad came home.' She looked at the detective for his approval of how she had presented the story.

'Much better . . . How do you think your grandmother felt about her husband returning?'

'She felt sorry for him.'

'Really – but didn't he do the wrong thing?'

'It wasn't as bad as what *she* did.'

'What did she do?'

Arching an eyebrow, Monty told him, 'She tried to have him killed.'

Josey was genuinely stunned by the matter of fact way she'd spoken, *is she playing me?* He kept his voice even when he asked, 'And that was because of the affair?'

'Yes.'

'So, what were the circumstances of him coming home, do you know?'

'He wanted to save her from going to gaol. He told her he wouldn't be pressing charges, and that he wanted to have a go at saving their marriage.'

What Monty was telling him could only have come from one person Josey decided. 'Is all this what your grandmother told you?'

She ignored the question. 'Gran told him he could forgive, if that's what he wanted to do, but promised he'd be getting no forgiveness from her. Two police officers were there listening. Everyone just stood in the doorway. It was like my gran was deciding if she should allow my grandfather even come into the house, let alone come home to stay.'

'And did she – let him come home?'

'Yes.'

'What happened with the police?'

'They just left. There was no more trouble about it after that. Well, not for *them* anyway.'

She hesitated . . . Josey waited.

'You know, Gran had a bad time at school she told me. The other kids teased her, saying cruel things like, your father can't keep his hands off his patients . . . he screws his nurse and your mother wants him dead.'

She'd made the point using her normal voice.

Monty's earlier behaviour was worrying, making it hard to tell if she was psychotic, or playing the detective to see what his reaction would be. Her eyes drifted upward to the right on several occasions, a trait that used to be recognised as body language suggesting a person is genuinely recalling a real memory.

Had Monty moved her eyes up to the right when she was playing the part of her grandmother?

Josey didn't think she had.

These days, physiological markers are the favoured way to determine if memories are real. At least that's what Josey had heard; he was no expert. But what he did know was; a memory can be very real to the person doing the remembering, yet at the same time completely wrong. It's also been known for people to be implanted with false memories by corrupt psychologists.

Josey wondered how much of a psychologist Margaret Pritchard was, and if she was, what could her motive possibly be?

It was time to get to the big question. He would have to tread lightly now, he was about to delve into whether or not Monty believed she had identified the rapist, or perhaps the murderer.

'Are you able to talk to me about what freaked you out when you were hypnotised?'

'How important is it for you to know?'

Her reluctance was still fully intact.

Josey shifted to the original driving force behind her mind-snap – the nightmare.

'Am I right in saying the man in your dream is the same man who murdered Alan Kelly.'

She held on him for a moment. 'All right, yes, who else would it be?'

Her answer was laced with attitude.

Josey skipped over it. 'You saw his face, that night in Kelly's flat.'

Her expression neither confirmed nor denied it. 'It was dark.'

'And the man you saw under hypnosis, was that the same man?'

Josey's question didn't sit well with her . . . she was hesitant, struggling to answer – *or perhaps not wanting to?*

He moved on. When did you first realise your mother had been raped – in the dream, or under hypnosis?'

Her eyes began darting around the room.

Josey picked up the necklace from the arm of the chair to draw her attention to it. 'At first, because of this trifling piece of jewelry—the very thing that frightened you in your nightmare—you thought the rapist was your grandfather. The question you have to ask yourself is which came first – seeing it in the dream, or seeing it in the old Cadillac?'

Monty couldn't see what he was driving at.

'Blaming your grandfather changed when you were hypnotised . . . was it at that point that you saw someone other than your grandfather, someone other than Brian's killer, or Alan's killer. And, just as we now know the man who shot Brian wasn't the man who shot Alan Kelly, it begs the question—who are all these people?'

'You're telling the story,' she snapped at him. *Attitude again.*

Josey didn't mind this icy reaction; it was sounding more like the real girl. 'Okay, it's fair to say you saw someone else's face, but you didn't know who it was.'

She was trying to read the detective's expression. 'What's this about? I sense you're trying to tell me something.'

He smiled. As he expected, she really hadn't seen a face at all, but what? 'First I want you to explain exactly what you saw in your bad dream—about your mother's rape.'

'Why not while under hypnosis? It was hellishly more terrifying,' she said defiantly.

A good answer again for Josey, this is what he was hoping to hear. 'I don't doubt you for a minute. Your mind probably had time to augment your nightmare.'

A frown left her forehead. 'Oh I see where this is going. This is all about *discrediting* me.'

'Monty, that's not true.'

'Then what – I really can't see the point of what you're asking me.'

'I had to be sure you weren't under the impression you'd identified who your mother's rapist is—'

'Rest your mind, Detective – I haven't.' She'd answered without hesitation.

'Can you explain what you *did* see?'

She looked trapped.

'Just tell me what you saw.'

She focused on her hands and said with a waver in her voice, 'I thought I was in hell – all I could see were hideous shapes surrounding me; writhing like devils–like—'

She sobbed into her hands, finally releasing indescribable swathes of guilt and fear. 'I became confused about what really happened to my mother.' Her eyes flicked onto Josey. 'I know I was wrong about Granddad, it's just the amount of stress I was under; trying to figure things out. In the end I felt conflicted about what was real and what wasn't.'

Josey didn't need to ask more questions. All that remained was to get on with the case. He saw no reason to delay it. 'Monty, you were right, I do have something to tell you, and I think you will find it very good news, albeit a double edged sword.'

She met his eyes expectantly, a tiny smile brightening her demeanour.

'I've made a breakthrough,' he announced with great satisfaction.

Her face lit up. 'Holly shit, really?'

There's that real girl again. He could hear the release of tension in her voice. He held back, savouring her moment of discovery—

'Well, are you going to tell me?' she demanded with an impatient titter.

'I know who the killer is—'

'Bullshit.' She'd said it with her *happy-face.*

'I also know who the rapist is.'

Her eyes formed saucers . . . 'Wait – what the hell?'

'Yep, two different people, in fact if you include the two killers we already know about—Kelly's and Brian's—the count comes to four, maybe more.'

Monty's mouth rounded open; hardly able to believe what the detective was saying.

He saw her uncertainty. 'I know what you're thinking.' He scooped up the necklace from the arm of the chair and stepped over to give it to her.

'I don't want that,' she told him emphatically.

'Keep it and give it back to your grandfather.'

She remained reluctant to take it.

'Monty, if you hadn't made the mistake of connecting this to your grandfather, I may never have uncovered the real rapist.'

The tarnished, unattractive ornament had little

going for it, and with no inkling of how Josey used it to find the perpetrator, she was at a loss to concede that it had somehow gained a newfound significance. She opened her mind and at the same time added a smidgen of impatience. 'All right,' she said taking it from him, 'now for shit-sake please tell me who these people are.'

He hesitated, annoyingly. 'You're going to hate me for this, but I'm afraid you'll have to wait until tomorrow when your grandparents arrive.'

She just looked at him—blank.

'I have a few questions for them before I can make my next move.'

She rolled her eyes. 'Oh, shit, how the hell am I supposed to sleep with this buzzing around it my head?'

'Sorry, I thought you'd waited long enough to see some light at the end of the tunnel.'

She looked at him suspiciously. 'Can you at least give me a clue?'

'That's all I'm saying until morning,' he told her closing the issue.

'Right, so that's it then.'

That's it. He creased his brow apologetically. 'A few more hours and you'll know.'

His answer disappointed her, but he had truly wet her appetite, raising excitement mixed with a considerable amount of frustration. She stood from the armchair, smiled, said goodnight and headed for her bedroom. She stopped at the door and thanked him.

Josey poured himself a wine and opened up his laptop in the office adjoining the kitchen. He added some new notes on the case and browsed over the old ones. It was difficult to connect what he had just heard with the idea her grandmother was behind her uncanny recollections, but definitely not out of the question. He revisited fact-and-fiction. His hunch was still intact. But experience taught him to consider all aspects of the case in search of critical evidence that might have been overlooked, or dismissed.

Of course there were certain facts—regarding events before Kristen Pool hired his services—that had been relayed to him by other people; some by Poole herself. One key was the dispute at the hospital over keeping Montana alive in a brain dead state. Poole hadn't been making that up, it was well reported in the press, and Josey even had Borcheck check into it unofficially via a friend at Poole's hospital. Although Poole managed not to incriminate herself in the telling of it, Josey knew she was bitter about the way Doctor Pritchard had snubbed her authority. Then of course there was the way in which she put the acid into Josey after he suddenly parted ways with her. Although a bit of a stretch, he had to consider she could easily have been the would-be killer.

By Monty's own admission, her grandfather was off the hook as her mother's rapist for the same reason as Brian Appleby; DNA had exonerated both of them. The DNA sampling that she instigated was as a result of her believing she'd seen something other than tangible suspects during her hypnotism.

Josey entered into his notes what he had learnt from Monty about her DNA tests and exactly how and when she had ultimately obtained samples from both Walter and Bee.

Within an hour of losing Josey on the train she had gone to the office of Australian DNA in Sydney to be tested against her father, who she knew had his DNA on file there. As for Bee, in spite of his belief she had tested his paternity before they met – it was flawed, and wrong. *How could she have gotten his DNA before they met?* She'd gained his sample from a cup at his unit shortly after they got together. She could have explained all this at the time—when he made the accusation at his parents' holiday shack on the Hawkesbury River—but she didn't want to cast a cloud over everything else that was going on.

Josey cast his mind back to the day he visited the Pritchard's first hideaway, and the subsequent conversation with Nurse Patricia Heath. It was clear, given she had lied in claiming the family were away, that she was prepared to do their bidding. Monty had explained how growing up in the secretive house of her grandparents had been made easier by the constant companionship of Nurse Heath, who she lovingly called, Patty. The phone conversation he had with her - in which she willingly helped him find Monty via Brian Appleby, was further reason not to suspect Heath. Although Josey had planned to keep everyone who knew Monty on the list, there was no reasonable reason to put Nurse Heath anywhere close to the top.

As for Margaret Pritchard; Josey viewed her as a very strange woman; at least in so far as what had been told to him recently by her equally strange eighteen year old granddaughter. Yes, Monty's recollections of paranormal conversations with her mother were categorically accepted by the grandmother, but Josey rather suspected they were instigated, and *encouraged.*

Looking at it logically, as he always did, everything that Monty reportedly told the grandmother about her mother's memories, were undeniably known by Margaret in advance. It wasn't hard to imagine she may have been inducing the three year old into believing the farce, power of suggestion.

Until he found out more, he could make no sense of such a subterfuge.

Perhaps she thought of Monty as a replacement for her dead daughter, possibility.

There certainly was no concrete reason to assume a connection to wanting her granddaughter dead, although she did have a history in that respect, given her extreme reaction to her husband's affair.

But still an unlikely suspect . . .

He thought about Kristen Poole again.

Could she possibly have been so vindictive as to want Monty dead in order to hurt her arch enemy, Walter Pritchard?

Josey decided she had been far too vocal in the

press to be that person. He had cancelled her out long ago.

Then there is the Applebys. Although Josey's theory about Mrs. Appleby and her son had been all but squashed by his new understanding about the assailant, it was still just as easy to assume Bee might have wanted Monty dead for the same reason as his mother. At one point he thought perhaps they really had planned it together. But then the theory had become decidedly muddy. He'd reminded himself about what Monty had pointed out the day of the shooting at the shack; she was clearly convinced the hit man was not the one who killed Alan Kelly, her motorcycling boyfriend. This meant someone was definitely hiring killers to do their dirty work.

Fits with my hunch; especially the motive.

Josey's summation that the stalker somehow knows about Monty's claim her mother was murdered, pointed to someone having a fear of connection.

Kill the informant.

The diary loomed large in the list of reasons the killer might have thought the book could be incriminating. He remembered thinking Monty's book could have been what the killer was looking for the night Allan Kelly was murdered.

Collateral damage . . .

Fact or fiction, Monty's insights married to his own findings about the brakes. He chose to waste no time pondering over her claims she knew her mother had been murdered. The fact is she never once connected the murder with the car or the brakes. The closest she'd come was associating her father's car with the rape.

Both events involve the two family cars, and that in itself was enough of a connection for Josey to set his investigative imagination in motion. He added these connections to one more, Beerwah, near Glasshouse, and figured she had gone there simply because that's near where the family lived when her mother was a teenager at school. As was already alluded to, *in times of trouble people often return to the place of their roots.* In her case, she was returning to where her family lived before she was born.

Whatever the catalyst, her decision coincided with his - a decision made on the basis of a photograph in which her mother appeared.

Question by question, Josey thought that he had answered them all. If it hadn't been so late in the night, he would have rang Brack right away to talk about the location they had unearthed, and to mull over the plan of insurgence. At least he could check out the place on the net and be ready to make a move in the morning, once the chopper arrived with the Pritchards. He felt certain there wouldn't be a problem convincing Borheck to provide quick transportation north once the party was informed of what had been discovered. He spent another half hour on the laptop before calling it a night.

On the way to his room he paused at Monty's door

to listen. He had an intense urge to check if she was okay, but didn't want to wake her if she was already sleeping.

The sound of movement drifted into the hallway.

'Are you all right, Monty?'

'Yes, I'm fine - thank you . . . goodnight.'

Josey smiled to himself. 'Night, see you in the morning.'

Satisfied she was in there and safe, he let-her-be and went to his room.

Sleep came almost instantly.

CHAPTER TWENTY
A Fly in the Ointment

Bruno Borcheck's house sat a kilometre away from the front fence of the property; there wasn't a neighbour for more than twenty. As the two guests slept inside, they were oblivious to the arrival of an uninvited visitor. There was no strong reason to expect a threat, Josey had told Monty that all the suspects that knew their whereabouts had all been cleared of any suspicion - he hadn't been entirely truthful.

With the moon blanketed by cloud, the figure's approach was concealed by a deep darkness that was well enhanced by a covering of overgrown shrubs and trees surrounding the building. The manner, in which the invader crept toward a side door and silently turn the handle, indicated vicious intent.

The door presented no barrier, opening up to allow

entry.

The figure, dressed in black for additional concealment, advanced into the house and stood still, allowing the gloom to adjust sufficiently to present a dim grey layout of the room. A set of stairs could now be seen spiraling to the floor above; to the bedrooms. Silent shoes traversed shiny tiles to reach the stairway and ascend. At the top, a corridor invited the visitor to select from ten doors. Ten bedrooms, only one were needed to locate the target.

Splatters of moonlight filtered into the targeted room, the black-clad figure entered, interrupting the pale patterns that waltzed across the floor. The mystery intruder advanced silently toward the bed, toward the sleeping *chump* who would soon be dead.

The nebulous menace reached the bedside and surreptitiously revealed a long bladed knife.

A shimmer of cold light climbed the edge of the steel vane as the weapon was raised high – with intent to kill.

The murderer plunged the knife downward with a powerfully vicious thrust—

He heard the thud as it entered his chest. Josey's beating heart exploded, intense pain waking him from a deep sleep. Sensing the assailant just inches away, he strained to make eye contact, but saw only dark hollows where eyes should be.

A sudden wind gust parted window shades, inviting a pale flickering glow to illuminate a felonious face leaning closer to gloat – it was, *Kristen Poole? . . .*

He tried to yell, but vocal cords refused to produce sound.

Gunshots rang out – it was *Fredie* firing at the intruder.

Josey tried harder to shout, finally expelling sound that took impossible amounts of effort to resonate into the real world—

His own voice woke him with a start for a second time, for real, the pain in his chest a fading memory, the assailant, Kristen Poole, *gone*, or to be more exact; *never there*.

The dream lingered long after ending, leaving the question; *why conjure a dream in which Poole seemed so real, so believably the killer. What's it telling me?*

The thought catapulted him from the comfort of his bed to the chill of the hall. As expected, no one was there. He quickly made his way to Monty's room and hesitated at the closed door for a moment before entering; he wanted to be sure she was tucked up in bed safe; and hoped not to freak her out if she awoke to see him standing over her.

Just a dream, he told himself.

But, the dream had rattled him, raising an illogical fear it had been some sort of forecast of Monty's abduction, he ventured further into the darkened room, pastel moonlight teasing his s to see. On reaching the bedside he found it to be empty. No longer certain the abduction idea was so crazy, he ran his palm across the crinkled sheets.

Cold . . .

Gone for quite some time, maybe she couldn't sleep and is downstairs raiding the refrigerator.

His concern for her safety reignited following a search of the kitchen, the bar and the rest of the house—calling out.

This is not good. 'This is not bloody good at all.'

He ran outside, out into the blackness beyond the glow of the lights he had turned on all over the house; and called until his voice was hoarse.

Am I still dreaming? . . .

The thought was as empty as it was impossible. He knew this was real, and he would have to face it. Face the family and tell them he had once again lost her. He ran back to the house and rummaged through draws and cupboards till he found a flash-light. He searched the property for an hour, continually calling out. *Nothing* - she was gone. He found himself preferring outrageous alternatives, chief among them that his dream *had* been real, and that he was dead. Logic quickly pushed such thoughts aside, he realised he was wasting energy worrying about his own skin . . .

. . . This is about her, dumb-cluck; snap out of it!

He went back into the house for one last look for her. *It's a big house, maybe I'll find a clue. Or maybe I'll find her on a floor somewhere, unable to sleep in a strange bed.*

He was clutching at straws, this was his second surveillance. It was then that a chilling thought came to mind. He darted back to the living room to see if he was right, to see if he had missed it . . .

The answer stared him in the face with alarming clarity—

The laptop he'd left on the table was *gone* . . .

She's got the location, and who she'll find when she gets there. Bloody hell.

The necklace, which he had returned to her, was nowhere to be found. This could only mean one thing – *she's taken it with her.*

He ran to the garage and realised his next fear, the one and only car was missing.

Armed with this new urgency, he did two things that had now become mandatory—with total abandonment, he called Maxine - then Brack.

CHAPTER TWENTY ONE
Close Contact

They reached their destination and pulled up with the headlights pointing toward the old house. The property looked to be about five acres of unworked land, the circa sixties timber house set a hundred yards back from a fence that had seen better days. Crudely lying at the base of the rickety fence was an aging timber sign with a street number and the words, *Ross Royal, Mechanic*, painted crudely in white. The sign looked like it had originally been nailed across the top of another that was still on one of the fence posts.

'Check these out,' Brack said drawing attention to the opposing signs, 'same number – different name.'

'Ross Skillion,' Josey read from the original sign.

'Looks like you've found your man,' the sergeant scoffed, 'except *someone* has beaten you to it.'

Knowing that it could only be one of two people, and that it may have been Monty, gave Josey a chill.

Brack killed the engine and doused the lights. The two men warily left the car and entered the property through where there used to be a gate.

Dawn had only just begun eating away at the last remnants of darkness. No lights were showing in the windows of the house.

'He could be in his workshop,' Brack told Josey as they got out and walked. 'We can't see it from here, it's out back.'

'You checked out the whole place?'

'Checked everywhere, the joint was locked tight. That's why we've been seeing him in town so much. Didn't see him earlier tonight, so I'm guessing he's here.'

Maxine's call to Brack had confirmed Monty had been sighted in Beerwah early in the morning, just hours after leaving Borcheck's house. Josey could scarcely believe she had risked coming to this place. The alert came from Richard the security man at the post office. Josey rescinded every bad thought he'd had about the guy – including his personal hygiene.

Being separated from Monty was definitely not part of Josey's master plan; it raised a very big possibility he wouldn't be able to prevent her from making the mistake he had feared all along. This was exactly why he didn't want to tell her the full story until morning. Now he had his laptop to blame, and his own carelessness for leaving it unattended.

First the hypnotism stuff-up and now this.

Maxine was probably somewhere in the area by now as well, *hopefully not right here*, he thought.

A hundred yards down the dirt driveway, and the remaining fifty metres across grass to the house, brought them onto the verandah near the front door. It was wide open. Not unusual if someone is at home, but *given it was still fairly dark and no sign of lights . . .*

Josey pulled a gun from under his jacket and looked at Brack for approval, 'Problem?'

'Only if you use it,' the off duty cop advised.

'Let's hope I don't have to.'

Brack's body language expressed discomfort at the thought.

They moved inside. Brack had a pocket-torch, which he shone around the room. No sign of anyone. Not in view at least. They followed the disk of light as it traced across the floor. They were hoping to find Skillion and surprise him, at the same time not find any bodies, not even his.

The room had two exits, one leading to a kitchen, and the other to what looked like the living area. The kitchen was clear. They moved into the living-room. *Clear*.

The rest of the house, which consisted of three bedrooms, stuffed to the rafters with car parts, proved fruitless as well.

'So far so good,' Brack quipped, 'no one's dead.'

'Yet,' Josey said, reminding him the search wasn't over.

'Through here,' Brack advised as he led the way to

a back door via a small laundry.

The first thing they noticed about the workshop when it came into view was that it had a light on, which as they approached, went off.

Someone's in there.

Brack turned off his pocket torch, put it away and joined Josey in arming himself with his service pistol, a weapon that would get him into a lot of trouble if he had to fire it.

They reached the shop's gaping door and hesitated, listening - *nothing.*

As stealthily as creaking boards allowed, they entered the mechanics greasy forest of cars and equipment, lit by a working light mounted on a short tripod. They couldn't help being drawn to the light and what it had to offer. Its main point of focus, a bright yellow, classic Mustang had its front end sitting high atop jack stands – void of wheels. The earthen floor looked to have been blackened by years of spilt oil, *what one might expect to see in a mechanic's workshop.*

Not so the rear end, which also appeared to have no wheels, and unlike the front end - no stands, just a hydraulic jack – released to its lowest point, resulting in the car's chassis resting hard against the black oily ground, which seemed to be disturbed by a fall.

The two men rounded the crippled car and bent to look underneath. From the raised front end, looking toward the back, they saw the legs of a man whose head, or chest, would amount to being level with the rear axle.

'Fuck,' Brack cursed as he tucked his gun away.

Josey housed his gun too, running to the jack to begin pumping—

The man underneath groaned.

S*till alive - that's something.*

Brack came round to the side of the car as it lifted and shone his torch, picking up the man's face. He had seen men close to death many times. This was one of those times.

'Is it him?' Josey asked as he kept raising the vehicle.

'It's him,' Brack answered, familiar with the victim's identity. Then, focusing on the trapped mechanic, asked. 'Hey, buddy, can you hear me? Did someone do this to you?'

He seemed unable to talk. He was obviously in horrendous pain.

Josey locked off the jack and came to see for himself the man who was thought to be the main focus in the case. Here was a man crushed beneath a car—the anonymous villain from the start. It would have been beyond callus not to feel sympathy for him in such dire straits. He was clearly in no state to be answering questions, but there was little choice, he was close to death. 'Who did this?' Josey asked, afraid the answer might be, *Monty.*

The grease jockey's eyes widened, aware he was living out his final moments. In his last breath, he told them. 'You're . . . too, late . . .'

A soft fading wheeze heralded his passing!

Josey really didn't need another body on his hands. He was glad he had Brack with him, a witness for when questions were asked later. His presence at crime scenes was growing, and it wasn't over yet.

'Shit.'

Brack faced Josey and found him staring at the ground. 'What's up?'

Josey picked something up and held it in the palm of his hand.

'What is it?'

'A necklace – it proves she was here.'

His copper friend didn't know the real significance of the necklace, other than it belonged to the Pritchard girl, but he could see Josey was upset that his worst fear had been realised. 'I'm sorry, buddy.'

'Yeah, me too.'

There remained one crucial element of the case that needed to be dealt with, and soon. Josey's hunch had another arm to it—Brack knew what it was, and so did Maxine, both beseeched to keep the secret under wraps until a resolution was reached.

Brack's problem of course was; how the hell was he going to explain what he was doing at the property in the wee hours of the morning, off duty, and with a service pistol. 'You do realise we're not alone here, Brack noted as he craned his neck around checking out the workshop.

'Right, our friend here couldn't have turned off the light.'

'I have to call this in,'

'I know you do,' Josey responded apologetically.

'Sorry to get you into this.'

Brack shrugged, he was already in serious trouble. *That's what you get for hanging out with Detective Josey,* he thought.

'What will you tell them?'

'The truth, so I suggest you get your hunch sorted *A-sap.*'

Josey seemed distracted.

'What now?' Brack inquired quizzically.

'Do you smell that?'

'Oil?'

'No something else.'

Brack sniffed the air like a hound-dog. It hit him. 'Chloroform,'

CLANG!

They froze. The noise came from the back of the shop.

Drawing their guns they cautiously set out to investigate, keeping a look out for any sign of movement. When they neared the back wall, Brack hesitated, motioning for Josey to do the same. He pointed to what looked like a small office that was perched on top of a crude loft supported by aging timber beams. Equally aged timber-stairs ascended to a closed door leading into the tiny room. Brack went to lead, but Josey motioned for him to follow instead. He didn't argue – reminding himself that if there were to be any shooting, it would be prudent not to fire his issued service revolver.

On the landing at the top of the stairs, a glass panel afforded them a sweep of the whole room. If anyone was in there, they were hiding.

Josey tried the door; it opened, heightening the chance that someone was already inside. The door was the type that could only be locked from the outside.

Brack tapped him on the shoulder and signaled to take the left side. Brack took the right.

The room was being used as an office, certified only by a small untidy desk that shared its crowded surface with oily car parts. The remainder of the area was just as crowded, providing little floor space. A monopoly of larger machines and parts were scattered around like the merchandise of a junkyard - plenty of tall objects to hide behind. The two men approached each resulting avenue of walkable space with cautious ritual, beginning with a pause, then a glance to make sure they weren't about to be jumped—*or shot*, and finally crossing to the next plausible object in which to hide behind. They had almost run out of places to look when a figure in overalls and a wide brimmed hat darted out the door they had come through—the only door in or out. They heard a click, saw the figure wipe across the window pane in a blur.

On their arrival at the door, they confirmed the click was the door being locked, effectively assisting the escapee's getaway. The window beside it was secured with iron bars. They took turns putting their shoulder into the premeditated barricade. It was the type that opened in, making the task all the harder and time consuming. The time it took to break out of the office allowed the runner to reach the exit, which they witnessed from the landing. While leapfrogging down the stairs a large engine could be heard kick-starting behind the shed. They hadn't noticed a vehicle on the way in, which led them to presume it had been parked out of sight on purpose.

'Out back!' Josey shouted.

They bolted across the workshop, out the door and around the side, arriving at the rear wall as a duel cabin four-by-four fishtailed around the corner, narrowly avoiding running them down. To have any chance of catching up they needed to make an Olympic sprint toward Brack's car.

They were no match for a vehicle at full throttle and receding from view at an alarming rate. By the time they reached Brack's sedan, the *Four-by-four* was a kilometre away.

Brack spun his sedan on the dirt and poured on the power, catapulting dust and gravel. Dust was his friend; the escapee's car was providing a constant plume to follow, locating the car as efficiently as any tracking device. It would not be so easy if it reached the bitumen, not to mention the added danger of other road users.

Brack was very used to these local roads, an advantage that brought him within a few car lengths of the source of the churning cloud. The obscuring dust also meant the escapee could not see the pursuing car in the rearview mirror, or see how close they were getting.

Brack's prowess in country driving allowed him to read the opacity of the preceding dust; consistency meant the vehicle in front was not deviating from the road, or slowing. For Josey, this felt like speeding with a blindfold.

Brack suddenly hit the brakes hard, sensing the veil was thinning. His sedan slid into a lengthy broadside, exiting the blanketing cloud moments later. A glance to the left revealed the four-by-four was heading off-road.

'That's not good,' Brack observed.

'Can we follow?'

Brack already had his car on the move to give it a try. 'Maybe for a while, it gets pretty rough up there.'

Up there, described a mountainous looking group of rugged hills.

Five minutes later the ill-equipped sedan was bouncing over uncharted territory at a frustrating crawl, having totally lost sight of the surefooted over-lander.

'Define pretty rough,' Josey prompted, hardly able to verbalise due to the tossing of the vehicle.

Brack hit the brakes hard again, spinning the car into a sideways slide on moist grass, the passenger's side coming to rest inches from the lip of a deep ravine. Josey's window provided him with the disturbing view—*the absence of solid ground replaced by thin air, and a thirty foot sheer drop—*

It didn't bear pondering over what would have

happened if they had been travelling faster.

The escapee had taken the vehicle around the ravine and was coming back into view, crossing a fast flowing creek at the mouth of the gorge.

The pursuit was over.

CHAPTER TWENTY TWO
The Revelation

B ack in Beerwah an hour later, Brack took Josey to Rick's den at the back of the post-office and they let themselves in via the open door, which had been kicked in.

'Officer Broom's work,' Brack explained.

Officer Broom, who was busy preparing the equipment for his boss, gave them a fleeting acknowledgement and continued on with his task.

It was 9am Saturday, and that meant Ricky would be unreachable, doing what he did every weekend, using his truck for deliveries that often took him miles away from town. They had no time to find out where he was, because Josey urgently needed to see what the Sergeant himself had already seen after Josey's early morning call from Borcheck's house. Rick's absence meant getting Broom to assist in gaining entry with the help of his size eleven boots.

Broom gave his Sergeant the nod, indicating the equipment was ready. Brack knew how to use the machines; he'd watched Rick a million times. He pointed at the monitor Josey needed to watch.

> The screen displays the front of the Beerwah Hotel, The time display shows it is 3am.

'The white Audi sedan,' Brack said drawing attention to it, 'parked directly in front of the entrance.'

It was Borcheck's car from the holiday home Josey noted. Someone can be seen in the driver's seat, but the windows are too dark to see the driver. He knows its Monty.

Brack hit the play button.

> There are no people or other vehicles on the street.
> The clock recommences counting, but the driver makes no attempt to get out.

'She sat there until the hotel opened around 8am,' Brack advised.

> The image stops at around 8am, leaving the driver frozen, half out of the car.

'That's her, right?' Brack asked Josey, seeking confirmation.

'Play,' Josey requested.

> The image moves forward in real time.
> Monty Pritchard continues getting out
> of the car.

'Yep, that's her.'

> She collects a small bag from the back
> seat and walks into the hotel.

'Okay, now let's take a look at the back of the hotel just a half hour ago. I've yet to see this myself. Go ahead, constable.'

Broom takes over the controls and finds new footage.

> The four-by-four that Josey and Brack
> had seen at Skillion's property, slides
> into the car park close to the rear
> entrance of the hotel and stops. The
> escapee from the workshop gets out,
> still dressed in overalls and wide
> brimmed hat, goes to the rear door of
> the vehicle, opens it—looks about to
> see no one is watching, and leans in.
> A moment later Monty appears- dazed.

Josey notes, 'She's suffering the effects of the

chloroform.'

'Hmmm, watch. It's coming up.'

Monty begins to struggle.

Brack hammered the stop button.

The picture freezes.

Josey was now not only able to identify Monty, but her captor as well—clear confirmation.

'That your Perp?' Brack enquired confidently.

'Indeed it is, and it's all the proof I need.'

His friend warned, 'Maybe so, but you probably don't need reminding I've given you as much rope as I dare. Please don't give me another dead body to have to deal with.'

It was a sobering thought, one that convinced him to continue with his plan post haste, and to bring this case to a head—carefully. He understood that Brack had every right to take over; storm into the hotel and make an immediate arrest, but was holding back in consideration of Monty's safety. Storming police officers often bring about unnecessary collateral damage. Josey's plan of attack was much more subtle, but still fraught with danger.

'Go on then,' Brack encouraged, 'Bugger off. I'll keep a watch from here, room five-zero-one. It faces the street, so if you find yourself in any sort of trouble over there, just come to the balcony. The moment I see you, the cops take over.'

Josey crossed the street and entered the hotel. He walked through the foyer knowing he wouldn't be approached, because the staff had been advised about what was going on. There wasn't a single person in the town that Sergeant Brack didn't have in his pocket, the hotel manager was no exception, so getting him to cooperate was a forgone conclusion.

Josey entered the lift and took it to the fifth floor.

501, left on the corridor.

It was hard for him to comprehend why he felt so nervous; he had been in potentially dangerous situations like this more times than he cared to remember. He put it down to worrying about Monty.

It's now or never.

Knock, Knock, knock.

'Who is it?' - came a nervous response from a female voice.

The door had no peephole.

'It's Cameron! Cameron Josey!'

There was shuffling inside and no immediate answer.

Finally – 'Just a minute!'

Josey took a punt and waited.

The door opened.

'Hello Meredith,' Josey said to his client, 'didn't expect you in Beerwah so soon.'

'I was about to call you,' she told him, sounding

more relaxed than when she'd answered from the other side of the closed door. 'Come in.'

So far so good.

Josey slid into the room and Meredith helped the door click closed.

'Would you like some coffee?' she said waltzing into the kitchenette.

'If you are,' he agreed taking up one of two lounges at a small table.

She poured two cups and joined him, sitting opposite. 'When Maxine and I met up and she told me what you had discovered about Pritchard's mechanic, it was totally unexpected, I was shocked.'

They both sipped their coffees in unison, happy to let the other person speak next.

'I sent a cheque to your office,' she finally offered.

'No hurry. Let's get this case wrapped up first.'

'It seems you've almost done that.'

'Still need to find Monty. You haven't seen her have you; since you got here?'

'No.'

She just lied through her teeth without blinking an eye.

'Maxine tells me she ran away again, such a silly girl.'

'She's hard to figure,' Josey affirmed convincingly, *two can play this game.*

They raised their cups, but Meredith aborted, realising they were again in unison. As Josey was throwing back all of his lukewarm coffee, she felt compelled to keep the conversation alive. 'What about the mechanic – Ross, um - Royal is it?'

Josey distractedly peered into his empty cup, keen to ask her if she was the one who ripped the fake name off the fence, but it was too soon.

She went to get up, but he sprang to his feet ahead of her. 'I'll get it,' he offered heading into the kitchenette.

She sat quietly while he went about pouring more of the tepid brew, waiting for him to answer.

He wanted to make her nervous. 'Royal is dead,' he told her bluntly, hoping he'd see an incriminating sense of relief as he returned to his seat.

'Oh no,' she said sounding innately calm and empathetic, 'We're too late.'

Didn't work - ramp it up.

He ran his eye over the layout of the apartment, concerned about what might be behind a closed door at the end of a short hallway. 'It's funny; we're-too-late is exactly what *he* said.'

She looked a little frozen. 'He spoke to you?'

'No more than those few words.'

She drained her cup, swallowed hard and said, 'I wonder what he meant.'

'Probably the same as *you*.'

She looked even more frozen, and puzzled. 'That Monty killed him you mean?'

'Do you think she did?'

'I have no idea. I hope not.'

Back off a little.

'Sorry, I didn't mean to sound like you would

know more than I do.'

'No, that's all right.'

'I may need your help on this,' he announced.

'What can I do?'

You could confess and end this he thought. 'Well, I'm in a pretty sticky situation right now, as you can imagine. I need you to talk to the police and explain our arrangement. Let them know I'm working for you, and that you hired me to find Monty. I think it will help a lot. Actually I'm very good friends with the local sergeant. He's offered to put in a good word for me . . .'

She's thinking. 'I'll do what I can, absolutely.'

'Good,' Josey responded sitting back in his chair as though a great weight had been lifted from his shoulders, and then proceeded to drain his cup yet again.

She shuffled to the edge of her chair and reached out to take his empty cup, 'Man, you're really thirsty,' she said feigning lightheartedness, 'can I get you another?'

'No I'm fine; actually I think your pot may have gone off the boil.'

She looked nervous. 'Can you excuse me for a moment?' she asked as she stood.

'Sure.'

Here we go, he thought as he shifted to the edge of his seat on the ready.

She made it to the door in the hallway and entered quickly – too quickly.

Immediately on his feet and pacing to the door he

heard it click closed, followed by a second click.

Something dropped inside the room.

With two sharp kicks he separated the door from its hinges and barged in to find Monty squirming on the bed, Meredith leaning over her. She was administering chloroform via a cloth in one hand and holding a pistol on Josey with the other. He couldn't tell if it was hers or Monty's.

'You don't look too surprised,' she observed, 'you had this worked out before you even came in here; didn't you?'

'I worked out you were in love with, Royal, or should I say, Skillion - if that's what you mean.'

No denial – just annoyance.

'Looks like I gave you less credit than you deserve. How'd you work it out?'

'The how was fairly easy toward the end. I just went over the facts.'

'Which were?'

The brakes and the rape pointed to someone who knew the family, someone who had access to both cars. The Pritchard's mechanic, Ross Skillion came up trumps. So, I got my buddy, Sergeant Brack, to nose around; found out you and Skillion were an item when you both lived in Melany, which of course is not far from Beerwah.'

'How did that implicate me?'

'A simple bit of research on Skillion's whereabouts at the time of the other murders showed that he was nowhere near the crime scenes.'

'He could have hired someone.'

'Thought about that - problem was his phone records indicated no contact was made with the felons. The cops can work that sort of stuff out more than you know. You weren't the only other suspect I was considering, but you were the best fit.'

'All right Einstein, tell me why.'

She looks ready to fire - what about the noise - she's past caring - psychotic.

'When Montana got pregnant to him,' Josey began, using the time to figure out a plan to disarm her, 'jealousy and rage drove you to kill. In spite of the fact he raped her, you decided you'd take your vengeance out on Montana rather than him, because you still loved him.'

'That's a hell of an assumption, Detective.'

'Not when you consider he bought you a diamond friendship ring.'

'You *have* been poking around town haven't you.'

'It's what I do.'

'Hmmm, there you were, poking around like *Dick Tracey,* doing what you do best—But, pray tell, how did all this equate to my killing Montana?'

'You'd been with Skillion long enough to know your way around cars and you were presented with an opportunity to take care of Montana without getting caught. There was no guarantee the sabotage to the car would be found—and as we know it wasn't. I'll take full credit for turning that scenario on its head.'

'You are a fucking prick, Josey.'

'Thank you. Anyway, if the sabotage did get

noticed, Skillion would be the one getting charged with tinkering with the brakes. Let's face it; he'd have a tough job proving otherwise. Of course you lose him to the *big house* if that happens, but hey, if you can't have him, then you've just made sure no one else can. How am I doing?'

'What'd I do wrong?' she asked feeling more than a bit peeved, 'had to have been something stupid.'

'It kind of was. You brought yourself undone when you claimed to have called the ambulance for Alan Kelly. I checked. It was a man who put in the call.'

'Very clever, but you're not going to stop me doing what I started. This little bitch should never have been allowed to live. I blame Pritchard and the rest of those meddling do-gooders for that.'

It's time to alert Brack.

She sensed Josey was about to make some sort of move. Pulling Monty by the collar, Meredith dragged her half unconscious victim from the bed and along the floor like a chaff-bag.

Too late to get Brack.

Josey pulled his gun.

She fired, hitting him in the side, he faltered, providing her with time to reach a small balcony that overlooked the main street.

True to his promise, Brack saw this playing out on the monitors at the Post Office. He was already running from Rick's control room as he kept his second promise, calling in his men. 'Make your move *now,*' he barked into his radio. 'I want two guys inside hotel room 501, the rest on the street, a-sap—haul arse!'

Restricted by pain and uncertainty, Josey tried several times to make his way onto the balcony to foil whatever plan was developing in Meredith's deranged mind. Seeing as there was nowhere for her to go, he had to assume she meant to throw Monty over the edge, perhaps even jump herself. Each time he came into her line of sight he was fired upon. He didn't need reminding he'd already been shot once; blood was seeping through his fingers faster than he would have liked.

Brack arrived on the street; thought about going into the hotel himself—heard shots—saw what was happening on the balcony. With precious little time to prevent Monty plummeting from the fifth floor he positioned himself directly below.

In that instant, just as Josey feared, Meredith succeeded in launching Monty over the rail. Three uniformed men from the station arrived at their Sergeant's side as she fell into their collective arms. Brack caught a glimpse of Meredith leaving the balcony to return to the room. The other two cops, who had intended going into the hotel as ordered, diverted to the footpath to check on the status of the injured.

They found Brack holding his arm like it might be broken. 'I'm out,' he told them.

One of the men had a tear in his shirt exposing a gash to his shoulder. It was hard to immediately tell who in the rest of the crumpled entourage might be hurt, and how badly.

Monty was splayed out on top in an unnatural pose, at best incommunicado, possibly fatally hurt, or at worst - already dead; against all attempts to prevent it, her head had slammed hard into the pavement, leaving a substantial circle of blood splatter.

'Get upstairs!' Brack barked at his men.

Another shot rang out from the hotel room, enforcing the urgency of his order. They ran into the hotel with guns drawn. Staff cowered behind the front desk. Patrons took to crouching on the floor, or gaining refuge behind couches or any other solid object they could find.

When the officers got to the room they found Josey alone and bleeding from his gunshot wounds. One cop stayed with him while the other went to the balcony and yelled down to his boss. 'The shooter's gone, Sir, and we've got a man down.'

'She's got wheels out the back!' he yelled frantically. 'Get after her!'

The cop from the balcony breezed past the officer tending to Josey and told him to stay with the victim.

When he reached the street, a patrol car that had just arrived skidded to the curbside and picked him up.

Meredith's four-by-four bounced into view from behind the hotel and raced away from their position. The police siren wailed as the patrol car spun away in pursuit.

Meredith pushed the big vehicle as fast as it would

go in a careless attempt to escape, as would an animal being hunted down by predators. Her life depended on getting free from those who would destroy her.

Did I succeed—?

There was no time to stick around and find out.

Five floors would kill her . . . wouldn't it?

Yes. She's definitely dead, just like her stinking mother.

When this is over I'll come back and kill the rest of the fuckers - and that fucking detective. He was supposed to help me do this.

Meredith was so entrenched in her twisted thoughts; she didn't see the logging truck crossing directly in the unswerving path of her unfaltering vehicle.

Doomed, it slammed into the side of the massive stack of logs at full speed, sliding beneath the load with such unrestrained force that it tore the top of the vehicle clean away, severing it at the window sills. The lower half continued for a hundred yards before swerving and striking a roadside tree, setting off a massive explosion that raised a fireball that could be seen for miles around.

The cabin of the truck rocked marginally, but the driver just figured one of the wheels had dropped into a pothole. Barely hearing the noise over the roar of the big engine straining in low gear, he only became aware something had happened when he saw the inside of the cabin glow red. He looked out his side window and saw the sky burning. A second explosion sent flame and shrapnel cartwheeling as he brought his rig to a halt. He felt a projectile's wind as it speared through the cabin, taking out the windscreen.

He jumped down from the truck and saw the top half of the wreck wedged at a weird angle beneath his cargo of logs. He knew that whatever poor soul had been inside was well and truly beyond help.

People from the town, drawn by the noise, slowly overcame their shock and moved closer to the gruesome scene to see if anything could be done. There was nothing. Judging by the amount of blood spilling from the entanglement, some-or-all of the victim had to be in there, but most certainly dead.

'Wouldn't have known a thing,' the truck driver said to a nearby onlooker, managing to find the positive in what had happened.

Someone asked, 'Does anyone know who was in it?'

'Whose vehicle is it?' another person enquired nervously.

No one knew.

A few people thought to take a closer look at what was left under the logs, but their imaginations held them back.

CHAPTER TWENTY THREE
Licking Wounds

B risbane's Carmel-Care Hospital became the mandatory meeting place for almost everyone connected with the Monty Pritchard Case. As planned, Borcheck used his air ambulance to fly Margaret, Walter and Andrew—who had to be transported on a stretcher bed—from Sydney to the Sunshine State. Brack was missing though; he had chosen to stay in Beerwah for the treatment of a broken arm.

The Pritchards were put up in Bruno's private quarters on the hospital grounds. Andrew had picked up an infection in the gunshot wound he received courtesy of his niece. He found himself side by side with Josey on the third floor.

Josey's injuries; also gunshot wounds, both from Meredith, were a through and through just above the hip on the right side, and a six centimetre nick to the neck.

None of the patients were confined to bed.

Rebecca and Molly were on their way back to Australia following Josey's call to let them know what was happening. He tried to stop them, but they wouldn't listen.

Unexpectedly, Maxine finished up in the hospital too. She was laid up on the fourth floor, room 406. Her punk-hairdo had undergone a savage trim to make way for a dozen stitches to her scalp. It hadn't been learnt till after Meredith's accident that Maxine had made her way out to the mechanic's property only to run foul with Josey's crazed client. Max was later found by locals, dazed and roaming the countryside. Once Bruno was made aware she was at another hospital, he had the poor girl transferred so that she could be with the others.

Josey sat by Maxine's bedside listening to what happened.

'Following your distress call in the middle of the night,' Max explained, 'I followed Meredith to Queensland like you told me. When I arrived at the property I couldn't see where the two women had gone. I went around to the workshop and was about to go inside. I thought I heard a noise at the back. I could smell chloroform. I walked along the side wall till I reached the back edge of the building. I leant forward to look around the corner—when—lights out. When I woke up I found myself in dense bush with no idea where I was.'

'It could have been worse,' Josey told her. 'Thank

God you're all right.'

'Amen to that . . .'

Josey and Brack were unaware Max had been to the property because for whatever reason she hadn't been able to contact Josey on the phone to let him know. They later found out from Brack that the area is a mobile black-spot.

The injured and the non-injured alike formed a habitual pattern, all meeting in the hospital's community room to discuss their injuries—the case—and how lucky they were to be alive. They especially felt happy in the knowledge Monty lay in room 101 on the ground floor; recovering from her massive fall. The staff had been advised by Josey not to put her in any of the rooms that had balconies.

These daily discussions, which occasionally monopolised the tiny TV-come-reading-room, would encourage other people seeking relaxation to turn tail and find somewhere else to sit.

The best thing about everyone being at the same hospital was that Monty had a constant stream of visitors on hand. It allowed all manner of unresolved issues to be clarified and set to rest. In particular, Walter and Monty found a new understanding regarding living with their personal differences.

Visits from Margaret were awkward. Try as she might, she was not able to engage Monty in conversations about her gift. She finally had to accept that either the young girl didn't want to talk about it anymore, or—the gift was suddenly gone. In Margaret's mind, the latter was the most likely.

Walter and Andrew put it down to the knock she suffered to her head, but wanted it known it wasn't a professional diagnosis. At least that's what they told Margaret. They were just happy the nightmares were over, and that Monty could now move forward.

Uncle Andrew didn't broach the subject of her gift in any sort of depth; he restricted his conversations to Monty's wellbeing and the possibility of her coming home to be with the family, in spite of its history of dysfunctionality.

Forever the investigator, Josey was keen to know what happened between Monty and Meredith at Skillion's property. Monty was in hospital for over a week before he raised the question, but she assured him there was no problem in talking about it. Even *she* was beginning to feel the nightmare was in the past. In telling her story she had just one condition – she would only tell it once. This meant everyone was required to come to her room and form an audience. They brought chairs with them and circled the bed . . .

> Monty pulls into Beerwah at 3am in the morning, unaware she is being recorded by a security camera. It's cold outside and the hotel is closed, so she sits in the car with the motor running until the sun comes up. At 8am she gets out of the car, collects her travel bag from the back seat and goes inside the hotel, crosses the foyer and dutifully presents herself at the front desk.

'Jennifer Macintosh,' she announces to the attendant. 'Do you have a single room for the night?'

He flicks through the computer interface to check—.

'Well, hello.'

She turns to the voice . . .

'I was completely caught off guard,' Monty told Josey. 'As soon as I turned round and laid eyes on who it was, I thought to myself, this damned woman just keeps on showing up everywhere I go . . .'

'Holly shit, Meredith? What are *you* doing here?'

'There's a reaction I didn't expect, did you just get in?'

'Sort of, I've actually been sitting in my car outside since 3am.'

'I wish I'd known, I'm staying in the hotel – you would have been more than welcome to come up.'

'This is some coincidence,' Monty points out; given this is the third surprise visit from her mother's teenage friend, not to mention the circumstance of her timing.

'Why don't we talk upstairs in my room,' Meredith offers glancing at the attendant. 'Is that okay?'

The desk clerk nods with approval. 'Leave your bag with the Porter. I'll have it brought to your room once we allocate it. I can put you on the same floor with Ms. Northey if you like.

Meredith answers for her. 'Perfect.'

The two ladies take the lift to the fifth floor. Room 501. 'Come in, come in,' Meredith invites.

With little choice she accepts, still trying to work out what Josey's client is doing in Beerwah. 'I don't wish to be rude, but why are you here?'

'I was going to ask you the same question - is Cam with you?' . . .

'I realised I'd put my foot in it when she asked where you were. Thanks to running off, I didn't know you'd asked Maxine to bait Meredith by inviting her to come up for the *showdown* with the mechanic; that's what Meredith called it, which is why she was expecting us to be together.

'Anyway, Meredith told me what Max said about Skillion, that he'd changed his name to Royal. She put on this big surprise act, you know, to learn the mechanic was behind fiddling with the brakes . . .

'But of course, I knew all about Skillion from what I'd got from your computer.

'I asked her if I was right in thinking she might have known him; seeing as how she lived up here. She completely evaded the question at first, but when I pushed her she openly admitted she had, but said nothing about being in love with the guy – in love with my father as it turns out.' The thought of it brought forth tears . . .

'It's hard to believe I didn't connect that part of it before running up here halfcocked,' she finally told Josey apologetically.

Walter and Margaret shuffled closer together in support of each other, not unnoticed by their granddaughter, who seemed comforted by it.

'I started wondering how much you'd told her,' she said shifting back to Josey, 'you know – about the mechanic. She was making me nervous and I couldn't explain why. It seemed like she was sucking up to me. And, she had this unsettling interest in the necklace,' she told her family, 'which I was wearing.'

'Why?' Walter asked.

'Why was she interested?

'That too, but no, why were you wearing it?'

She turned to Josey for help.

'If it wasn't for that necklace, my investigation wouldn't have gotten off the ground.'

Their faces were telling him they understood, sort of, kind of. The necklace was still around her neck, which she fondled as one might a crucifix or some other meaningful memento.

'Go on with your story, honey,' Josey said bringing his attention back to Monty.

She took a deep breath and recommenced. 'So at this point, I'm completely unaware of what she's planning. It was almost a relief to have her with me in fact. I mean, I was already having second thoughts about committing murder. I still had no idea the man was my father. *Meredith* did, as you know.'

Monty's family was clearly bewildered by her account, horrified to realise the danger she had placed herself in; fraught with the fear of what could have happened.

'Anyway,' Monty continued, 'as far as Meredith had me believe, she was going to confront Skillion – my bloody father,' she rolled her eyes as she said it, 'and get him to confess to what he'd done to my mother's car. As I said, I had no clue about the love triangle, and she carried on making no mention of it; that is until we went out to the property.

'When we went into the workshop and found him working under the car, it all changed . . .'

'Who's there?' Skillion says, looking at the four female legs from his vantage point from beneath the car.

'It's me, Meredith,' she tells him, 'one of your old flames.'

Curiosity brings him sliding out on his lay-down trolley. He looks surprised - really surprised. Not by Meredith, but by Monty. It's like looking at Montana, the way she was when she was eighteen; the way she was the night he penetrated her against her will. He couldn't resist a subtle-sick-grin.

'I see you've recognised her,' Meredith says to him, sounding strangely sinister in Monty's view. 'But how about me . . . I know it's been eighteen years, but some people say I look ten years younger than I am.'

His fascination changes to annoyance. 'What the hell's this about?'

'It's about you admitting to Montana's daughter—*your daughter*—that you're a rapist.' She turned to Monty to gauge her reaction, a callous grin crossing her face when she saw the hurt.

Father and daughter meeting for the first time – collectively lost for words.

'That's right, sweetie,' she tells Monty as though enjoying the disclosure. 'I'm surprised you didn't work this part out. See, unlike some people I'm one of those who believes in your gift—'

What gift? Skillion wonders.

What's coming out of Northey's mouth is confusing him. 'What do you want from me, Meredith?'

The anger in her is intensifies. *'What do I want?'*

The words are full of hate, exiting her lips like vicious spit—

She pushes Skillion's trolley back under the car with her foot and screams –*'This!'*

Before he has a chance to roll free, Meredith dashes to the Hydraulic Jack and releases the lock on the handle, bringing the weight of the car plunging down onto the chest of her cheating lover . . .

The telling of this story was upsetting Monty, but with her family around her she felt a safety she hadn't experienced in a long time. 'I didn't miss that she hadn't called him a killer, just a rapist. That could only mean one thing. I had no idea what to do. The strangest thing was – I felt for him, crushed under that car like that. I mean, hours earlier, I was prepared to kill him myself. I could have killed my own father without knowing it.'

'Well, you didn't kill anybody,' Josey reminded her in support. He noticed tears rising. 'Are you okay to continue?'

She summoned control. 'Yes. I want to,' she said panning her eyes over her worried family. The questions hidden behind their faces ate at her, but she knew they wanted to hear the story as much as she needed to tell it. She went on. 'Meredith put her head down close to the ground so that she could actually watch him die as she spoke. The way she spoke, it was truly frightening. It was like I wasn't there . . .

> 'I gave myself to you, Ross, trusted you. But you decided to fuck that rich tart in the back seat of her father's car. You got her pregnant with this one, but I guess you only have to take one look at her to know that.
>
> 'Think back to that day, Russ, you never knew it, but I stood watching the whole

thing through the side window.' Her eyes swing onto Monty. 'Sorry I have to be the one to tell you, sweetie.'

Monty's mind is swirling, in the course of a few months she's gone from believing her grandfather has raped her mother, to finding out she is the daughter of yet another rapist altogether, who until this very moment she didn't even know existed.

Keeping her eyes on the distraught girl, Meredith said, 'I waited till she'd left, then I made out like I'd just arrived and let him fuck me in his office straight after.' She swings her vindictive attention back onto the quarry beneath the car. 'If I'd got to you a half hour earlier, this bitch standing behind me would probably be mine . . .'

Monty had diluted the worst of Meredith's foul language for the sake of her family. 'I couldn't take any more,' she told them in tears. 'I picked up a tyre lever and tried to hit her with it. She was too quick for me, so, I ran – I was convinced she might kill me as well. She caught me. The next thing I know, a rag or something was put across my mouth and everything went weird, I still knew what was happening, but I was powerless to stop it. I must have blacked out. The next thing I remember was waking up in the back seat of the car as we arrived at the hotel.

Josey figured Meredith must have put Monty in the

car and returned to Skillion's workshop for some reason, perhaps to make sure she hadn't left incriminating evidence. Or perhaps for one last look to make sure the mechanic was dead.

That must be when Brack and I disturbed her, Josey surmised.

This was all water under the bridge, and Josey saw no point in mentioning it, but he did fill them in on why Meredith couldn't find Skillion when she went looking.

'She didn't count on the name change,' he told them. 'It was only a week after Montana's car crash that she travelled to Melany to see Skillion, where he originally had his workshop, but found he had pulled up stumps already. She also discovered that he must have changed his name, because there were no Ross Skillions to be found on any register.

'When Skillion heard Montana had died in the car that he had recently worked on, he had an inkling Meredith was involved and that he might get the blame. It was most likely guesswork on his part, but, as we know, he was right.

'She tried for fifteen years to find him, before finally giving up and hiring me to inadvertently do her dirty work.'

It didn't worry Detective Josey too much that he had been used like that, because if she hadn't hired him it might never have been discovered Montana was murdered, let alone raped by the mechanic.

Josey was well aware certain members of the Pritchard family, including Monty, would be prepared to argue that Montana's murderer would eventually have been discovered anyway because of Montana's gift. That idea belonged to the pages of fiction as far as Josey was concerned, although he had to concede all aspects of her so called gift had not yet been explained away. Perhaps they never would be. That was okay too. Looking at Monty now, happy and relaxed with her family at her side, there was enough of a conclusion to call his case closed.

'It's all behind you now,' Josey told her. 'You can get on with your own life.'

She smiled and nodded, looking very content.

'We can thank Meredith for one thing,' Josey pointed out, 'Call it poetic justice if you like, but she inadvertently prevented you from becoming a murderer.'

Monty considered his comment and concluded, 'Do you know what, in the end, I don't think I could have done it.'

It seemed to Josey, she had accepted who and what her father was – rapist or not.

She confirmed it with a sentimental wisdom beyond that expected of one so young. 'Whichever way you look at it, he gave me life.'

*

Going back to the day of the hospital admissions, Josey had gotten bailed up by the Pritchards when they came to visit him at his bedside.

Walter was the most curious. 'How on earth did you manage to piece this together?' he asked, sounding in awe at last.

'Your father's anchor was the start,' Josey told him. 'That's no secret. The brake failure was the second clue. The secret to who was behind the killings and the rape had to somehow be connected to the two cars.' Josey looked into the storm of enquiring stares. The facts were less than ideal for the Pritchard family.

Margaret squirmed. Her expression was hard to read. Josey preferred to believe she was beginning to see that her granddaughter's double life was coming to an end. He wasn't sure what part she had played in all of it, but she could at least be credited with contributing to the outcome – they all had.

'Until I heard back from my friend Sergeant Brack,' Josey explained, 'and heard he'd located Skillion's property, or Royal as he was calling himself, it all seemed a little farfetched. That didn't worry Monty – when she delved into my laptop and saw the information I had on Skillion, she immediately went on the hunt. As you all know, Ross Skillion, was the only mechanic doing specialised work on classic cars when you guys lived up there. It all pointed to him.'

'I don't understand,' Margaret said, 'Montana and Meredith were such close friends. A love triangle seems too little a reason to kill.' She had no sooner said it when she realised she had once found herself in the same situation, the difference being that she had come to her senses and called the hit man off from killing her husband. She elected to remain quiet and listen to the rest of what Josey had to say.

'Unfortunately, Meredith just happened to see your daughter being raped. That's what drove her to do what she did.'

Margaret sucked in volumes of air and said, 'Dear God, I'm completely torn.'

Walter understood she meant between Meredith and herself, But, he had the appearance of a broken man, as though he might be carrying the guilt exclusively on his own shoulders.

'Skillion and Northey were our friends,' Andrew pointed out with deep disappointment. This was the first time he had spoken since Josey started his explanations. He was arguably more cut up about what happened to his sister and niece than anybody. He was the first to hear Monty's accusation that her mother had been raped in Walter's car.

Josey was thankful he had been oblivious to the culprit until now; otherwise there was no telling what he might have done to the perpetrator. He was also thankful it never occurred to Monty the murderous offender might be her father, until she'd come face to face with him.

Josey decided the demise of Skillion and Meredith was about as evenhanded as anyone could hope for, and Monty's gift aside, he accepted she deserved a large part of the credit for the natural justice that they received. It was an undeniable fact that her dream about what happened in her grandfather's

Cadillac turned out to be real.

One big question remained unanswered for Josey, *what actually contributed to the dream?*

The answer may lay with Margaret, a loving grandmother who suffered the loss of a teenage daughter way too early, and the destructive infidelity of a philandering husband.

CHAPTER TWENTY FOUR
Conclusions

As everyone expected, endless questions were asked about the string of dead bodies left in the wake of Josey's investigation.

Thankfully, there was no shortage of people vouching for the private detective, chief among them his friend and confident, Sergeant Barry Brack of the Beerwah Police. Brack was able to satisfy the authorities that Josey had conducted himself in a proper manner, never once firing his licensed pistol; a fact backed up by forensics.

Forensics also had no trouble attributing the death of Brian Appleby to the assassin, who as it turned out, was indeed hired by Meredith Northey. The death of the Hawkesbury assassin, although clearly shot by Monty Pritchard, was deemed self-defense.

Had it not been for the fact Meredith herself shot

Allen Kelly, Monty's male friend and an assassin himself, Monty would have at the very least found herself under a cloud of suspicion. No one was more surprised than her to learn Alan's killer was a woman, let alone Meredith Northey.

Monty had asked Josey what he thought about Meredith choosing to do the killing herself rather than hiring other people as she'd done at Hawkesbury.

His answer made sense. 'The night Kelly was killed, Meredith wasn't yet sure she would ever find Skillion, and after seeing you so chummy with Kelly at the cafe–the man who was meant to kill you–she needed to take out her anger immediately, on both of you. Basically she couldn't cope with the analogy of losing her hired assassin to a Montana lookalike.

Finally, the psychotic behaviour of Northey in her final hours in Maleny and Beerwah, witnessed by many townspeople, cleared all those connected to the case of any wrong doing. They found her gun amongst the wreckage – and not much else, which for Josey, answered who's gun Meredith was using at the Beerwah Hotel, because Monty had given *her* gun to her uncle just after the family got back together at Bruno's hospital.

Bruno Borcheck, although never officially charged by the authorities for the illegal use of his air ambulance, did face an investigation by the board, of which he was a member. Their investigation was never going to end in his dismissal for one very powerful reason; Walter Pritchard, who was the hospital's major ongoing investor, threatened to pull out unless they backed off.

Less than three weeks after the events in Beerwah, the Pritchards, including their son, but not their granddaughter, found yet another abode well away from prying eyes - on the west coast of Australia.

Shortly after the family's latest disappearance, Sergeant Brack received a cheque for a million dollars for his part in saving Walter and Margaret's granddaughter. Josey, who obviously was never going to see a penny from his dead client, received two million. It was the single most money he had ever been paid.

Monty Pritchard found her Shangri-La in the Blue Mountains above Sydney, returning to one of her old hideaways. She was brought up in and around the mountains of Queensland, but couldn't bring herself to stay in a place with so many memories, bad and good - *her memories*.

She hadn't thought about her mother's mediumistic memories since being in hospital. She was no longer sure they were actually her mother's. That part of her life seemed so unreal now; she decided to leave it all behind.

Benjamin Shephard was very excited about Monty's return to the mountains, because he was sweet on her, sexually, and believed the afternoon delights with her would be back on. What he didn't count on, was that Monty's head had moved into a different space. She still didn't know what she was looking for in life exactly, but it wasn't him, and it wasn't casual sex. More than once, if she saw him through the blinds approaching the house, she pretended not to be home. He eventually gave up coming around.

So as not to allow her mother to drift too far from her mind, a picture of her at the age of eighteen stood on watch nearby. It was the license photo that Barry Brack had found for Josey, *the somewhat fictitious poster.* Anyone who saw it could be forgiven for thinking it was Monty in the picture, not her mother. And, she let them think it. The days of explaining were over.

Josey returned to Sydney along with Maxine, whom he had given a month off work. He stayed away from the office himself for a few weeks, because along with his wife Rebecca and daughter Molly, they completed the overseas trip that they had aborted. With two million dollars in his pocket, so to speak, he could afford it. He even took Max.

By the time Maxine and Josey resumed work, her hair had grown back to normal, and its colour, back to abnormal.

Josey had already acquired his next case. He closed the Pritchard folder and labeled it,

MIND-SET

Maxine opened the door to her boss's office and found him discussing the new case with his dead partner.

The detective had his back turned and didn't notice she was listening to his rhetoric . . .

'This next case could be a doozy, Fredie,' he

mumbled. 'A missing person – not unusual except that my client, who we'll name, Mulder, claims the avowed missing person has been having *doomsday* dreams.'

Max stifled the urge to laugh, rolled her eyes and quietly left him alone to work things out with his dead partner.